Judgement

Book Three

Norma Hinkens

Published by Dunecadia Publishing, California

ISBN 978-0-9966248-4-8 (ebook)
ISBN 978-0-9966248-5-5 (print)

For Sandy Blackwell and strong women everywhere.

Author's Note

Parts of this novel are set in Idaho. I have taken liberties with the geography of that state, including names of places.

Judgement: *the ability to make considered decisions or come to sensible conclusions after careful thought: the end of the matter.*

Many that live deserve death. And some that die deserve life. Can you give it to them? Then do not be too eager to deal out death in judgement. For even the very wise cannot see all ends.

J. R. R. Tolkien

Chapter 1

I've barely had time to think since we toppled the Craniopolis. It took the best part of three days to burn all the bodies, including the participants from Sektor Sieben. To their credit, the scientists oversaw the entire operation, and I never, had to venture down to the Crematorium. Disposing of the participants didn't seem to faze the scientists, but cremating the bodies of colleagues they had worked alongside for years proved a more gruesome task. We gave them no choice but to finish what they'd started—a fitting penance for their involvement in the atrocities that took place under their watch.

"Ready, Derry?" Trout says, barging into Jerome's office where I'm scribbling down my half-incoherent thoughts for the meeting we've scheduled to elect a council of survivors. Tucker raises his head from his paws momentarily before flopping back down beneath the desk.

"Ready as I'll ever be," I say, crumpling the sheet of paper in my hand into a ball. "I'm putting my name on the ballot too. I can't assume everyone will agree to me leading the Council and all the factions."

Trout perches on the edge of the desk and studies me from beneath his shaggy brows. "If you put it to a vote, we're doomed. The Ghost will take control of the Council at the first sign of weakness."

"Isn't that what I'd be doing—seizing power?"

Trout shakes his head. "You brought the factions together and led us to victory. You earned the right to lead the Council. People expect as much."

I lean back in Jerome's chair, gripping the arms. I've come to rely on

Trout's common sense perspective on most everything of late. He hasn't left my side since we overthrew the Sweepers. Without him, I'd have no one to help me figure out the resettlement issues bubbling beneath the surface of our newfound peace. Big Ed always has a nugget or two of wisdom for me, but the events of the last few days have taken a heavy toll on him–he's been bedridden since Panju's funeral.

We carried Panju's remains back to the city and buried her in the little cemetery behind the riders' barn. Trout was adamant about not leaving her ashes behind in the Craniopolis. I understand, more than most. I've been carrying the pouch with Mason's ashes around for weeks now. I thought about laying him to rest beside Panju, but I still need some part of him with me to give me the courage to keep going in our struggle for freedom.

Big Ed presided over a makeshift funeral service for the Undergrounders we lost. He didn't preach revenge like some had hoped, especially after they learned about the sovereign leader's deception and the existence of the outposts.

"We'll hold the scientists accountable, but revenge ain't a vision worth rallying behind," Big Ed insisted.

I suppose he's right. At some point, we will all have to let go of past wrongs and learn to forgive, but until the Sweepers have been stopped, we won't give up the fight to save those who can't save themselves. *I* won't, at any rate.

I'd hoped Owen would have been on board, but he's a lost cause. He and Nikki spend every minute together, oblivious to anyone else around them. I suspect they're both too traumatized to be of much help anyway.

I haven't seen much of Sven since we got back to the city. His hands are full with integrating the new residents and overseeing the cleanup of the Craniopolis. At least I tell myself that's why he's keeping his distance. The truth is, I think we're both afraid of what might happen between us now that we finally have a chance at a relationship.

Finding out that the sovereign leader is alive shook the Undergrounders to the core. Everyone assumed he had died in the meltdown. The revelation that he was in communication with Lyong all along, and sanctioned what was going on in Sektor Sieben, shocked and nauseated us. The mega ship he's been transmitting from was built years before the meltdown, which means the world government knew the earth's core was overheating long before they issued that fateful thermal radiation warning. The Undergrounders can't accept that the sovereign leader abandoned them to their fate on a crippled planet. There's been a lot of debate in the city about how to locate the ship, the *Megamedes,* as we've started calling it. There's no doubt now in anyone's mind that the sovereign leader is the black heart of the Sweepers' operation, and that heartbeat must be stopped.

"I'll ask a representative from each faction to serve on the Council with me," I say to Trout. "Everyone should get a vote in how things are run, even the deviations."

Trout raises his brows. "How's that working so far?"

I give a resigned shrug. It still startles people to pass a clone or a deviation in the street. Trout and I try to engage them, but the rest of the Undergrounders, the Rogues, and even the riders keep their distance. The Ghost has made it clear that the deviations have no place with us. He's leery of the military clones too, convinced they'll turn on us and annihilate us in our sleep. Truth be told, I'm more nervous of The Ghost exercising that option. I don't think he's forgotten that Rummy escaped under my watch. He might even have guessed that we had made some kind of a deal. The only reason any of us have co-existed peaceably over the past seventy-two hours is because we had one agenda—to bury the dead.

"Not everyone wants a vote in things around here," Trout says, getting up from the desk.

I draw my brows together. "What do you mean?"

"Now that the Craniopolis is immobilized, some of the Undergrounders are talking about moving out of the city, starting over with their own land."

A flicker of disquiet seeps through me. "We don't know yet if it's safe."

"Safer than it's ever been. No sweeps, even with the Superconductor turned off."

"But if there are other outposts, the sweeps could resume."

Trout scratches the back of his neck. "If they exist at all, they could be on the far end of the globe for all we know."

I straighten up in my chair. "What about the transmission from the Megamedes that the scientist intercepted?"

"That was a year ago. Everyone on the ship could be dead by now." Trout furrows his brow. "Including the sovereign leader."

"I still think it's too soon to start a new settlement outside the safety of the city." I tap my fingers on the arms of the chair. "If there is a Megamedes, and other outposts, we need to find them and eliminate them first."

"Remember that freedom you fought so hard for? "Trout gives me a reproving look. "It's theirs, too. You can't hold people here against their will."

I twist my lips and get to my feet. "Then let's hope they'll listen to reason."

From the stage in the main hall inside the courthouse, I survey the seating arrangement in front of me with a sinking feeling–it's not exactly the integrated community I dreamed of after our victory at the Craniopolis. The deviations are nestled around Jerome at the back of the hall like frightened young. Rogues line the peeling walls around them, striking a decidedly hostile stance, accentuated by their scrunched lips and scowling eyes. Riders and Undergrounders occupy the front rows of splintered pews as the city's rightful residents, and the scientists sit stiff-backed behind them, unsure of their place or role in this new world order. The clones are crammed into the back rows–an impressive lineup of strength, agility, intuition, and intellect, all ticking down to their expiration dates faster than we can rebuild the city. The segregation in the room grates on me, but now's not the time to address it. There's a familiarity in it that soothes the factions' suspicions of each other. Suspicions I need to eliminate before we can build a real and lasting community.

Jerome welcomes everyone and goes over some updated housing arrangements, before nodding to me to proceed. I slide my chair back and get to my feet.

"Today marks a new beginning for us. We've laid to rest all those who died for freedom. Each one of us here is a survivor, and we will always have that in common, despite our differences. With freedom comes a responsibility to others. The time has come for us to elect a Council of survivors to lead this city. Within these walls, we welcome all who wish to contribute in whatever way they can. Those who can't will be cared for. Those who won't are free to leave."

The Undergrounders and riders stare back at me with skeptical expressions, while the scientists trade wary glances with one another. The Rogues scare me the most. One careless word out of my mouth could be the match to ignite whatever boils beneath their dangerously bored expressions. The Ghost rubs his fingertips back and forth across his lips like there's an aftertaste of something repugnant from my speech on them. But I won't back down. He may not like what he's hearing, but I suspected all along that The Ghost would resent playing by any rules other than his own.

When I catch Blade's eye, he taps his tattooed knuckles to his chest in a familiar gesture of intimidation. Knowing him, he's taken what I said about people being free to leave as a threat.

I focus my attention back on the rest of the room. "Some of you are eager to leave the city and begin homesteading. Many of you left possessions you wish to retrieve from bunkers. But it may not be safe yet to settle beyond the barricade."

A murmur of disapproval ripples through the front rows where the Undergrounders are seated.

"Who says it's safe here?" a bearded Septite calls out, gesturing toward the sullen lineup of Rogues.

"We're thankful for what you did, overthrowing the Sweepers and all," a red-headed woman calls up. "But we don't want to live here with all these strangers. We have our ways and they have theirs."

"I understand your concerns," I say, "but first we need to send out scouting parties and make sure it's safe. In the meantime, we can find a way to make things work here. We'll begin tonight by setting up a Council to represent all the factions."

"What's there to be afraid of out there?" the bearded man calls out. "The sweeps are over."

I grimace. "The intercepted transmission from the Megamedes for one."

"No one's heard from the ship in over a year," he replies. "If the sovereign leader didn't die in the meltdown, he's probably dead by now."

Several people clap in response.

I raise a hand to quell them. "We can't make those kinds of assumptions. If the Megamedes is out there, it won't be long before the sovereign leader discovers the Craniopolis has been compromised."

The beaked-nosed scientist who intercepted the transmission from the sovereign leader stands and steps out into the aisle. He runs a finger nervously over the distracting mole on his cheek. "Maybe he doesn't have to find out. We can monitor the CommCenter in the Craniopolis for transmissions. If the Megamedes makes contact again, we can respond as if we are still an operational base."

"But Lyong's dead," I say. "The sovereign leader will want to communicate with him directly."

The scientist shifts from one foot to the other. "Lyong's own notes document his self-inflicted cell damage when he attempted to reverse the DNA structure of the aging process. I could report his death as a direct result of his experimentation."

I throw a quick glance over at Trout. He raises his brows in a subtle gesture of approval. If nothing else, it would buy us some time to figure out our next move. It would be easy enough to house a small group of scientists in the Craniopolis to scan the CommCenter for any incoming transmissions. Now that the clean-up operation is over, what's to stop us from using the Craniopolis for own purposes? Or the Hovermedes, for that matter.

As much as I detest everything the Craniopolis stands for, the truth is it may turn out to be a better housing option for the deviations anyway. The city's proving to be full of hazards for them—even the sight of a horse spooks them, and a simple neigh or whinny sends them running. They're struggling to adapt to sunlight and wide open spaces, and they aren't sleeping properly, which makes them even more agitated.

Dividing the city into zones is an option, but it goes against everything I had hoped to accomplish. Moving the deviations back to the Craniopolis temporarily might be for the best, especially if it stops a mass exodus of Undergrounders from the city.

"I'm willing to return to the Craniopolis and man the CommCenter," the scientist offers.

"What's your name?" I ask him.

"Viktor Kozlov."

"You seem to be an expert on communications." I give an approving nod in his direction. "I want you to put together a rotation of scientists to monitor the CommCenter. We'll also need a communications line set up between the city and the Craniopolis. Can you handle that?"

He nods. "Give me a couple of days. It shouldn't be a problem."

"Good. Let me know when you're done." I turn back to the crowd. "It's time now to vote in our new Council."

When the results come in there are no big surprises. Just as Trout anticipated, I am asked to govern the Council. Jody is elected to lead the riders' faction, and Sven to lead the military clones. The Ghost takes the Rogues' unanimous vote–although I suspect none of them dared vote otherwise. Trout is chosen to be the Undergrounders' spokesperson because Owen wanted no part of it. Jerome is selected by the deviations, and the scientists pick Viktor as their representative.

"I'll put the elected Council members to work on housing arrangements and schedules right away," I say. "Tomorrow, I'll lead a search party to comb the bunkers for any other survivors. We'll give them the option of joining us in the city. With the Superconductor turned off, we can stay here as long as we want. Once the search party returns, we'll make plans to locate the Megamedes and resettle the land. Until then, I ask you to be patient. Thank you all for your efforts over the past few days. Go home now and enjoy some well-deserved rest."

The crowd converses among themselves for a few minutes, and then begins to trickle out of the courthouse. Trout gives me a quick wave and disappears after them. I have a hunch he's heading over to Panju's gravesite. It was emotional for him to be elected to represent the Undergrounders.

Panju was an integral part of the original Council and he's bound to be wrestling with memories of the time they spent together.

When the room empties out, Sven and The Ghost join me on the stage.

"I'll go with you to search for survivors," Sven says. "I can leave Rocco in charge here. He's one of the best military clones I trained with."

"Not this time," I say. "I need you to keep peace in the city while I'm gone. I'll take Trout instead."

"Trout?" The Ghost mocks. "He doesn't know where the raided bunkers are." He tightens his lips into a half-smile. "But I do."

"*You're* offering to help?" I scour him with a skeptical look.

"You said you were looking for survivors. So am I." He leans in closer. "One in particular."

I flinch as his foul breath washes over me. *Rummy.* My heartbeat falters. I narrow my eyes at him. "This isn't the time to rehash personal scores."

A scowl twists across The Ghost's features. "You let him walk. I take *that* very personally."

"You were going to kill him."

The Ghost's face contorts in a mask of hatred. "He's a deserter and he took my men with him."

"I don't know what went down between you two, but like it or not, Rummy's a free man now. I'm going out tomorrow to search for survivors who need our help. Unless you have the same agenda, we're not travel partners."

Sven folds his arms across his chest and takes a step closer.

The Ghost throws him a dark look and walks off.

Sven stares after him, a strained expression on his chiseled face. "I don't trust him. He held a knife to your throat not that long ago."

I rub my fingers over my forehead in small circles to relieve the mounting pressure. "But he knows where the other bunkers are. We could save a lot of time if he leads us there."

"You could take Jerome's map. He was documenting the raided bunkers on it."

"It's incomplete."

Sven places his hands around my waist and draws me to him. "What if The Ghost's real agenda is to take revenge on you for letting Rummy go?"

I look up into Sven's amber eyes, a dizzying array of emotions arresting my senses. It's the first time he's touched me since we arrived back at the city. There's nothing to keep us apart now that the battle is over, but we're wading into unknown waters. I suck in a breath as I listen to the thud of Sven's powerful heart beating next to mine. This is real. And it scares me. I want to be with him, but I can't bear the thought of watching him ossify one day soon.

"Maybe I'm kidding myself to think I can trust The Ghost," I say. "But he came through for us in the Craniopolis. He deserves a chance."

Sven lets his hands slide from my waist and tucks a strand of hair behind my ear. My skin tingles where he touched me. I shake off the feeling, reminding myself that he has an expiration date, which is a good reason not to get attached. I've lost too many people already.

"I need to pick Tucker up from Jerome's office on my way back to the riders' barn," I say. "I'll grab that map just in case The Ghost's a no-show when the search party is ready to head out in the morning."

Sven nods. "I'll help Jerome escort the deviations back to their accommodations."

Jakob is back from his shift at the clinic and fast asleep by the time Tucker and I reach the riders' barn. Tucker immediately trots off to find Big Ed and curl up with him. I toss my pack down and prod Jakob awake. He props himself up on one elbow when he sees me. "How was the meeting?" he asks, rubbing his eyes.

I grimace. "Jury's out. No one seems that interested in building a community together. Some of the Undergrounders want to leave, they're scared of the Rogues and freaked out by the clones and deviations. The clones aren't all that excited to be here, even though they promised to help rebuild the city. The deviations are freaked out by the horses. And that offends the riders." I let out a heavy sigh. "And The Ghost's still obsessed with finding Rummy and carving him up."

Jakob frowns. "It takes time to build trust. You're expecting too much from everyone too soon."

"Maybe." I stifle a yawn. "We'll see what tomorrow brings. I think I managed to talk everyone off the ledge for tonight at least. Go back to sleep. I'll check on Big Ed."

Before Jakob can respond, the wooden door to the barn swings wide and Jody bursts through, eyes half-crazed like flickering bulbs.

Chapter 2

"They've gone!" Jody gasps, leaning on the doorframe.

I jerk to my feet, adrenaline flooding my veins. "Who?"

"The Rogues!" Her face tightens with grief. "They've taken the horses and fled the city."

I stare at her in disbelief. After the way the meeting went I wouldn't have been surprised if the homesteaders had packed up and gone. But the Rogues? My heart squeezes in my chest. The broken look on Jody's face is enough to tell me the Rogues have taken her horse, Condor, too.

I pick up my pack and swing it over my shoulder. "We'll go after them. They won't get far," I reassure her. "They don't know the first thing about riding horses."

"Most of them will be on foot anyway," Jakob adds, reaching down for his boots.

"If anything happens to Condor–" Jody's voice chokes as she shoves the barn door wide and strides back out, her thick ponytail swishing behind her.

I swallow hard. It's not difficult to imagine what she's going through. Just the thought of the Rogues taking Tucker away from me is enough to make my skin crawl. We have to move quickly. Knowing the disdain The Ghost has for any life but his own, he won't hesitate to put a bullet in a horse. As for Blade, I don't even want to think about what he'll do to a spirited steed that refuses to cooperate.

I shrug my jacket on, sick to my stomach. I wouldn't be alive today if it weren't for those horses. They're heroes like any one of us. No matter the risk, I'll do whatever it takes to bring them back.

"Hold up, I'm coming with you," Jakob says.

"No! The wounded need you here." I shoot him a pleading look. "And I need someone to keep an eye on Big Ed. Let Jerome and Sven know what's happened. We'll be back as soon as we find the horses."

Jakob gives a reluctant nod.

Outside, a light rain is falling, but the gathering clouds are knitting into something more menacing. It's hazardous to head out in the fading light with a storm coming in, but this can't wait until morning. On our way to the main gate I pump Jody for more details.

"We left the horses tied up outside the courthouse while we were wheeling wagonloads of food to the clinic to feed the wounded," she explains. "When we got back, they were gone."

"Who opened the gate for the Rogues?" I ask.

She gives a frustrated shake of her head. "There was no one on duty. Jerome has been preoccupied sorting out housing for everyone. Things are lax now that the Sweepers aren't a threat."

I grit my teeth. One more reason to put the Council to work right away. Someone needs to oversee security, and water and food distribution, and all the other things it will take to keep us from descending into chaos.

An Undergrounder walks by carrying a bucket of water, and I shout over to him to get some guards to the gates. He stares at me, a befuddled look on his face. "Is something wrong?"

"The Rogues have taken the horses," I say. "Our open door policy just ended."

He drops the bucket and takes off running.

When Jody and I reach the main gate, the other riders join us, their faces drawn, but resolute. I eye the additional weapons strapped to their backs and their laden packs, no doubt well-stocked with ammo. They have no intention of returning without their horses, which means there's more blood to be spilled.

"Let's go," I say, leading the way. I wish Sven was coming with us, but he's at the far end of the city helping Jerome with the deviations, and we don't have time to waste looking for either one of them.

We exit through the container gate and begin making our way through the rubble-strewn city outskirts. I shiver as the damp takes hold of my weary bones. I only hope we can keep up a brisk enough pace to stay warm once night falls.

"I don't understand why the Rogues took the horses when they can't even ride," Ida says.

"I think The Ghost was sending me a message," I say. "He took the horses so we couldn't leave without him. He's trying to force us into helping him track down Rummy."

Jody scowls. "From now on we let those tattooed freaks have at each other. I don't offer protection to horse thieves."

"I'm okay with that," I say, lengthening my stride to match her pace. "They just blew their chance of sanctuary in the city."

We follow the horses' trail into the forest and over a thick bed of leaves and fallen twigs. The Rogues don't have much of a head start, and it won't be long before we catch up with them. We need to work out a plan to recover the horses. I furrow my brow as I trudge forward, the straps from my laden pack digging into my shoulders. Our best bet is to wait until the Rogues are asleep–that way we'll only have the guards to deal with.

A twig snaps somewhere to my right. I still my breath and listen. The steady pattering of raindrops on leaves fills my ears. Another snap, this time, louder. I jerk my head around and hold my hand up to halt the riders.

"Did you hear that?" I whisper to Jody.

She nods, frowning. "Do you think some of the Rogues circled back around?"

I slide my gun off my shoulder. "It's possible. They must have known we'd come after them. Let's spread out and hide so we're not easy pickings."

Jody signals back to Ida and the other riders. We part ways and disappear into the thick, damp foliage. I scuttle beneath some low-hanging limbs, and wade deeper into the undergrowth as quietly as I can, searching for a spot to hole up in and monitor the trail from. If it's a lone patrol, I can take him out from the cover of the deep ferns. I stiffen at more rustling sounds behind me. It sounds like someone is closing in on me. Heart pounding, I dive beneath a thatch of ferns and lie there listening to a flock of scolding crows in the tree above. For a long time, I don't move. I scarcely dare to breathe. I can't hear any rustling in the undergrowth anymore. Whoever was following me must have gone in a different direction. Cautiously, I relax my stance and stretch out my cramped limbs.

A cold drop of rain trickles down a fern frond and splashes on my face. I shiver and wriggle backward out of my hiding place. A wiry arm snakes around my neck, but before I can scream, a hand closes over my nose and mouth. I kick and flail, but the hand squeezes tighter, and my movements weaken as the air leaves my lungs.

When I come to, I'm lying on my back. I frown, wondering why I can hear the sound of rain when it's not raining on me anymore. I turn my head sideways and suck in a breath. Rain peppers the glass I'm looking through and slides down the other side of it like meltwater. Green fronds swish up and down the filthy glass like windshield wipers. I feel like a fish in a bowl. I blink. Am I hallucinating?

I close my eyes and swallow. My throat is dry like sandpaper. *What happened?*

"Are you okay?" a gravelly voice asks.

The arm around my neck! My eyes fly open. I jockey myself up on my elbows and stare at the sallow-skinned, statuesque woman towering over me. "Who are you?" I ask, throwing a darting glance around. We're in an old camper van, and by the looks of things, someone's been living here for a long time. The seats have been reconfigured to accommodate a wood stove in the center. Dried meat hangs from hooks in one corner.

The woman gives a wry grin. "It may not look like much, but it's home." I'm Lou Perinsky."

"Derry Connelly." I maneuver my way to the edge of the seat, eying her warily. "Do you want to tell me why you kidnapped me and almost suffocated me?"

"Yeah, about that." She reaches behind for a jug of water and hands it to me. "There were a couple of Rogues hot on your tail. One of them was staked out not far from your hiding place and you were about to crawl right out into his line of sight. You were too feisty to reason with, so I did what I had to do to keep you quiet."

I glug the water while I study Lou's weather-beaten face framed by wispy gray hairs spilling from a loose braid. No tattoos, so she's not with the Rogues. And a mountain woman wouldn't live in an abandoned van. She must have come from the city.

"How long have you been here?" I ask.

"Since the meltdown. I fled the city once the evacuation order was issued."

I rumple my forehead. "There was an evacuation order?"

"Day of the meltdown. The world government said there was unidentified thermal activity. Everyone was supposed to assemble on the east side of the city, get on buses."

My jaw drops. "Did they get out?"

Lou shrugs. "Not everyone believed the threat was real. I did my own thing and headed north into the mountains. No way I was getting caught up in some cattle transport to a government camp."

"Going it alone was risky too," I say, looking around the cramped space. "You'd have been safer in a bunker, and more comfortable."

Lou presses her fingers against the glass and stares at the raindrops. "Long as I don't have a snout and claws I'm not living underground."

I laugh. "I can relate."

Lou turns and smiles at me. I'm fascinated by her cheekbones. She's a beautiful woman even at her age which I'm guessing is around fifty.

"You must have been lonely at times," I say.

She purses her lips. "I bumped into Undergrounders hunting here and there. Got my fill of their griping."

I scrape a few loose strands of hair out of my face. "Speaking of Undergrounders, my friends will be looking for me."

Her face creases in concern. "If the Rogues didn't get to them."

"They're trail riders, familiar with the woods. I'm willing to bet they evaded the Rogues' patrols."

Lou jerks her chin toward the window. "It's pounding down out there. Sure you don't want to wait it out?"

"I can't. We have to catch up with the Rogues. They snuck out of the city early this morning with our horses."

Lou's face clouds over. "Rogues in Shoshane City? I thought it was well fortified."

"It is. It's … complicated." I stare at her, wondering how on earth I can summarize everything that's happened over the last few days.

She studies me for a moment. "Sounds like you have news I should know about." She takes a seat opposite me and leans forward expectantly.

I give her a condensed version of everything we've been through. I can't help but notice her eyes moisten when I describe Panju's burial and Big Ed's eulogy. I wonder who she lost. She interjects a question or two, but for the most part, she listens in silence.

When I'm done, she sits back and rubs her hands over her face. "So the sweeps are over?"

"Haven't figured that part out yet." I reach for my pack. "As soon as I've stabilized the city and the Council can handle the different factions without running the risk of riots, I'll send out some scouting parties. But if I don't get those horses back, I can count on the riders being the first to go on a rampage."

Lou raises her brows. "I'd think a teenage girl would sooner face a rider rampage than pick a fight with the Rogues."

I shake my head. "It's not an option. The riders risked their lives, and their horses' lives, for our sakes. We have to get them back. We'll wait until the Rogues are asleep and then strike."

"How are you planning to pull that off?" Lou asks. "If you shoot the guards you'll wake the rest of the camp. And you don't strike me as the silent assassin type slitting throats from behind trees."

I shrug. "We'll work something out. First, we have to find the Rogues."

Lou sets her jaw. "I'll help you find your friends, but I'm steering clear of stirring up a hornet's nest of Rogues around my home."

"This isn't your fight, I get it," I say. "Just take me back to the riders." I sling my gun over my shoulder. "If you change your mind about the hermit thing, you're always welcome to join us in the city."

Lou smiles. "I appreciate the offer."

She yanks open the rusted van door. "Rain's easing up. We're in luck. Follow me." She jumps out and ducks beneath a canopy of greenery. I hustle after her, amazed at the grace she moves through the forest with despite her height.

Smudges of charcoal sky peek through the tree tops. It's hard to tell if it's already dusk, or more storm clouds plotting a course. I've no idea how much time I spent passed out in Lou's camper. I swat a sapling out of my way and concentrate on matching her lithe movements as she forges a steady path through the brush. She leaps like a deer across a muddy stream and disappears into the undergrowth on the other side. Halfway across the stream my foot slips on a rock and I teeter off balance before stomping down in a mud puddle all the way up to the top of my boot. I almost holler to Lou to wait up, but I don't want to risk being overheard by the Rogues. I reach for a branch to steady myself while I jerk my mud-caked boot free. No sign of Lou on the other side. She must have kept going. I hop across the rest of the stream and plow my way into the undergrowth. I come to a halt and pan the forest in every direction. There's no indication of which way Lou went. Surely she wouldn't abandon me when she knows I have no idea where I'm at. I adjust my pack, pushing down the niggling fear inside as I begin bushwhacking my way forward. What if she ran into the Rogues?

I freeze at the sound of thudding footsteps heading toward me. Heart racing, I melt down into the brush and load a round in my gun.

Chapter 3

The footsteps draw closer. It doesn't sound like a lone patrol. I'm guessing there's five, possibly six of them. Pinpricks of sweat form above my brows. The Rogues must have ambushed Lou. Did they see me cross the stream too? I don't know how many of them I'll be able to take out from my vantage spot, but I can't leave Lou to her fate after she risked her life to save me.

I peer cautiously out from behind a pine tree and line up my shot. I steady my breathing as the first figure comes into view.

Jody!

My fingers shake so hard I almost drop the rifle.

"Over here!" I call out.

Seconds later, the brush parts. Relief floods across Jody's face. "Are you okay? We've been searching for you for hours."

"I'm fine." I swat a fern out of my face and get to my feet. "Did Lou tell you I was here?"

"Who's Lou?"

"She was helping me look for you. Tall, sallow-skinned woman. You didn't see her?"

Jody turns to the other riders and shrugs. "We haven't seen anyone."

"She's a loner. Probably took off once she saw you." I pick a leaf out of my hair and brush myself off. "She hid me from the Rogues in her camper van."

"A camper van here?" Jody creases her brow.

"Says she's been living in it since the meltdown. I asked her to come with us, but she's not overly fond of company." I ram my rifle into my pack and throw one last glance around on the off chance that Lou is peering at me from behind a tree somewhere. "Let's get back on the Rogues' trail."

"They're moving north," Jody says. "Headed to the mountains."

I grimace. "My hunch is that The Ghost thinks Rummy's hiding out in one of the bunkers."

"I don't care about Rummy. I just want Condor and the other horses back before anything happens to them."

I tug on the straps to tighten my pack. "I don't care about Rummy either, but if there are survivors in the bunkers, they're in danger. Once we rescue the horses we need to gallop ahead to warn the Undergrounders."

"How are we going to find them?" Jody asks.

I reach into my jacket and pull out the folded-up map from Jerome's office. "We can start with this."

Jody leads the way north and we soon settle into the rhythm of zig-zagging our way through the forest, avoiding walking in the Rogues' trail in case there are rear guards.

Before long, a cold wind kicks up and the forest's shadows begin to close in around us. My clothes are still damp from the rain earlier, and I shiver at the drop in temperature. I'd trade almost anything for a chance to warm my hands by a fire, but it's not an option.

"The Rogues will have to break for camp soon," I say. "We need to be careful we don't run into a—"

"Shhh!" Jody grabs me by the wrist. "I heard a whinny."

I stand rooted to the spot, breath on pause, but all I can hear are crickets tweeting and the occasional squirrel chatter.

"I'll check it out," Jody whispers to me.

"I'm coming with you," I say.

Jody motions to the other riders to hang tight. We pad forward, parting the foliage as quietly as we can. I flinch when I hear a snort. The Rogues must be closer than we realized. My ears are warm and buzzing, my senses electrified as I search the deepening shadows for a silent patrol.

Jody nudges me and points up ahead. An untethered horse stands half-concealed in a grove of trees, munching on a few scrubby tufts of grass.

Jody gestures to me to go to the left, then she circles around to the right.

I grip the barrel of my gun and tiptoe forward, keeping my eyes peeled for the slightest movement. The horse lifts its head, still chomping, but quickly loses interest in me and returns to the grass. I loop around and meet back up with Jody. "No sign of any guards," I say.

Jody grins at me, her eyes aglow. "It's Bandido, Ida's horse. He must have got away from them." She whistles softly and the stallion pricks up his ears and trots over to her. He nuzzles Jody's neck and she rubs his head for a few minutes before leading him over to a tree stump. "Let's get out of here," she says, vaulting from the stump onto his back. I clamber up with considerably less grace and grab a hold of Jody's waist.

"Relax," she says. "We won't be galloping in here."

I tighten my grip. "I want to be prepared for the whiplash getaway if we run into Rogues."

Jody chuckles. She nudges Bandido into the undergrowth and steers him back to where the other riders are waiting.

Ida's eyes widen on our approach. She runs to meet us and falls on Bandido's neck, whispering in his ear. "Where did you find him?" she asks, blinking back tears.

"Grazing in a grove of trees," Jody says. She dismounts and helps me down.

"He always was a rebel," Ida says, a note of pride in her voice. "Probably bolted when they went to tie him up for the night."

"Which means the Rogues are camped out close by." Jody frowns. "We'll have to hide Bandido here. We can't risk the Rogues hearing him."

I watch as Ida leads Bandido over to a clump of spruce trees. She takes a rope from her pack and secures him to a trunk. "I'll be back soon, Bandido," she says, running her hand over his mane one last time.

I take a few swigs of water while the riders don their packs. My teeth chatter. The lure of starting a fire is growing stronger, but creature comforts will have to wait.

We trudge through the woods for another quarter mile or so before voices drift in our direction, interspersed with harsh laughter. The unmistakable smell of meat roasting above a flame taunts my nostrils. I scoot over next to Jody to make sure my voice doesn't carry in the night air. "Let's get our bearings, figure out the sleeping arrangements, where the horses are tied up, that kind of thing. Once the Rogues are passed out, we'll make our move."

Jody relays the information back to the other riders. Like specters in the night, we merge into the foliage to scout out the perimeter of the Rogues' camp.

Once I'm close enough to get a decent view of the activity, I flatten myself on a bed of pine needles and peer out from under a canopy of ferns. A large campfire crackles in the middle of the clearing and several kills are roasting on a spit above it. Saliva pools beneath my tongue. My stomach rumbles and I squeeze it tight to quell the sound. The last thing I want to do is alert The Ghost that he has unexpected company for dinner.

Beyond the flames, small clusters of Rogues lean against their packs, limbs stretched out, jawing with one another. Some are dozing. It's too dark to identify them. Any one of them could be The Ghost. There's no sign of the horses and I don't hear any whinnying, so I'm guessing they're tethered in a grove on the far side of the camp. Luckily for us, the Rogues didn't want the odor of steaming horse droppings anywhere near their kitchen. It will make our job that much easier.

A tall, thin Rogue strolls back and forth along the perimeter in a leisurely manner, exchanging a few words here and there with the men seated around the camp. He's heavily armed but he doesn't seem overly concerned about threats. Maybe the Rogues are naive enough to think the riders wouldn't be able to track them down this quickly. I hug my jacket around me and rub my arms trying in vain to keep warm. There's nothing more we can do until the Rogues bed down for the night. That's if I don't freeze to death first.

I pull myself up and make my way gingerly through the dense cover along the camp perimeter to look for Jody. An owl whoops and flaps past my head hunting down fresh rations. I take a deep breath to calm my racing heart and continue creeping my way around until I spot Ida tucked behind a large cedar tree.

"Where's Jody?" I whisper.

Ida points to her right. "She went that way to find a tree to climb. She wants to see how many Rogues are guarding the horses."

"I'll go check on her." I peer upward into the leafy canopy. Twilight is closing in and I can't make out much more than the shape of the leaves networked above me. I'm not sure I'll be able to find Jody, but maybe she'll see me. I tiptoe forward for a few minutes until a loud neigh startles me. I freeze in position. My first thought is that I've been spotted by a patrol on horseback. My heart thuds as I wait for a search beam to pick me out. But it doesn't. I slip behind a tree trunk and take a deep breath. I guess I'm closer to the horses than I realized.

I sweep the forest in front of me for any sign of Jody. She must have climbed a tree already. It's not a bad idea for me to do the same. Safer than prowling around and spooking the horses before we're ready to make our move.

I suss out a tree that looks relatively easy to climb but is still tall enough to give me the perspective I need. Planting the heel of my boot on a nub, I push off and pull myself onto the lowest branch. The next one is too flimsy to support my weight, so I stretch a little farther to reach for the branch beyond it. I grit my teeth and feel with my foot for a crevice in the tree trunk. I push off again, but my boot slips, and my pack swings sideways, yanking me hard to the left. I scramble to catch hold of the branch below me and manage to grab it at the last minute. Weak with relief, I drape my body over it, then watch in horror as my water canteen tumbles from my pack, clips a branch, and lands with a dull thud in the pine needles below.

I stare down at it, blood pounding in my temples. No one in the camp could have heard it fall. But I need to retrieve it in case a patrol comes by and spots it.

I glance around at the neighboring trees, but there's no sign of Jody and I'm not high enough up to spot the horses. I wipe my clammy forehead and adjust my pack for the descent. I lower my right leg down and balance the toe of my boot on the branch below me. I'm getting ready to let my weight drop when a drunken voice belts out, "Whoa, livin' on a prayer."

Chapter 4

I meld with the tree trunk, my pack protruding like a swollen stick insect. It must be a patrol.

"Take my hand an' we'll make it I swe-ar."

He's coming this way.

The rough bark scrapes my cheek when I turn my head to get a better look. He's not in view yet. The only real cover is higher up in the tree, but there's no time to scale the next few branches. I'm dead anyway if he finds my water canteen. In desperation, I grab a pine cone and hurl it as far as I can into the brush. The footsteps come to an immediate halt. I hold my breath and listen. I don't know if I've bought myself enough time to make a run for it, or only prolonged the inevitable.

The Rogue mutters something to himself. He thrashes around like he's looking for something. I hear the sound of a cartridge being slammed into a gun. I swallow hard, my brain ticking over like a time bomb, as I scramble to come up with some avenue of escape. I'm fast, and he's drunk, but if I try to outrun him, I might lead him straight to the other riders. My only other option is to take him out. I reach over my shoulder and slide my rifle out of my pack.

The thrashing sounds stop. Then a rasping laugh cuts through the shadows. "*There* you are. Perched up in them branches like a scared bird with its wings all tucked in."

The nape of my neck prickles. My fingers curl with a life of their own around the trigger.

"Shimmy on down now, cowgirl, before I shoot you clean out of that tree."

Cowgirl?

I hesitate. There's a prolonged beat of silence. Several trees over, the leaves rustle and part.

"Hold your fire," Jody says. "I'm coming down."

I clamp my lips together to keep from screaming out loud. I peer tentatively into the shadows and catch the glint of a gun. I lean out a few more inches and spot the Rogue grinning up into a tree. Jody's leg dangles down from the leaves as she reaches for the branch below her. I cock my gun and take aim at the Rogue's chest. The shot will alert the camp to our presence, but I have no choice. I can't let Jody fall into The Ghost's hands.

Before I pull the trigger a whistling sound goes by my ear. The Rogue keels over with a heavy thump. Jody freezes, one leg in midair.

Heart pounding, I vault to the ground and run to her.

"Jump!" I hiss, gesturing at her to hurry.

She snaps back to life, half-sliding the rest of the way down from the tree.

She embraces me and then turns to the fallen Rogue. "Is he dead?"

I give a somber nod. The arrow protruding from his chest hit its mark with unerring accuracy. "Did you see anyone?"

She shakes her head. "It came out of nowhere."

I swivel slowly, searching the shadows for any sign of an archer. My mind races to piece it together. Could Lou have had something to do with this? Did she follow us to the Rogues' camp, despite what she said about not wanting to get involved? I didn't see a bow in her camper van, but she had venison drying, so she hunts with something more substantial than snares and traps.

"We need to hide the body," I say, repressing a shudder.

Jody points to a dense patch of ferns behind us. I grab one leg, and she reaches for an arm, and together we haul the lifeless Rogue beneath the leaves and throw enough broken boughs over him until even the wild turkey feathers on the end of the arrow shaft are covered up. I scatter several handfuls of leaves and pine needles over the drag marks. "It won't be long before the

Rogues realize he's missing. We'll have to strike soon."

"There are only two guards stationed by the horses," Jody says. "Between us we can handle them, but we won't make it out alive if we strike before the rest of the camp's asleep."

I nod. "Let's head back to the others and work out a plan."

We give the Rogues' camp a wide berth on our return trip to ensure we don't encounter any more patrols. I keep a watchful eye out for Lou, but she doesn't show herself. If she was the one who shot the patrol, she still has no intention of being drawn into our horse thieving exploits.

When we get back to the riders I fill them in on what happened and sum up our predicament.

Ida is dubious about our chances of untethering the horses and making our escape while the Rogues are still awake. The rest of the riders indicate they'll go along with whatever decision we arrive at.

"If only we could find this Lou woman and ask her to help," Ida says. "She could take out the guards for us with her bow and the Rogues wouldn't hear a thing."

I rub my brow. "It may not have been Lou. There could be any number of mountain folk living alone out here for all we know."

"So we look for *whoever* it was who nailed the Rogue and enlist their help," Jody says. "If we wait any longer to strike, we run the risk of the Rogues discovering that a guard's gone missing."

I raise my brows. "It won't be easy to find Lou if she doesn't want to be found."

"Let me save you the trouble."

I let out a yelp as someone lands on the ground behind me.

I spin around and stare at Lou. "You scared me half to death. You're like a ghost on steroids."

She smiles and leans her bow against a tree trunk. "I get plenty of practice stalking wildlife. You learn to become one with your surroundings."

I grin back at her, shaking my head in disbelief. "I knew it was you. Thanks for helping us out."

She shrugs. "You had him. But it would have been a shame to wake the rest of those thugs when I had my bow handy." She reaches into her pack and pulls out my water canteen. "This yours?"

I grimace. "Thanks, totally spaced on it." I take it and stash it in my pack. "So now that you're in the neighborhood, do you want to help us get those horses back?"

Lou folds her arms in front of her. "I don't do property disputes. I only shot the Rogue to save your lives."

"Stealing a cowgirl's horse is as good as leaving her for dead," Jody says, a dangerous glint in her eyes. "It was a hanging offense in times past."

Lou strokes her chin with her thumb and forefinger, letting her gaze travel over the riders' faces. "My corner of the woods is starting to feel more crowded than I'm comfortable with. If getting those horses back moves you on, I could be persuaded to lend an arrow to the cause."

Jody's face breaks into a smile. "I promise you won't see us for dust afterward."

Lou reaches for her bow. "I'll look for a good tree to shoot from. As soon as the guards are down, make your move. I'll cover you in the event one of the other Rogues hears something. Don't look back. I can slip through these woods like a spirit and they'll never catch a whiff of me."

"Thank you for everything." I level my eyes at her. "And I meant what I said before. You're welcome in the city anytime."

Lou nods. "I'll keep that in mind."

We follow her through the undergrowth, steering well clear of the camp's perimeter on our way to the grove where the horses are hidden. When they come into view, Lou hunkers down and studies the guards' movements for a few minutes. When she's satisfied, she selects a tree as her vantage point to shoot from. She scales it silently and efficiently, disappearing into the dark canopy above.

The riders and I creep around to the back of the grove and conceal ourselves behind a cluster of gnarled juniper trunks about thirty feet from the horses. A large chestnut mare, tethered on a short rope to a lodge pole pine, lifts her head and looks in our direction, then nickers and turns away. One of the two Rogues walking the boundary of the grove, throws a disinterested glance our way, then kicks a rock out of his path and continues on.

"Once the guards are down, stick close to me," Jody whispers. "Don't stand behind any of the horses while we're untying them. They'll be stressed and unpredictable."

I nod and settle down to wait, my breathing fast and fluttering. I glance across at the other riders, tense and ready to charge as soon as Lou's arrows find their mark. My heart pumps double time as the minutes go by. The guards make several passes back and forth along the perimeter and still nothing happens. My frustration begins to mount. What's Lou waiting for?

I shift my position and shake out a cramp in my leg. The two Rogues pause and exchange a few words before resuming their patrol. One of them stifles a yawn, and that's when the first arrow hits its target. The Rogue crumples to the ground with a muted bleat that barely reaches our ears. His partner swivels, aims his gun into the shadows, and catches an arrow straight through the heart. He pitches over and rolls down a small ridge into a hollow beyond the grove.

"Now!" Jody says.

Adrenaline spurts through my veins. I leap forward, tailing Jody as she pounds across the clearing toward Condor. He startles, then whinnies excitedly as we converge on the grove. The other horses paw the ground impatiently as the riders' fingers work to unravel the knots.

Jody flings the rope aside, grabs a stick and pole jumps onto Condor's back. "Let's ride!" she yells, extending a hand. She yanks me up behind her with a powerful tug. Before I have time to snake my hands around her waist we're off, veiled in the thick cloud of dust the agitated horses ahead of us are whipping up. We ride like the possessed, ducking beneath branches, weaving between trees, flying over downed logs and granite boulders. Behind us, I hear a cacophony of confusion and shouts, and a burst of gunfire, but it comes too late to stop the horses who seem to have sprouted wings.

In no time at all, we reach the spruce trees where Bandido is tethered. We pull up short and trot over to him, heaving for breath, but euphoric.

"Where's Ida?" Jody asks, looking around at the other riders as they canter into the clearing one by one.

We turn our heads in unison as the last horse limps into view. Behind the distraught rider, Ida's body sways back and forth like a broken reed.

Chapter 5

Jody leaps down from Condor's back and races over to help the other rider lift Ida from the lame horse. I slide clumsily to the ground and rush to their aid.

"Ida, can you hear me?" Jody pleads, smoothing a hand over her clammy cheek.

Ida groans in response.

"We couldn't ride out of there fast enough," the other rider explains. "She caught a bullet in her thigh."

"We need to get her to the clinic," I say. "We'll have to go back."

Jody knots her brow. "If you want I can send a couple of riders on to the bunkers to warn the Undergrounders."

"No, it's too dangerous to split up. Let's get that wound tied up and get out of here." I pull a shirt from my pack and tear it into strips.

Jody works to secure the makeshift bandage around Ida's leg.

I wipe the sweat from my face with what's left of the shirt and look across at the rider examining the lame horse.

"What's wrong with her?" I ask.

"Could be a torn ligament," he says. "Her leg is badly swollen. I'll take her back to the city at a pace she can handle. The rest of you go on ahead with Ida."

"I don't want to leave you behind," Jody says.

"Ida's lost a lot of blood," he says. "You need to get her to the clinic before it's too late."

Jody gives a reluctant nod. "Thanks, Curly. Watch your back out there."

The moon lurks behind a webbed fog on our return trip and visibility worsens with every step. We position Ida as best we can in front of Jody on Condor's broad back and set off. Our lead-footed pace is unnerving, especially now that we've stirred up the hornet's nest of Rogues Lou predicted. Between Ida's injury, and the shadowy hazards on the forest floor, we'll be lucky to reach the safety of Shoshane City before dawn. I hope for Curly's sake that the Rogues don't pursue us. He won't stand a chance on his own if they find him.

I adjust my rifle strap on my shoulder and fix my eyes on the murky trail. I might as well scratch The Ghost off my shrinking list of allies. He showed his true colors when he stole the horses out from under us. And after pulling off this stunt to retrieve them, I'm right up there with Rummy in the most-likely-to-be-eliminated category. My stomach twists with fear. Part of me knew this day would come. The idea of someone like The Ghost settling down in the city and taking orders from the Council is so far removed from reality that I don't know why I ever thought it would work. His agenda will always trump the common good. He did save Izzy and Brock, so he's not a total scumbag, but maybe only a child can move his heart.

The horizon is flush with an ambient ruby light by the time we arrive at the outskirts of the city. To my relief, the container gate swings wide on our approach, reassuring me that we have a guard rotation back in place. We make a beeline for the clinic and Jody and I carry Ida straight back to one of the examining rooms.

A moment later Jakob appears, dressed in scrubs. "What happened?" he asks.

"Gunshot. Where's the doctor?" I ask.

"I sent him home," Jakob says. "He's been on his feet for seventy-two hours."

Jody clenches her fists, her eyes fixed on Ida's pale, trembling lips. "Get him back here right away. We need him."

Jakob lays a hand on Jody's arm. "I can take out the bullet. Hannah will help me." He gestures to the door as a young fair-haired Septite woman walks through with an armful of freshly laundered sheets.

Jody's eyes dart to me. I give her a reassuring nod. "He knows what he's doing."

I watch as Jakob unwraps the makeshift bandage on Ida's leg and rattles off a list of supplies for Hannah to gather up. Jody smooths a hand over Ida's forehead. "I'm right here with you. You're going to be fine."

I tap Jody discreetly on the shoulder. "I need to find Jerome."

"He's gone," Jakob says, without looking up. "He left with the deviations."

I stare at his back in disbelief. I've been gone less than twenty-four hours and already the city's inhabitants are defecting. Even though we agreed it would be in the deviations' best interest to return to the Craniopolis, I didn't expect it to happen while I was gone. It still stings that my vision of a blended community is fragmenting around me faster than I can process it. "Where's Sven?"

Jakob steals a glance in my direction. "He's with Trout at the courthouse."

"I'll be there if anyone needs me," I say. I give Jody a quick shoulder squeeze in passing. "Ida's in good hands. I'll look for you back at the barn."

As I make my way to the courthouse, my stomach flutters in anticipation of seeing Sven again. I wonder what goes through his head when he thinks about us. Does he dare to dream of a future together? We haven't talked yet about what he said in the Craniopolis.

Without an expiration date, you ... I ...

So much was happening around us at the time that I convinced myself it didn't mean anything, but the truth is I knew exactly what he was saying.

I push the thought of a future with Sven to the back of my mind like I do every time it surfaces. I keep telling myself it's a moot point, but it draws me back in like a siren's call. *What if he didn't have an expiration date?*

The Septites think it's unnatural that a human would be attracted to a clone. And I suspect by the wary looks the military clones give me when I'm with Sven that they don't approve either. A human can't–shouldn't love a clone. Big Ed might disagree, he's hip to whole the idea of clones being God's creatures just like the rest of us. I know what I see when I look into Sven's eyes. He's capable of love like any other man.

On a whim, I decide to stop by the riders' barn first and check up on Big Ed, although mostly I need some perspective before I see Sven again.

I spot Big Ed dozing in a chair in the corner, his gray beard draped over his chest like an old, knotty fishing net. I take a few hesitant steps toward him, reluctant to wake him, but Tucker jumps to his feet when he sees me, barking a raucous reunion that startles Big Ed awake. He peers up at me, eyes rheumy with sleep, then smacks his gums together and pushes himself up in the chair with a grunt. "You're back. All good?"

"We found the horses. Ida took a bullet in the leg, but she's going to be all right. Jakob's taking it out right now."

Big Ed stares at me for a moment, before hefting a shaggy brow upward. "Something else on your mind?"

I sigh and pull up a chair beside him. "It's about Sven. You saw what he did for me in the Craniopolis—he offered to sacrifice himself to save Owen. I know he loves me and I want to be with him, but with an expiration date hanging over his head, what kind of future would we have?"

Big Ed puts a finger behind his spectacles and rubs his eyelid like he's waking up his thoughts.

I fidget on the edge of my chair.

He clasps his gnarled hands in his lap and looks over at me. "You get him 'til death do you part, same deal any of us get. There are no guarantees."

"But, Sven's a clone." I rake my fingers through my hair in frustration. "I'm not even sure if he's human. A lot of people are going to be weirded out by that."

Big Ed cocks his head to one side. "There weren't no natural union of man and woman in his making, but it ain't my place to say he's any less human than you or I. A man willing to sacrifice his life for you is a man capable of love."

I groan. "So you don't know if he's human either?"

Big Ed smiles. "If it helps any, he sure looks like he's made out of skin and bones same as you and me."

I grin back at him. "Which might explain why I'm falling for him."

He pats me on the knee, eyes drifting to half-mast. "In that case, don't you have someplace better to be?"

Heart fluttering with anticipation, I jog up the courthouse steps and run right into Rocco. He throws a quick glance behind him, and then grabs my arm and pulls me aside, a tad too roughly for my liking.

"Take your hands off me," I say, glaring at Sven's right hand man. "What do you think you're doing?"

He releases me, his eyes steely. "Sven wasn't expecting you back so soon."

I frown at him. "Is something wrong?"

Rocco runs a hand across his jaw. "We're relocating to the Craniopolis tomorrow. Sven's in Jerome's office finalizing a security plan with Trout."

My stomach knots. "What? Why?"

"Sven thought it would be for the best. He planned to be gone before you got back."

I clench my fists. "Sven would never leave without telling me unless he was pressured into it. Did someone warn him to stay away from me?"

Rocco shrugs, a blank look on his face.

I narrow my eyes at him. "*You'd* better not have had anything to do with this!" I elbow past him and march down the corridor to Jerome's office.

Sven and Trout look up, startled when I storm in.

"Hey!" Trout grins at me. "I take it you found the horses?"

I give a curt nod. "Ida's been shot. Jakob's taking out the bullet."

"We didn't expect you back so soon," Sven says, an uneasy look on his face.

I throw myself down in a chair. "I'm beginning to think I should never have left. Half the city is upping and moving out." I stare accusingly at Sven until he drops his gaze.

"Rocco and some of the other clones are unhappy here. They want to go back to the Craniopolis. I agreed to accompany them."

No wonder Rocco wasn't happy to see me. He's been agitating the military clones. "Well, *I* haven't agreed to anything," I retort.

Trout's brows shoot up, his eyes darting between Sven and me.

"I need to talk to Sven alone for a few minutes," I say, frowning at Trout until he gives a one-shouldered shrug and exits the office.

I wait for Sven to say something, but he won't even look at me

"Is it true?" I ask, trying to curb the emotion in my voice. "Are you leaving because of me?"

He lets out a heavy sigh. "I'm leaving because I have an expiration date and no hope of the kind of future you deserve."

"There's always hope," I say. "Overthrowing the Craniopolis was only the beginning. Lyong had a whole team of scientists working on resolving ossification. He was motivated, for his son's sake. He said he had found the DNA sequencing that caused it. What if the cure is in the research files?"

Sven shakes his head. "I can't offer you what you deserve. I can't even promise you tomorrow."

"You aren't listening to me! What if the scientists can fix you? With your enhanced immune system, you might end up living longer than any of us."

Sven smiles at me sadly. "Listen to yourself, Derry. *What if this? What if that?* I'm a clone. I can't change my destiny." He stands and swings his pack over his shoulder. "You need to be with your own kind."

"I know what I need, and it's you," I say, tears prickling my nose. "You're scared, I get it. I'm scared of my feelings too, but you make me come alive someplace deep inside. When I left the bunkers, more than anything I wanted to feel alive again."

"You and I are a fantasy," Sven takes my hand and raises it to his lips. "One day very soon I'll ossify. I can't bring any more pain to your life than you've already suffered." He kisses my hand, then turns and strides out of the room.

"Wait! Sven!" I get to my feet and grip the edge of the table, my knees too weak to support me. I sink back down in Jerome's chair and bury my head in my hands, my brain fogged with pain. I've never told Sven before how I really feel about him, never even admitted it to myself, but I meant every word I just said. If there is any possible way Sven and I can be together, it's worth fighting for with every atom of my being. My stomach tingles with a strange mixture of apprehension and exhilaration. I don't know how to make it happen, but at least I'm sure now of what I want—to be with Sven no matter how soon the end comes.

Chapter 6

It's almost noon the following day when I wake from the deep sleep I tumbled into back at the riders' barn. My mind casts about for a moment or two before I find my bearings and everything comes rushing back. I roll over and sit up, a knot of pain coiling inside me. Maybe there's still time to talk Sven out of leaving. I need something that will convince him we have a shot at a real future together. I tug my fingers through my hair and get to my feet. One of the scientists must know something about Lyong's ossification research. If there was a breakthrough of some kind, Lyong wouldn't have been able to keep it a secret from everyone in the Craniopolis. Maybe Viktor can help me get to the bottom of it.

An enticing aroma of spices toys with my senses as I pull on my boots. I stand and make my way out to the main living area. To my surprise, Owen and Nikki are seated at the far end of the dining table, deep in conversation. Tucker sits on his haunches beside them, no doubt enjoying the odd tidbit for his patience. When he sees me, he trots over and wags his tail. I ruffle his neck and he promptly drops and rolls over. I laugh and give him a quick belly rub. Owen and Nikki eye me with guarded looks when I pull up a chair. "Glad to see you're here," I say. "We haven't talked in days."

"Nikki and I had a lot of catching up to do." Owen glances in my direction, but he doesn't quite meet my eyes.

I hike my brow. "You've barely exchanged two words with me or Trout since you got here."

Owen stares down at Nikki's hand curled inside his own. "It's time Trout and I went our separate ways. I'm not a member of the Council, and I don't want any part of leading the Undergrounders anymore." He raises Nikki's fingers to his lips and kisses them. "I have another chance at a life I thought was over, and I don't want to lose it again."

"You can still be together and be a part of the community here." I look to Nikki for support, but she averts her gaze.

Owen turns to me, a resolute look in his eyes. "Nikki and I are leaving with the homesteading group."

My jaw drops. "What?"

"Some of the Undergrounders are planning to head out to the Deadwood River basin to begin homesteading. They're worried about residual radiation from the Superconductor."

"And it hasn't helped to have all these clones and deviations milling around either," Nikki adds. "Not to mention the Rogues."

I frown. "The Undergrounders did a good job of chasing the deviations out of town already."

Nikki throws me a dark look. "They're happier in an environment that makes sense to them."

I want to point out that we didn't do a very good job of helping them make sense of anything, but I bite my lip. "What if another outpost resumes the sweeps?"

"Lyong could have been jerking our chain about the outposts," Owen says. "Even if they do exist, they could be halfway around the world. We might never see another Hovermedes. We can't live here in limbo forever."

I stare at him, at a loss for words. Everything we sacrificed for is fracturing around us, but maybe this is how it's meant to be; survivors forging a new path. We fought for freedom, and now I get to see what it looks like up close. Messy, discordant, experimental. I can't dictate what people should do or where they ought to live.

"Jakob and Hannah are coming with us," Nikki adds.

I raise my brows. I did wonder if there was something more than a working relationship between them, but I'm happy for them. They suit each other.

"You should think about joining us," Owen says.

A vision of a Septite homesteading future flashes before me. Whatever life units Sven has left, I can't imagine him spending it herding goats and growing vegetables. I feel a certain obligation to Owen. He was everything to me when Ma died and Da took to the bottle, but I don't owe him the rest of my life. I want to spend it with Sven. "I've made a commitment to the Council," I say. "I'm going to stay here and help rebuild the city with the military clones."

Owen raises his brows, but before he has a chance to respond, an Undergrounder walks over and plants a pot of stew and a stack of bowls in the middle of the table.

"Thanks," I say, grabbing the ladle. Several more Undergrounders drift over to the table. I dish out a serving for each of us, grateful for the distraction. I gulp down my stew, eager to escape the dining hall before the topic of Sven comes up. Owen may suspect that Sven is the real reason I don't want to leave the city, but I'm not ready yet to admit to my brother that I'm in love with a clone.

"Catch you guys later," I say, shoving my chair out from the table. "I need to speak to Viktor before he leaves for the Craniopolis." Tucker jumps up, tongue dangling in anticipation of a hunt or a run. I toss him a lump of fatty rind and leave him in Owen's care.

I make my way across town, pushing down thoughts of losing Owen again. I can't go with him and the other homesteaders. My heart is with Sven now. I need to find a way to help him before it's too late.

Viktor and the rest of the scientists are housed in a former office building in an old section of town close to Nikki's apartment. The boarded-up block is an unappealing square of soot-colored brick, retrofitted with plywood boards to keep the warmth in, but the light out–a fact that doesn't seem to bother the scientists. Most of the time they're more content to sit in darkness than mingle with the Undergrounders and enjoy the sights and sounds outside. Big Ed says they're traumatized now that they're out of Lyong's clutches and able to process what they were a part of all those years.

I yank open the makeshift plywood entry door, and step into the foyer.

Inside, the air is stuffy and smells of old boxes of newspapers and years of mold. It takes several minutes for my eyes to grow accustomed to the dusky space. Three shadowy figures, seated in office chairs with broken wheels, stare in my direction. I shiver. The place has the feel of an abandoned asylum.

"Is Viktor here?" I call over to them.

One of them points to the stairway at the back of the foyer.

I smile a quick thank you at their expressionless faces and hurry up the splintered flight of stairs.

Viktor is seated in a corner of what was once a communal office kitchen. He's clutching a closed book in his hand and staring at a spot on the floor in front of him. His face twitches when he sees me, almost as if I've caught him doing something wrong.

"I wanted to talk to you before you leave for the Craniopolis." I slip my rifle off my shoulder and rest it against the wall.

His beady eyes are watchful as I sit down opposite him. "What about?" He brushes a finger down his beaked nose.

"What do you know about Lyong's research on ossification?"

Viktor tenses. He purses his pillowy lips. "It was classified."

I lean toward him, our knees almost touching. "Perhaps you stumbled across something?"

His eyes flash with fear. "It's dangerous to ask such questions."

I give a bewildered laugh. "Why? Lyong's gone."

"His eyes are everywhere."

"Trust me, they're not in here."

He casts a discomfited glance over my shoulder, then edges forward in his seat. "There were rumors of a breakthrough at another outpost. I hacked into Lyong's files. He was working out some sort of arrangement to take his son Sook there."

I churn the information over in my brain for a moment. "So the only way to reverse ossification in the clones is to take them to this other outpost?"

Viktor blinks. "If the rumors are true, then yes."

"Where is this outpost?"

"I don't know."

"But you could get the coordinates?"

Viktor furrows his brow, a sheen of sweat glistening on his upper lip. "I could try and contact them, but it's risky. If they find out what happened at the Craniopolis—"

"They won't. You only have to secure the coordinates."

Viktor gives an unconvincing nod.

I have a feeling he's holding something back from me. But he could just be afraid of what might happen. It's a risk to contact the outpost, but it's worth it if it means there's a chance of revoking Sven's expiration date.

"When will the communication line between the Craniopolis and the city be operational?" I ask.

"Everything's set up on this side," Viktor says. "I'll activate the signal once I'm at the Craniopolis."

I reach for my rifle. "I'll wait to hear from you."

A light afternoon breeze has picked up by the time I get back to the main street. A hawk hang-glides overhead, charting a course north to the mountains. I walk briskly past the Aquaponics Center in the direction of the riders' barn. I want to try to catch Sven before he leaves and tell him what I've found out so far. If nothing else, I need to make him understand that he doesn't have to resign himself to an imminent expiration date.

I round a corner and frown at the crowd gathered a short distance from the container gate, an uneasy mix of clones and Undergrounders engaged in a heated exchange of words. I can't tell from here what's going on, but it looks like they're standing around someone or something.

I increase my pace, eager to put a swift end to any disagreement that could lead to a fight between the factions. When I reach the group I shoulder my way to the center and pull up short. Lying in their midst is an ossifying clone, his skeletal fingers curved upward like beckoning talons, his taut skin a charcoal-still-life gray. I watch with horror as the remnants of his skin crumble to powder and drift to the ground like dirty snow.

A paunchy, flat-faced Undergrounder beside me shoots me a repulsed look. "We don't want this in our city. It's unnatural, keeling over and dying like that. It's freaking the children out."

"We didn't ask to die this way," one of the military clones retorts. "Just like you didn't ask to have your DNA canned for cloning. The Sweepers are the monsters behind this. Why don't you haul the scientists out in the streets right now and take your revenge on them?"

The rest of the clones pin me with steely gazes that demand my backing.

"You know as well as I do the scientists who are here were against what was going on in the Craniopolis," I say. "They wanted out."

"Or they wanted to end up on the winning side when they realized the writing was on the wall," another clone says.

"He's right," the flat-faced Undergrounder chimes in. "We don't know what their motives were for coming out with us." He glares at the military clone. "Or *your*s either."

The clone grabs him by the neck and lifts him several inches off the ground. The Undergrounder makes a choking sound, scrabbling with his hands to work himself free.

I pull out my gun and point it at the clone. "Let him go!"

He drops his hostage and backs away scowling. Before I have a chance to say anything more, a horn sounds and the gate to the city groans open in front of us. My heart sinks when a riderless horse limps through.

Chapter 7

Something's happened to Curly.

The Undergrounders and the clones throw me questioning looks, but I don't offer any explanation. I don't want to sound the alarm yet that something's wrong. I walk up to the horse and take it by the reins. "Take care of the clone's remains. I'll handle the horse." I lead it off in the direction of the rider's barn, a sickening feeling building inside me with every step. There's only one reason Curly didn't come back with the lame horse. The Rogues must have caught up with him. He could be dead by now, or The Ghost could be planning to use him to barter with me if he suspects that I'm hiding Rummy from him.

The walk from the city gate to the barn has never seemed longer. I'm not sure how I'm going to break it to the other riders that Curly didn't make it back. I brace myself as I head inside the stable. A young rider by the door jumps to his feet. A look of alarm flits across his face. Wordlessly, he takes the reins from me and leads the horse into a stall to examine her leg. "Where did you find her?" he asks.

"At the main gate. She came back alone."

He nods, his lips pressed together as he prepares a poultice.

We leave unspoken what we both fear most, that Curly has fallen into the Rogues' hands.

Minutes later, Jody arrives back from the clinic. Her face blanches when I give her the news. "First Ida, now this," she mutters, sinking down on a stool.

Nothing I can say will make this any easier for her. Just the thought of what The Ghost might do to Curly is enough to send chills down my spine. He's not going to be in a merciful mood after we took the horses right out from under the Rogues' noses.

"I'm going to ride back out there and look for Curly," Jody says. "He wouldn't leave one of us behind."

I nod. "I'll go with you. Give me a few minutes. I'll meet you at the main gate."

I stop by the sleeping quarters at the back of the barn first, hoping to catch Trout, but no one's seen him all morning. I leave a note for him on his bunk, naming him interim chief in my absence, to be made permanent in the event I don't return. I'm not under any illusions about our chances of rescuing Curly without casualties. A few riders are no match for the Rogues. Maybe I can talk Sven and the military clones into coming with us instead of returning to the Craniopolis. Anything to keep him with me a little longer.

"Have the military clones left yet?" I ask when I make my way back out to the stable.

Jody shakes her head. "Sven's heading over to the courthouse to pick up some things Jerome wanted from his office."

My mood is somber as I jog back to the courthouse. The Ghost knows we're not going to leave Curly behind. He'll be expecting us. This is a doomed rescue attempt unless I can swing the odds.

I take the courthouse steps two at a time and corner Sven in Jerome's office. He jumps up when he sees me. "Derry! What's wrong?"

"The Rogues captured Curly. The lame horse arrived back at the gate a few minutes ago without him."

Sven stares at me, expressionless, only the throbbing pulse in the side of his neck betraying whatever emotion he's fighting to control.

"The riders risked their lives for us. We owe it to them to attempt a rescue. Please, Sven, this isn't about you and me. Curly needs your help."

He blinks and inhales a sudden breath as if coming to. "I'll round up the military clones. Rocco can escort the scientists back to the Craniopolis and then return to the city. The military clones will have to stay here in case the Rogues attack."

I shoot him a heartfelt look of gratitude. He takes a hesitant step toward me and then stops, as though he still suspects me of somehow staging the whole thing to keep him here. "I'll meet you at the gate in five minutes," he says, exiting abruptly.

I grab the binoculars from Jerome's desk and tuck them under my arm. They could come in useful if we're trying to spot Curly in the Rogues' camp.

We ride hard out of town, the fleet-footed military clones easily keeping pace with the horses. When we reach the forest we avoid the trail and begin thrashing our way through the dogwoods and ferns. We hike for several hours at an increasingly halting pace until we reach the location where the Rogues made camp. A disquieting chill settles over us. All that remains is an ominous ring of stones and cold ashes.

Jody quickly pinpoints the Rogues' departing trail. The recent rain has softened the dirt and the heels of their heavy boots have left their imprint in the mud, even tracking it over the logs they stepped on. Jody examines the telltale signs and tosses a few broken twigs aside, her face grim. "The bracken here is smashed to a pulp. They're not trying to cover their tracks. They want us to find them."

"So we're walking into a trap," Sven says.

I take a deep breath. "The Ghost wants me. He can't get past the fact that I let Rummy escape." I look around at the others, my heartbeat tripping in my throat. "He'll take me in exchange for Curly. No one else has to get hurt–"

Jody cuts me off with a sour look. "Don't even go there. I don't make deals with horse thieves," she snaps, before disappearing beneath a thick, dark canopy of trees framing the trail.

I'm fairly certain by the looks on the other riders' faces as they fall in behind her that they would have taken the deal if Jody hadn't cut me off. Sven gestures to the military clones to go ahead of us. I throw him a grateful look. This could be my only chance to bring him up to speed on my conversation with Viktor before the military clones return to the Craniopolis. We walk along in silence for a few minutes before I build up the courage to broach the topic. "I talked to Viktor earlier. Lyong was telling the truth about resolving ossification. There was a breakthrough at one of the other outposts."

Sven's stride falters, but he keeps his eyes forward.

I grab his sleeve. "Sven! You know what this means. They can fix you, you and everyone else." I gesture to the clones on the trail ahead of us.

He presses his lips together, his expression strained. For several minutes he continues pounding his way through the brush, and then he comes to a halt and turns to me. "How does Viktor know about this?"

"Same way he intercepted the transmission from the Megamedes. He hacked into Lyong's files."

"All speculation," Sven says. "The scientists at the outpost could have been exaggerating their progress."

"I don't think so. Lyong was planning to take Sook there."

The dubious expression on Sven's face morphs into one of curiosity.

I bite my lip, trying to keep from grinning wildly. "Viktor's going to secure the outpost's coordinates."

A deep flush creeps over Sven's face. His amber eyes lock with mine. For one dreadful moment I think he's going to tell me that I'm wasting my time, chasing a fantasy, that we should give up on the dream of growing old together, but before I realize what's happening his lips are pressed to mine, smooth and potent, an explosion from which I know I will never recover.

When he releases me, the fragments of my brain slowly resurface, and I become aware of a pair of military clones observing us in icy silence. I steal a harried glance at Sven. He lifts his brows, somehow asking my forgiveness while looking remarkably unrepentant.

"You fell behind," one of the clones says, staring at me. "We came back to check on you."

Cheeks burning, I beat a hasty retreat after the rest of the group, savoring the lingering taste of Sven's lips on mine.

We follow the Rogues' trail for a couple of hours until we reach a fast-flowing stream where we break to let the horses drink. Jody wanders off and comes back a few minutes later. "We're closing in on them," she says. "We should go on foot from here. There's a copse up ahead. It's not far from the trail, but well-concealed. We can leave the horses tethered there."

"We need to work out a plan to rescue Curly," Sven says.

"We won't have the advantage of Lou's arrows this time," Jody says. "We'll have to wait until nightfall to rescue him."

I furrow my brow. "That's exactly what The Ghost will be expecting us to do. We need to think more along the lines of ambush."

Sven folds his arms across his chest. "What kind of ambush?"

"Something that will make them scatter and give us a chance to get Curly out," I say. "We'll attack on two fronts. Once they're camped for the night, half of us can push ahead on the trail and climb up into the trees and wait for them. When they come through, we'll pick them off, while the rest of us strike from the rear. The Rogues will be confused and forced to split up to defend themselves, and that's when the riders swoop in and rescue Curly."

"I like it," Sven says.

Jody massages her brow. "We'll need to do some recon before the Rogues break for camp. I want to find out how they're transporting Curly, how many guards are assigned to him, that sort of thing. If Curly's on his feet, it will make our getaway easier. If he's injured, it will complicate things."

"I'll come with you," I say.

Jody nods. Without another word she turns and slips into the brush.

My eyes linger on Sven's for a moment, before I follow Jody into the undergrowth.

A pair of squirrels exchange a burst of sharp chatter and disappear with a flick of their tails up into a nearby pine tree as we go by. The ground is still damp, muffling the sound of our footsteps, but we tread with caution nonetheless. Even a snapped twig would be enough to herald our approach to a patrol so we take the time to weave around obstacles in our path.

Visibility is hampered by the copious undergrowth and the canopy of greenery up above, beyond which I can make out a few smudges of a silver-gray sky. I wipe my sleeve over my sweaty forehead and reach around to the side pocket of my pack for my water canteen.

All at once Jody drops and motions to me to do the same. I flatten myself beneath the understory and peer out, searching for any sign of movement. Minutes tick by before the faint sound of voices drifts toward me. Jody crawls lizard-like over to me. "They're east of us," she whispers. "If we climb up on that ridge we can get a good look." She points at a steep slope, slick with soggy half-mulched leaves and patches of rotten bracken. A few stringy roots offer the only helping hand up.

"We'll have to take a run at it," I say. I rummage around in my pack for Jerome's binoculars and hang them around my neck, before tossing my pack to one side.

Jody rests her pack up against mine. "Ready when you are."

Together we charge the slope and reach for the roots. I dig my toes into the wall of dirt and pull with all my strength to work myself up. My wiry contortions beat Jody to it and I realize with satisfaction that I've grown stronger in the past few months.

We take a minute to catch our breath and then jog up a more gently sloping section to the very top of the ridge. I kneel and train my binoculars on a clearing on the trail up ahead. Within minutes, the first Rogues emerge from the trees. They tromp along, single file, rifles slung casually over their shoulders. I spot The Ghost almost at once, his casual gait belying the cunning that lurks inside his whip-thin frame. Blade follows a few feet behind him, a wool cap pulled low over his eyes. The nape of my neck prickles at the sight of him. "The Ghost's near the front," I whisper to Jody, all too conscious of how far my voice might carry from the ridge top.

"Any sign of Curly?" she asks.

I shake my head, keeping my binoculars trained on the ant-like procession. I count seventeen Rogues go by, before I finally spot him, staggering along on a leash behind a short, pudgy Rogue with a duck-like stride. "Got him!" I shove the binoculars at Jody.

She grimaces. "Looks like he's limping."

"How many Rogues are behind him?" I ask.

"Two … three … I think that's it. No, here come a bunch more."

Jody thrusts the binoculars back at me. "I don't want to wait until morning. Curly's not in good shape. I say we take our chances and attack as soon as it turns dark. Even if they're waiting for us this time, we'll have the advantage with the military clones and their enhanced vision."

Without waiting for my response, Jody turns and strides off down the slope. I jump up, still clutching the binoculars, and break into a jog after her. My heel slips in the loose dirt and I tumble forward, grasping in vain with my free hand at a branch just out of reach as I careen down the mulch-covered slope to the forest floor below. I land with a soft thud in a bed of leaves and pine needles and scramble to my hands and knees, unhurt, but shaking with fear. I stretch out my fingers for the strap of the binoculars and pull them toward me, heart pounding. Did the Rogues hear me fall? I grab my pack and gun and hunker down in the brush. A few feet behind me, a woodpecker hammers furiously on the bark of a nearby tree. I jerk my head in the bird's direction and freeze when a tattooed face peers back at me.

Chapter 8

Rummy!

My thoughts zap around in my head like I'm being electrocuted. Should I run? Shoot before he does? Yell to warn Jody? I take a shallow breath, toxic fear flooding my lungs. I can't wait for him to make the first move. My fingers tighten around the barrel of my gun. When I raise it, Rummy puts a finger to his lips and flattens himself against the trunk of a tree.

A swishing sound stills my heartbeat. The thud of footsteps. Someone's moving through the understory toward us. The hairs on my clammy skin stand on end. The Rogues must have heard something. I squeeze my eyes shut and listen. The rustling stops, and I hear the sound of someone relieving himself in the bushes only a few feet from me. I hold my breath until the swishing resumes and the footsteps fade away.

When I dare to peek out again, Rummy has disappeared. I scan the surrounding trees and peer nervously over my shoulder, but I can't spot him anywhere. I wait for what seems like an eternity before crawling out from my hiding spot. One eye on my surroundings, I brush the worst of the mud and leaves from my clothes. Jody appears at the top of the ridge, and I signal to her that it's safe to come down. She turns away from me and makes a graceful descent, using the roots for support as she lowers herself back to the ground.

"Lucky break," she says. "I thought for sure the patrol was on to you."

"We're not out of danger yet," I say, throwing a nervous glance over her shoulder.

She frowns. "What's wrong?"

"Rummy's here. Hiding out. He must be trying to contact Blade."

Jody's eyes widen. "Did he see you?"

"Yeah, but he won't give me up. The last person he wants to talk to is The Ghost."

"No telling what he might do to save his own skin." Jody furrows her brow. "It's too dangerous to try to rescue Curly now with the patrol lagging behind and Rummy nosing around. We should stick to our original plan and set up an ambush."

I pull my lips into a tight line. "Rummy better not mess this up." I shoulder my pack and give the straps a quick tug to secure it. "If he makes his move before us, he'll put the Rogues on high alert, and whatever chance we have of rescuing Curly will be shot."

Sven looks visibly relieved when we show back up. "I was about to go searching for you. What took you so long?"

"We had a close call," I say. "Turns out Rummy's following the Rogues too."

Sven whistles. "He doesn't want to leave without Blade."

I nod. "That's my guess."

"It could complicate things for us," Jody says.

"I'll tell the clones to keep an eye out for him," Sven says. "What do you want us to do if we spot him?"

"Take him alive," I say. "He may agree to help us once he hears our plan. It would be his best shot of getting Blade out of there."

We load up our gear and continue tracking the Rogues from a safe distance until the dappled green light on the trail fades to dusk and the patchworked forest floor assumes a nighttime pall. Amidst the shadows, we creep silently closer to where the Rogues are setting up camp. From beneath a dense patch of ferns, I watch the activity through binoculars. The campfire in the center flickers and snaps to the sound of muffled chatter. Several armed guards patrol the perimeter. I grimace. The Ghost isn't about to make the same mistake twice.

I turn to Sven. "We should split up now. I'll take half the military clones ahead on the trail and scout out the best spots for sniper positions."

"I'm coming with you," Sven says. "My men can handle the rear attack."

I'm still shaken from my encounter with Rummy so I don't argue with him. This time, I want Sven at my side. "Tell your men to follow the Rogues as soon as they break camp in the morning. No one's to fire off a shot until we confirm Curly's position. We can't take the chance of him being hit in the crossfire."

Sven wastes no time dividing the clones into two groups. "Wait for my signal to attack," he instructs the group that will strike from the rear.

I turn to Jody. "You and the rest of the riders flank the Rogues from the east and get Curly out of there as soon as they scatter."

Jody gives a curt nod. She turns to go but then hesitates. "Whatever happens, thank you for coming. Curly would have done the same for any of us in a heartbeat." She reaches for her pack and gestures to the riders to follow her.

Sven and I take the first group of clones on a circuitous route around the Rogues' camp, clambering over downed trees and traversing streams to avoid any chance of encountering a patrol. Once we're a safe distance ahead on the trail, we start searching for the best section of forest canopy to conceal ourselves in. We need to be situated far enough back from the trail to be protected from random shots, but close enough to allow for accuracy when it comes to picking off the Rogues.

After some debate, we settle on a dense patch of oak, birch, and hemlock trees of varying heights. "We might as well eat first and rest for a few hours before we get into position." I toss my pack down. "We won't see any action until morning." I offer some jerky around, but the clones decline and pull out sachets of lyophilized food.

"You can't live off that stuff forever," I say. "Jerky's a much more rewarding experience anyway—gives you something to chew on."

A smile tugs at the corners of Sven's mouth. He's become accustomed to real food, but it took some time for his stomach to adjust. I can't help but wonder what he'd think of a pint of chocolate chip ice cream, or a giant bag of nacho cheese-flavored chips. Saliva pools beneath my tongue. I wet my lips, caught off guard by a slew of forgotten memories triggered by my senses.

After we eat, Sven assigns the first shift to two military clones, and the rest of us bed down in the foliage, burrowing into the thick layers of half-mulched leaves to keep warm. I shiver, eying the shadowy canopy above with sleepy eyes. My thoughts turn to Rummy. Stumbling across him earlier was a shocker. I don't know why he didn't make tracks out of here days ago and put as much distance between himself and The Ghost as possible. Does he really think he can talk his brother into deserting? That might be why The Ghost is keeping Blade close by his side—he's using him as bait to draw Rummy in. I yawn and shift around to make myself more comfortable, the Rogues' tattooed faces gradually blurring together in my mind.

When I wake, only half-lucid, Sven towers over me. "It's almost dawn."

I sit up and wipe the sleep from my eyes. "Where are the clones?"

He points above my head. "They're in position. I tried to wake you earlier but you were so groggy that I took pity on you."

I run my hands through my tousled hair.

"There's a decent oak tree over there with plenty of perches," Sven says. "Room for two."

I throw him a wary look. "Sounds cozy, but we'll be more effective if we spread out. I don't need you to cover me."

"No, but you are gonna need a leg up." He grins. "The lowest branch is head height, *my* head height."

I take a quick detour into the brush before making my way over to where Sven is standing beneath a sprawling oak tree. He's not kidding about its height. The trunk yawns upward as far as I can stretch my neck to see, its girth easily ten feet across. The tree's dense, wide-spreading branches and plateaus of leaves create a colossal living umbrella, ideal for concealing several people. Clustered around it are hemlocks, the drooping, feathery ends of their branches adding another layer of seclusion to our hiding spot.

Sven gives me a leg up and I begin a painstaking ascent, securing the heel of my boot with every step before I push off to the next branch.

By the time I reach a height that allows me a full view of the trail, snatches of streaky bacon sky are peeking through the foliage. Any time now the Rogues will be heading north again. I crawl into a generous fork between two boughs and balance precariously against the trunk, the thick, irregular scales of bark protruding into my back. I resign myself to the most uncomfortable wait of my life. At least the pain will keep me from nodding off and tumbling to the ground below.

I run through our plan again in my head. Everything depends on the element of surprise. And for that, we need Rummy to lie low. If we can wreak enough havoc on the Rogues and force them to scatter, it will give the riders an opportunity to get Curly out of there. But if the Rogues decide to fight, we could be in for a bloody battle with the same men who, only days earlier, fought with us against the Sweepers. It all seems so pointless. If only The Ghost could forget Rummy and let the past go.

I stiffen at muffled voices. A moment later someone barks out an order that carries through the tree tops. I signal to Sven, but the clones are already on alert.

Their enhanced faculties are a huge advantage in a situation like this.

I can't gauge how far away the Rogues are. I get into position to shoot, but my muscles quickly cramp up and I stretch back out, listening for footsteps. Before long, the sound of a large number of people moving through the brush reaches my ears. When the first Rogue strides into view, I clench my jaw and line up my sight. Four, five, eight armed men go by. A trickle of sweat inches its way down one side of my nose but I don't dare move a finger to swipe at it.

Several more Rogues appear and then I spot The Ghost and Blade. I signal to Sven to get ready.

Another handful of Rogues march by, scanning the brush on either side of the trail. Still no sign of Curly. My nerves are beginning to unravel. He was limping yesterday. Maybe they moved him to the back of the pack so he doesn't hold them up. Not a safe position once the second group of military clones attacks from the rear.

My apprehension turns to dread when the last of the Rogues march by—followed by a heavily armed patrol. I throw a quick glance in Sven's direction.

He raises his brows questioningly, and I signal to him to hold his fire.

The Rogues bootlace through the trees until they're out of sight and their footsteps have deadened. My pulse hammers in my temples. Did they kill Curly? Or leave him somewhere for dead? Either way, we're going to have to backtrack and look for him. I whistle like a wood thrush to signal to the clones that we're retreating. Ignoring Sven's offer of assistance, I jump from the last branch and land with a soft thud in a thick carpet of moss. A moment later Jody and the riders emerge from the forest. "What happened?" Jody asks. "We waited for your signal."

"I exhale. "He wasn't with them."

Jody's eyes burrow into me. Alarm works its way across her face. "We have to find him."

"We will, but you need to … prepare yourself."

She sways gently back and forth as if reeling from the insinuation that Curly might be dead. Her eyes moisten. "If they killed him, we might never find him. They could have buried him anywhere."

The brush behind us rustles. A sinister laugh sets my skin on fire. "Curly ain't two foot under yet."

Chapter 9

Jody and I spin around in unison. The bushes part and Rummy steps through, shoving a disheveled Curly in front of him. "This the cowboy you're looking for?"

Jody takes a step toward him, but I lay a hand on her arm when Rummy reaches for his gun.

"What do you want?" I say.

A sneer flicks across his lips. "Out o' the kindness of my bleedin' heart I'm gonna give you what y'all's looking for and I ain't asking for nothin' in return." He nudges Curly in our direction. Jody and another rider rush over to him, grab him by the arms and help him over to a granite boulder.

"Where did you find him?" Sven asks.

Rummy's eyes narrow to glassy slits. "Them dawgs left him tied to a stump. Figured he'd decompose right along with it."

"I guess we owe you one," I say with some reluctance. Rummy doesn't give favors for free. My biggest fear is that he'll ask us to help him get to Blade.

"This one's won't cost you, Butterface." He slings his rifle over his shoulder. "I ain't cashing in yet, but I know where to find you." He turns and winds his way back into the brush until he's lost from view.

I take a few deep breaths before turning to Jody. She stares back at me in stunned silence.

Curly shakes his head. "Why did he help me?"

"Because I helped him escape from The Ghost once," I say. "Let's go before he changes his mind about cashing in."

It's mid-morning by the time we reach Shoshane City. The container gates swing wide on our approach and we trot through, weary and overcome with relief. Shouts of excitement ring out from the watchtower when the guards spot Curly. They sound the horn to alert the city. Jody waves up at them and then makes a beeline to the clinic with Curly.

"I'm going to do a quick check of our security around the barricade," Sven says. "We've been lax of late, but with Rummy and The Ghost roaming free again, we'd best be prepared for anything."

I exchange a few words with the watchtower guards before heading over to Jerome's office at the courthouse. Trout's face lights up when he sees me. We embrace briefly before I collapse into a chair opposite him.

"I couldn't believe it when I read your note," Trout says. "What were you thinking going after Curly without me?"

"I couldn't find you," I say.

His face falls. "I went to Panju's grave. By the time I got back to the barn you were gone."

"Is Tucker all right?"

"Snug as a bug curled up with Big Ed," Trout replies. "I heard the horn. So you found Curly?"

I cock an eyebrow at him. "Rummy did. And he turned him over to us no strings attached."

Trout's eyes widen. "Where's Curly now?"

"At the clinic. He twisted his ankle, but thankfully the Rogues didn't rough him up too much."

"And Rummy?"

I trace my fingertips over my brow. "He's still tracking the Rogues, hoping to lure Blade away from The Ghost."

Trout leans back in his chair. "Maybe that's not what Blade wants."

"That's what I'm afraid of. He might turn Rummy in."

We fall silent for a moment or two. There's a good chance The Ghost's playing Blade for a fool. Rummy's a doomed man if he doesn't give up on this insane quest. He should have taken the chance I gave him and disappeared.

"Did Rocco escort the scientists back to the Craniopolis?" I ask.

"Yeah, he's back already," Trout says. "Been quiet around here without you. Some of the homesteaders are packing up."

"When are they leaving?"

"Week or two, I'm guessing. It's a big operation. They're transplanting seedlings from the vegetable gardens into wagons and building a portable fish tank to set up an Aquaponics system." Trout peers at me from beneath his brows. "You know Owen and Nikki talked Jakob and Hannah into joining them."

I nod. "They'll be good additions, with their medical knowledge. Any word from Viktor?"

Trout shakes his head. "Not yet. He should have a communications line up and running by tomorrow."

I chew on my bottom lip. "Viktor told me Lyong was planning to take Sook to the outpost with the ossification breakthrough. If the rumors are true, it means they can fix the clones."

Trout lets out an amused snort. "You mean, *Sven*."

I throw him an irritated look. "Sven and the rest of them."

A hint of a grin comes across Trout's face. "I still think it's weird, him being a clone and all, but he really likes you and I gotta hand it to him, it was a brave thing he did in the Craniopolis, offering to take Owen's place." He leans across the table. "If they can override his expiration date, does that mean Sven's not a clone anymore? You two could hook up for real then."

"Shut up, Trout! This is important. It could change everything for the clones."

"Just saying, it's *way* weird."

We spin around when an Undergrounder bursts into the office. "The Craniopolis just made contact with the Superconductor."

Trout and I exchange surprised looks. Viktor made quick work of setting up a communications line. A ripple of unease goes through me, but I dismiss it. Viktor works for us now. I have to trust he's not in contact with anyone else.

"Let's head over there," I say. "I need to talk to Viktor and Jerome."

Trout gets to his feet. "What about?"

I hesitate. He knows how I feel about Sven. What's the point in hiding the truth from him? "I want to know if Viktor's made contact with the outpost yet. Every day that goes by is one less I have to spend with Sven."

Trout gives a sympathetic nod. Despite all his joking around, he understands better than anyone after losing Panju.

"And we still need to figure out what the scientists' role will be now that Sektor Sieben and the cloning operation are shut down," I add. "Supposedly the scientists were involved in all sorts of research to benefit humankind, not all of which would have had Hippocrates turning over in his grave." I push myself out of my chair. "They're gonna need something to keep them busy."

"Out of trouble you mean," Trout says, following me out of the room.

On our way to the Superconductor, we bump into Jakob leaving the clinic. "Glad you made it back safely," he says, hugging me. He slaps Trout on the shoulder.

"How's Curly?" I ask.

"Beat up and dehydrated. He sprained his ankle, but he's going to be fine."

"Believe it or not, Rummy saved his life."

Jakob raises his brows. "So I heard. Could mean trouble headed our way. Sven has increased security all around the barricade to be safe."

"Rummy's tracking the Rogues, trying to lure Blade away from The Ghost. I don't think he'll bother us anymore." The empty words echo through my head. Something tells me we haven't seen the last of Rummy.

"Where are you off to now?" Jakob asks.

"The Superconductor," Trout says. "Viktor's got a communications line up and running. He's transmitting from the Craniopolis."

"I just finished my shift at the clinic." Jakob sticks a thumb in his overalls. "I'll walk over there with you."

My smile freezes. I don't particularly want Jakob privy to my desperate bid to help Sven. Neither he nor Hannah approves of our budding relationship.

I shrug. "Whatever."

Trout winks at me in my perplexity. I reward him with a scathing look.

The main street is chock full of half-loaded wooden wagons as we walk by. I stare curiously at the caravan of supplies piled high. Some of the carts are built like large flats to house a variety of seedlings, others are outfitted with sides and rails to transport goats and chickens. The whole scene has a pioneer nostalgia to it, except in this case the threat on the trail will be tattooed subversives and possibly a Hovermedes or two.

I rub the back of my neck as I survey the assembled wagons. I still have a couple of weeks to talk Owen and Nikki out of leaving. We can't play settlers until we've secured the land, and that will take time.

"We're almost ready to pull out," Jakob says, grinning over at Trout and me. "Hannah and I are building a medical cart to bring along."

"Does it have sirens?" Trout hefts a shaggy brow upward.

Despite my frustration, I can't help but laugh. What would I do without Trout to lighten the weight I carry?

We make our way across the city and past several boarded-up office blocks. Charred billboards festoon the few buildings still standing in this hard-hit section of town, the random words in the advertisements too disfigured to decipher. The asphalt was ripped from the road during the meltdown and tossed about like regurgitated entrails. Gaping fissures yawn their way to the center of the earth and apocalypse-tolerant weeds hide in cracks between concrete walls snapped in half like crackers.

"Check this out!" Trout kicks aside a chunk of signage with faded Chinese characters on it. "I just hit the motherlode." He digs out a moldy cardboard box filled with fortune cookies—crushed crumbs for the most part—still sealed in plastic.

"Who wants to know their future?" he asks, waving a handful of cookies at us.

"Later," I say. "Let's grab some and eat them later. Viktor's waiting on us."

We each snatch a handful of cookies and stuff them into our jackets, then clamber through the rest of the debris until we reach the perimeter chain link fence surrounding the superconductor.

The metal entry doors to the facility swing wide when I activate the keypad. The cool interior wraps itself like a shawl around me and a low-level harmonic humming fills my ears, a pleasant alternative to the charged snapping sound when the superconductor is running. A scientist sits in front of a large touchscreen, rapidly repositioning strings of code as her fingers fly across the screen.

She startles on our approach and clears the screen with a flick of her finger.

"Everything okay?" I ask, frowning at the blank screen.

"We had a minor hiccup with the communications line," she says, with a hollow laugh. "The good news is it's all straightened out now and you can talk to Viktor whenever you like."

I let my gaze travel over her face. *And so can you.* My gut tells me she was up to something. And that might mean Viktor's up to something too. After all, he was the one who picked which scientists stayed at the Superconductor and which ones returned with him to the Craniopolis. It makes sense he would leave someone behind whom he trusts.

"Get Viktor on the line now," I say, exchanging a wary look with Trout and Jakob.

The woman walks over to the CommCenter and twists a couple of knobs. A loud crackling erupts.

"What's wrong?" I ask.

"Bear with me," she says. "Viktor is working out some bugs on his end." She makes a few adjustments and a moment later an image materializes on the screen. Viktor's face blurs in and out of view several times and then comes into focus.

"Can you hear me?" he asks.

"Loud and clear," I say. "Congratulations. You made short work of connecting us."

Viktor bows his head, an odd, turtle-like movement that allows him to scan the entire room. I swear his eyes flick some coded message to the scientist behind me. My scalp prickles. On the Richter scale of suspicious, this is scoring a nine point five.

"How are the deviations settling back in?" I ask.

"They're relieved to be back in familiar surroundings," Viktor replies. "Jerome is overseeing their reintegration."

"Can we get Jerome on this line too? I want to talk to both of you."

Viktor swishes a finger over the mole on his left cheek. "Jerome is tied up with some resettlement issues. The deviations are traumatized by everything that's happened." He gives an apologetic wave of his hand. "Jerome's the only one who can handle them."

The niggling feeling in my stomach harmonizes with my prickling scalp. It doesn't make sense that Jerome can't spare a few minutes to talk to me. "All right," I say, with some reluctance. "Have him contact me as soon as he's able."

Viktor does that irritating pigeon dip with his head again.

"Any more transmissions?" I ask.

Viktor's beady gray eyes fixate on me. "As a matter of fact, I intercepted a transmission earlier this morning."

My heart begins to thump wildly. "Did you secure the coordinates?"

"It wasn't possible."

"Why not? You said you could nail down the outpost's position if they made contact."

"It wasn't the outpost."

I frown at him. "What are you saying?"

Viktor's voice drops an octave. "It came … from the Megamedes."

Chapter 10

My lips part, but I can't dig up a response. I glance around at the others. Trout and Jakob look equally flabbergasted. There's a strange glint in the female scientist's eye that I can't decipher. For a moment, she almost looked furious, but her expression quickly toggled back to neutral. Why would she not want Viktor telling us about the transmission?

My mind races in several different directions. If we can pinpoint the coordinates of the Megamedes, we might be able to land a Hovermedes on it. Lou talked about an evacuation order the day of the meltdown. If the buses were transporting people to safety, there could be civilian survivors on the Megamedes. The question is whether the world government was really saving people, or selecting subjects to take with them so they could continue their research. My stomach churns at the thought of all those people piling into transport buses like sheep to the slaughter.

"Are you sure it was the Megamedes?" I ask, staring at Viktor's face on the screen.

"No doubt about it," he replies, fingering that wretched mole again. "I tracked its circuitous magnetic path. The ship's over a thousand feet long, impossible to mistake."

"What was the transmission about?" Jakob asks.

Viktor blinks. "The Megamedes wants to send a delegation to the Craniopolis."

An icy tremor runs through me. "What for?"

Viktor twiddles with his collar. "We haven't issued any reports in the past few days. They've ordered an audit to ensure we're at optimal capacity."

"You mean … clone production?" Trout interjects.

Viktor nods. "And research quotas … participants."

"When are they arriving?" I ask.

"They estimate a week."

"The Craniopolis will never pass an audit," I say, rubbing my forehead. "Not with Lyong dead, and Sektor Sieben non-existent, not to mention the tunnels we blew up. That's three red flags right there that something is wrong."

"Lyong's death can be explained away easily enough," Viktor says. "As I mentioned already, we have documentation of his experimentation on his own DNA. An egocentric scientist overreaches himself. Perfectly plausible."

"It still doesn't explain the caved-in tunnels or why Sektor Sieben has closed up shop," Trout says.

"And Lyong's not the only important figure missing from this equation," I say. "Won's dead too. Anyone who sets foot inside the Craniopolis will know the facility was attacked." I rub my aching temples as I contemplate our options. Maybe there's a way to use the situation to our advantage. I turn my attention back to the screen. "Doctor Won ran Sektor Sieben, right?"

Viktor's brows slant inward. "Yes, he was Chief of Cybernetics. What are you getting at?"

"Won and Lyong disliked each other intensely. The world government would have known as much if Lyong was in contact with them. What if we claim that Won staged a coup? Blame everything on a dead egomaniac who isn't here to defend himself."

Viktor's eyes widen.

"It might work." Trout throws me an appreciative look.

Jakob adjusts his trucker cap, a troubled expression furrowing his face. "Too risky."

"I think it's worth the risk," I say. "The surviving scientists can greet the delegation. We'll pose as scientists too. If we can fool them, it would be a chance to find out more about the Megamedes."

I cast a furtive glance in the scientist's direction. I'm almost certain she knows more about the Megamedes than she's letting on. She ignores me and stares at Viktor.

"What if the delegation sees right through us?" Jakob says. "All they'd have to do is ask one of us a question. We don't know the first thing about science."

Trout grins. "Tell them you skipped school for a few years. They'll give you a free pass."

Jakob throws him a disgruntled look.

"You don't have to say anything when the delegation's conducting the audit," I add. "You can be a mute deviation if you like."

Trout bursts out laughing, and I look away to keep from doing the same. At least I can still make someone crack a smile.

"It's settled then." I turn back to Viktor on the screen. "We'll claim that Won tried to take over the Craniopolis after Lyong threatened to shut down Sektor Sieben. A bunch of clones died in the coup, the deviations were traumatized–some lost their ability to speak." I wink at Jakob, and to, my relief, he shakes his head and gives a crooked grin. He really is like a brother to me, and I hate it when we're at odds.

"How do you want me to respond to the transmission?" Viktor asks.

"Acknowledge it and comply with the audit. Don't alert them to the coup yet. The last thing we want is hordes of Schutz Clones arriving to restore order. We'll inform the delegation after they arrive. In the meantime, put whatever clones are available to work on cleanup and rebuilding the damaged tunnels. We need to look like we're fully invested in becoming a functional base again. I'll be there tomorrow to help."

Viktor bobs his head, and a moment later the image on the screen flat lines.

"The best this does is buy us some time," Trout says. "If we don't resume clone production after the delegation returns to the Megamedes, the Sweepers will come back. We won't be able to hide the truth from them forever."

"If we live through the audit, we'll work on phase two after that," I say.

Jakob raises his brows. "What's phase two?"

I grin. "Getting on board the Megamedes."

He gasps. "Are you out of your mind?"

"If the Megamedes is the heart of the Sweepers' operation, then that's where we'll strike."

"Impossible." Jakob shakes his head. "There's no way to get near it."

"We don't have to," I flash him an oversized grin. "They're bringing it to us. We just need to make sure that when the delegation returns to the ship, we accompany them."

"How are you planning on pulling that off?"

"I have an idea." I flick my eyes in the direction of the scientist. She averts her gaze and pretends to be engrossed in shutting down the CommCenter. "We'll talk about it later."

Back at the rider's barn, we bring Sven up to speed on everything over a hearty dinner of chicken, dumplings, and rice. Trout leaves me to do most of the talking while he shovels down his food.

"So you think the Megamedes exists?" Sven asks.

I shrug. "It's the second transmission Viktor has intercepted."

"Can we trust him?" Trout asks through a mouthful of food.

I trace the back of my nail across my lip. "He's up to something, but I don't think he's lying about the existence of the Megamedes. He can't exactly conjure up a delegation."

"What do you make of the scientist at the Superconductor?" Jakob asks.

"She's in on whatever Viktor's up to," I say. "Maybe they're planning on going back with the delegation."

"Why would they want to rejoin the Sweepers if they were sickened by what they were doing?"

"I'm not sure." I stare into my empty bowl. I can never seem to eat enough to satisfy my hunger these days. "But I intend to find out. In the meantime, we need to make plans to return to the Craniopolis tomorrow and begin staging the place for the delegation's arrival."

"What do you have in mind?" Trout asks.

"Some of the military clones can pose as Schutz Clones," I say. "And we'll need some warm bodies in the Intake Sektor to show that we're still conducting sweeps."

"Warm bodies?" Jakob's brows shoot up. "You mean Undergrounders?"

"It would only be for a few hours during the delegation's visit."

"Good luck with that," Trout says. "No Undergrounder's going to volunteer for that."

"Then we'll just have to be persuasive," I say.

"What are we talking about here, conscription?" Trout asks.

I shrug. "More like an ultimatum."

"Let's hope it's enough to convince them," Trout says.

I get to my feet. "We're about to find out. I'm calling an emergency meeting."

I'm met with disbelieving stares from the riders and Undergrounders when I break the news about the delegation. I don't blame them. They've just cleared the city of clones and deviations, and for the first time in years they were living without the fear of extraction hanging over their heads. Now I'm asking them to volunteer to return to the Craniopolis as live subjects in a Sweeper audit.

"If we can convince the Sweepers that Won was behind the coup we can buy ourselves some time," I explain. "Lyong's own records prove that he was in a weakened state. We can claim that Won took advantage of the situation. If we don't try it, the Sweepers will unleash a fleet of Hovermedes to hunt down those responsible for what happened at the Craniopolis."

Fear and confusion cloud the faces in front of me. "So who's with me?" I ask. "I need at least twenty volunteers to pose as extractees in the Intake Sektor." The Undergrounders' stares morph into expressions of horror. I slowly scan the room, waiting for someone to jump on board.

Minutes tick by and I'm met with stony silence. Owen gets to his feet. "No one's returning to the Craniopolis," he says, scowling. "We've suffered enough. You're pushing it too far, Derry."

I swallow down my bitter disappointment that Owen has chosen to go against me when he knows I need his support to make this work.

"If the Sweepers come looking for us, they'll bring every resource at their disposal," I say. "They'll destroy us."

Uneasy murmurs ripple around the room.

"And if your crazy scheme doesn't work, then what?" Owen glances around at the worried faces observing our standoff. "I'll tell you what happens. We'll all end up in Sektor Sieben as participants."

"Owen's right," one of the Undergrounders pipes up. "We can't fool the Sweepers. We'll end up as science projects if we go anywhere near the Craniopolis."

"You're wrong," I raise my voice to make myself heard above the discontent. "If we pull together we can make this happen. The clones, scientists, even the deviations, will all play their parts. But if we do nothing, the sweeps will resume and we'll be forced to turn the Superconductor back on. We'll accomplish nothing but death by radiation."

The room erupts. Undergrounders and riders face off, arguing heatedly with each other. One woman with a child in her lap puts her hands to her face, and rocks back and forth, weeping while the child works to pry her hands free.

I look over at Trout for inspiration, but he gives an apologetic shrug. I bang on the table with my rifle for silence. The room gradually quietens, all eyes settling on me.

"If we want to win this war, we need to know who is on board the Megamedes before we attack. Until then, our best bet is to dupe the Sweepers into thinking the Craniopolis is an operational base and buy ourselves more time."

At the far end of the room, Owen folds his arms across his chest, face set like flint. Nikki leans against his shoulder. The Undergrounders look with uncertainty from me to him. I clench my fists at my side. I lead the Council. I won't let him split the city.

"We leave tomorrow," I say. "I need twenty volunteers at the main gate by dawn."

Owen is the first to exit the room, Nikki hurries out after him. It's not good for morale that we put up a divided front at a moment of crisis, but Owen should have backed down. He didn't want to be a part of the Council so this wasn't his decision to make.

Jakob walks over. "I need to go to the clinic and check up on Curly. I'm sorry about Owen. He should have supported you."

"Thanks." I force a smile. "I don't expect you to come with us to the Craniopolis. You're needed here."

Jakob nods. "I'd do a miserable job of faking a role anyway."

"We'll need as many of the military clones as possible," I say, turning to Sven. "The riders can help handle things here while we're gone."

Sven nods. "We'll be at the gate by dawn. I'll leave Rocco behind to oversee things here."

I exit the courthouse and make a quick detour to check on Big Ed and Tucker, before heading back to my bunk and calling it a night. After a few minutes, Tucker appears and curls up on my legs. I sink my fingers into his fur and slowly begin to relax for the first time in days.

I wake the next morning with a start, almost bumping heads with Trout who's shaking me awake. A solitary finger of light streams through the cracks in the boarded-up window a few feet from my bed. I stare at it for a moment before it hits me. *I've overslept.*

"What time is it?" I ask, scrambling to throw aside the covers.

Trout brushes a hand across his unshaven jaw. "Never mind that. There's something you need to see."

Chapter 11

Something about his tone stops me in my tracks. I stare at him searching his face for answers. My heart thumps so hard it hurts. "Is it Sven?" I whisper.

He frowns. "No!"

I tug on his sleeve. "Big Ed?"

"No! Nobody's dead," he says, but he doesn't look me in the eye.

"What is it then?" I ask, pulling on my boots.

"You'd better come see for yourself."

I grab my pack and gun and follow Trout outside. I don't know why he's being so evasive, but at least it's not what I dread hearing most—that Sven has reached his expiration date.

The sky is overcast, crows scolding up above. Not a good omen for our return trip to the Craniopolis, but I brush it off and tromp down the street after Trout. My stomach rumbles, reminding me that I skipped dinner last night. "Where are we going?" I call to Trout.

He ignores me and turns onto the main street.

"This is stupid, Trout. Just tell me—"

My heart jolts. The caravan of wagons and carts that lined the road yesterday is gone.

I throw a harried glance at Trout.

"They left in the middle of the night," he explains.

The breath leaves my lungs. Owen must have talked the homesteaders into pulling out after our showdown in the courthouse. After everything we've been through together, my own brother betrays me like this. I sink down on a slab of cracked concrete and drop my head into my hands. He didn't even say good-bye.

"Did all the homesteaders go with him?" I ask.

"I guess so."

"Owen hasn't been himself since the Sweepers extracted him," I say. "I should have tried to talk to him about what happened to him, but he's been avoiding me."

"He barely talks to me anymore either," Trout says. "I never know what's going on in his head."

"*Nikki* is in his head," I fume. "She's the reason he's shutting the rest of us out."

Trout scratches the back of his neck. "Or maybe she's the reason he's holding it together."

I blow out a frustrated breath and get to my feet. "Neither of them are in a good place. They're not fit to lead the homesteaders to the Deadwood basin."

Trout rubs his one-knuckled finger and stares off into the distance. "We need to go. Sven's waiting on us."

"How many Undergrounders showed up at the gate?" I ask, falling in step with him.

He clears his throat. "You don't want to know."

I roll my eyes. "Just spit it out. This morning can't get any worse."

He frowns. "Five."

"Five!" I groan. I was hoping for at least fifteen or twenty.

"There were eight earlier," Trout says. "But three of them bailed when they heard the homesteaders left. They might be planning on going after them."

"The Ghost and his men will clean their clocks if they come across them. And they'll be easy pickings for a Hovermedes if they set up camp in the Deadwood Basin."

"With any luck, the Rogues are a long way from here by now," Trout muses.

I kick at a clod of dirt in my path. "Either way, we can't worry about Owen anymore. He made his choice. We need to stay focused."

We fall silent as we approach the main gate to the city. Sven and the military clones stand in formation, guns holstered, their expressions schooled to neutral. An elite force, bred for war as The Ghost once reminded me. To their left, a small group of Undergrounders monitors my arrival with skepticism.

I let my gaze travel over their faces and attire, cataloging what we've got. One woman and four men. The woman's hair curtains her face like overgrown weeds, and she's dressed in a frayed skirt that reaches to her ankles. Not an ideal ensemble to weave through the dense undergrowth in.

Maybe my disapproval shows in my face because the man standing next to her puts his arm around her waist and fixes me with a hard stare in return. I turn away, my stomach knotting. *Four* volunteers, and a fifth wheel who didn't want to be left behind. Great. Those two will be too wrapped up in one another to be of real use, but at least they're warm bodies. And right now I only have five of them to fill the Intake Sektor with.

A few spits of rain land on my face and I shiver.

"What do you want to do?" Trout asks. "We're never going to convince the delegation we're an operational base with only five extractees."

"We'll figure something out once we get to the Craniopolis." I wave up to the guards to open the gates.

We follow the squad of military clones through the debris that litters the outskirts of the city. We're underway only a short time before the disgruntled clouds offload their fury on us. Icy rain sleets down at a sharp angle, and I throw my hood over my head and bend into the deluge to protect my face. For some reason, I think of Lou and the raindrops sliding down the glass of her camper van. I was hoping she would have changed her mind about living alone, but I guess she really does prefer her solitude. The worsening visibility hampers our progress, and as the rain builds, I realize it's possible we may not make it to the Craniopolis by tomorrow.

My thoughts gravitate to Owen. He's picked the worst possible time to lead a group of vulnerable Undergrounders out of the city. I know only too well how quickly the tide can turn when people become disillusioned and start looking for a scapegoat. I hope for Owen's sake that this storm doesn't drive his band of wet-behind-the-ears homesteaders to abandon him.

I pull my jacket tight around me and increase my stride until I catch up with Sven. The wind is increasing in force, whipping up the forest litter into freakish figures. All around us tree limbs creak and moan.

"It's too dangerous to keep going," Sven yells to me. "We need to look for shelter."

I nod in response and signal back to the others.

We veer off the trail and begin bushwhacking our way through the webbed understory. I can't see three feet in front of me, but Sven's enhanced vision is an advantage even in this deluge, so I stick close behind him as he plows on.

The wind grows stronger until I can barely withstand the force of it. I'm dragging my legs behind me like wooden fence posts when Sven comes to a halt. He leans down and shouts in my ear. "There's a shack up ahead. We can hunker down inside for a bit."

I nod, eyes scrunched against the icy raindrops pummeling my face. Sven grabs me by the hand and pulls me forward.

Numb, and half-deafened, I don't open my eyes again until the bitter gusts suddenly abate and my face stops stinging. I'm standing in the doorway of a one-roomed, splintered wooden cabin that's buckling at the knees, but in one piece, at least for now. The clones and Undergrounders pile through the ramshackle door after me, drenched and miserable. I do a quick head count to make sure we're all here, before shrugging off my pack and sinking down in the dust with my back to the knotty wall.

A dead ringing reverberates in my head from the merciless pounding of the rain. I hug my shoulders in a vain attempt to trap whatever body heat remains. We won't be able to start a fire in here, and everything in my pack is as wet as I am. My fingers are too raw and frozen to poke around for something dry to put on anyway.

"You okay?" Trout asks.

"Yeah," I say, my teeth knocking off each other. I flick my eyes in the direction of the Undergrounders, staring morosely at the floor. "How are they holding up?"

Trout gives me a rueful grin. "I'll bet they're kicking themselves for showing up at the gate this morning. I'll go talk to them."

Sven wanders over, swiping at the water dripping from his hair.

"We can't stay here long," I say. "If we don't show up at the Craniopolis tomorrow, Viktor might take matters into his own hands. I don't entirely trust him."

"Once the wind lets up, I'll send one of the clones out to check on the condition of the trail." Sven pulls out some jerky and offers me a piece. "Might as well eat something while we're waiting."

"I'll trade you." I rummage in my pocket. "Ever tried a fortune cookie?"

I hold out a handful of packages in the palm of my hand.

Sven stares at them curiously. "What are those?"

"They used to give them out at Chinese restaurants before the meltdown," I say. "There's a piece of paper wedged inside with your fortune on it. They're a bit crushed, but, hey, they make a change from jerky."

Sven takes one and sniffs the package. "Is it a meal?"

I burst out laughing, then quickly compose myself. "It's not lyophilized food. It's a cookie—cookie *crumbs*." I tear open the plastic and taste a piece. Saliva spurts up from under my tongue. "They're stale but sweet. Try one!"

Sven rips the plastic with his teeth and pours the contents into his mouth.

"Wait! Don't eat the paper!"

He turns aside and spits on the floor. "Yuck! Disgusting!" He wipes the back of his hand across his mouth.

"You just spat out your fortune." I rip open another packet and hand him the paper inside. "Here, read this."

He unfurls the fortune with his giant fingers and furrows his brow.

"What does it say?" I ask.

"The greatest risk is not taking one." He glances at me, crumpling the paper in his fist.

"What? You don't like your fortune?"

"I already knew it." He smiles sadly and stuffs the paper into the pocket on his cargo pants where he keeps Won's remote device. "But I'll hold on to it to remind me."

I drop my gaze, a slow burn traveling up my cheeks. I reach into my jacket and pull out a fistful of cookies. "Give these to your friends," I say, shoving them into his palm.

"Thanks, but I can't imagine they'll enjoy them any better than I did." He gives me an apologetic grin. "I'll send one of the clones out to check on the trail in a minute. I think the worst of the storm's over."

I elbow Trout and we watch the clones' reaction as Sven hands out the fortune cookies. They treat them with even more suspicion than he did, sniffing them dubiously, and electing to read each other's fortunes without as much as a taste test.

When they're done, one of them gets to his feet, grabs his gun and heads outside. He's not gone five minutes before a blood-curdling scream lifts the scalp from my head.

Chapter 12

There's a frozen moment of disbelief before we scramble for our guns and dash for the cabin door. I'm the first one through, and I leap from the wooden porch and take off running as soon as I spot the clone's huge footprints in the sodden ground. Icy drops of rainwater shower me as I run. The trail beneath me is slick with mud, and saturated leaves skate out from under my feet. I flinch at another spine-chilling scream as I push through the foliage. The Rogues must have caught the clone. I don't dare picture what they're doing to him to make him scream like that.

I skirt around a massive granite boulder and come to an abrupt stop. My stomach slides into my throat. The clone is writhing on the ground in agony, his leg clamped in a steel-jawed bear trap. I drop to my knees at his side. "We'll get you out of this, I promise," I say, staring in horror at the rusted metal spikes driven mercilessly through his flesh. Big Ed showed me once how to open a bear trap, something about standing on the flat spring and setting the release lever, but I can't even see it for blood.

I glance up at the sound of thudding footsteps. Sven and the others come tearing around the boulder and pull up short, their faces taut. Sven immediately drops to the ground at the clone's feet. He grips the iron trap in his bare hands and pulls it apart with a loud roar. The Undergrounders exchange frightened looks and back up several paces, glancing dubiously around at the other military clones. A shiver goes down my spine. How did Sven do that? My heart races. Despite how I feel about him, he's not exactly human. He's something more.

"How bad is it?" Trout asks, peering over my shoulder.

Sven grits his teeth and examines the wound. "The bone isn't fractured thanks to his tensile strength, but he's bleeding profusely. We have to get him to the Craniopolis." He pulls out a grubby shirt from his pack and rips the sleeves from it.

"We should wash the wound first," I say. "That trap was badly rusted."

"His enhanced immune system will fight any infection." Sven tears several more strips from the shirt and begins wrapping the clone's leg. "But if he loses too much blood, there's an increased risk of ossification. We'll stitch him up once we reach the Craniopolis."

I silently hand Sven another shirt from my pack. Back in the city there were times I could almost forget that he's a clone, but in these never-ending moments of crisis, our differences are glaring—frightening even. His extraordinary vision, his enhanced immune system, the constant threat of ossification, his looming expiration date. Am I ready to set that all aside for love?

Sven helps the clone to his feet and he attempts to hobble forward.

"We'll have to carry him," Sven says to the military clones. "I'll take the first shift."

They help him lift the injured clone onto his shoulders and adjust his weight.

"Let's make tracks," Sven says.

"We're going to have to push through the night," I say to Trout as we make our way back to the cabin to gather up our gear. "Let me know if the pace becomes too fast for the Undergrounders."

I pull the rickety door to the cabin shut behind us, and we hit the trail, grimly determined to reach the Craniopolis before the injured clone ossifies on Sven's shoulders.

It's early afternoon the next day when we arrive at the secret tunnel that leads inside the Craniopolis. My legs are so tired I feel like I'm tromping through quicksand in concrete shoes. The sounds of the forest around me are dampened and fading, a muted background my exhausted brain can barely hold onto. I wait until all the clones and Undergrounders descend into the tunnel before I flick on my flashlight and slide down into the dirt after Trout. A centipede scuttles across the floor in front of me. The darkness closes in around the dime-sized beam from my flashlight, and the damp, familiar smell of the underworld fills my nostrils once again.

I push through my fatigue, imagining my aching limbs sinking into the soft, cushiony matrix of the pod chairs in the Biotik Sektor. If I have any energy left, I might even swallow a lyophilized roast beef dinner capsule before I collapse into a coma.

I've lost all track of how long I've been in the tunnel when voices drift toward me, coaxing my brain back to life. I shine my paltry beam along the dirt walls and spot the ladder leading up to the Biotik Sektor. I force myself toward it, my legs almost going into spasm from exhaustion. I reach for the ladder and pull myself up, rung by torturous rung, until a meaty arm yanks me the rest of the way out.

"Are you all right?" Sven asks, a worried expression on his face.

I nod, swaying back and forth on my feet. The room spins around me. Sven sweeps me back up and plants me in a pod chair next to Trout.

"We're taking the injured clone to the Medical Sektor to stitch him up," Sven says. "You and Trout wait here with the other Undergrounders. Get some rest. We'll hunt down Viktor and Jerome when we get back."

I let my gaze travel over Sven's muscled neck and shoulders. *No ordinary man* is the last thing I remember thinking before I drift into oblivion.

I wake to the sound of raucous laughter. I wrinkle my brow and stare blankly up at the ceiling, unable to place what planet I've flown to.

"Derry!" Trout hisses at me.

I bolt upright and look around in horror at the tattooed faces milling about the room. *I'm in a nightmare.* I rub my eyes, but it doesn't rid the room of the Rogues. They're sprawled out everywhere, sampling the endless menu options from the food dispenser and wreaking havoc with the pod chair controls. My eyes widen when I spot The Ghost heading my way.

"Rough night?" he asks, leering at me.

I shrink back in my chair. "How … what are you doing here?"

"Looting, pillaging, stocking up on some of those lyophilized steaks that don't need skinning when a man's hungry." His eyes bore into me, then narrow to slits. "Or maybe I'm tracking down horse thieves." He curls one corner of his lip at me. "I see you've been busy resettling the Craniopolis without me. What exactly are you up to?"

I throw a quick glance around hoping to spot Sven and the military clones.

"You seem antsy." The Ghost sneers at me. "I would have slit your throat in your sleep by now if I'd come for you."

I sit up and scratch my scalp hard to get the blood flowing.

"What do you want?" Trout asks.

The Ghost rubs his jaw, his eyes glinting. "That traitor Blade."

I frown. "I thought Blade was with you."

"Not anymore. He disappeared during the storm. And he came this way. Figured you could shed some light on it seeing as you're in the habit of poking around in my business."

A shiver tingles down my spine. So Rummy pulled it off. Hopefully, now he has his brother back he'll disappear for good. But I'm still left with The Ghost, and to say we have unfinished business would be an understatement.

"We haven't seen him." I reach behind for my gun.

The Ghost twists the gooseneck on a pod chair and sinks down opposite me. "Blade's no loss." He gives me one of the psychotic grins that accompany his rapid mood shifts. "I'm glad to be rid of him *and* those dang horses. I could even be persuaded to forget all about that little horse-thieving incident if you let me in on whatever it is you got cooking here. My men tell me you're shoring up the tunnels we destroyed."

Trout shoots me a wary look.

I raise my brows a fraction and give him a reassuring nod. My mind is racing with a daring proposition. I can put the Rogues to good use now that they're here. But first, I have to snag The Ghost's interest.

"One of the scientists intercepted another transmission yesterday," I say.

The Ghost leans forward in his chair, his breathing slow and shallow. "What kind of transmission?"

"It was from the Megamedes. The Sweepers are sending a delegation here to do a productivity audit." I pause and lower my voice. "This could be our chance to strike at the heart of their operation."

The Ghost's penetrating stare bores into me as he digests the news. For the longest moment I don't think he's going to bite, and then his lips split in a wolfish grin. "Tell me you weren't fixing to hijack the galaxy's only luxury superliner without me?" His eyes glitter with a hint of recklessness.

"Don't get ahead of yourself." I frown to hide the fact that I'm weak with relief. "First, we have to pass the audit."

Trout turns to The Ghost. "If we work together we can fool the Sweepers into thinking the Craniopolis is operational and buy ourselves some time to figure out how to infiltrate the Megamedes."

"This place look operational to you?" The Ghost throws back his head and laughs. "So where are you gonna tell them Lyong's at? On a white sandy beach somewhere using up his vacation days?"

I scowl at him. "Shut up and listen. The story is that Won tried to take over the Craniopolis. The records show that his Cybernetics program was a dismal failure. Lyong was losing patience with him."

The Ghost rubs his forefinger and thumb across his jaw. "Never gonna fly. Not without Schutz Clones or extractees."

"Sven and the military clones will stand in for the Schutz Clones," I say. "There's no way to tell who's under those helmets. As for the extractees," I grin across at him. "You couldn't have come at a better time."

The Ghost narrows his brows. "You want my men as live bait?"

I level my gaze at him. "You pay to play if you want a share in that luxury superliner. If it eases your mind any, Trout and I will be in the Intake Sektor too with some of the Undergrounders." *All five of them.*

"I want something in return," The Ghost says, after a moment's contemplation.

"What?"

"Land. Time you and I worked out a deal to go our separate ways." He pulls his lips into a disturbing smile. "I want everything east of Deadwood River."

My throat constricts. Trout and I trade uneasy glances. The homesteaders are on their way to the Deadwood River basin. I can't promise The Ghost what Owen has already claimed. The knot in my stomach tightens. Maybe The Ghost knows that.

The doors to the Biotik Sektor retract, saving me from having to commit. The military clones storm in and take aim at the Rogues scattered around the room.

I jump to my feet. "It's okay." I raise my palms in the air. "Don't shoot!"

Sven strides over to us, his expression grim. "What are they doing here?"

"They tracked Blade here," Trout says. "He disappeared during the storm."

"I told The Ghost about the transmission and he's agreed to help us," I add.

The Ghost sneers. "Bail you out, you mean."

Sven reaches for The Ghost by the throat. "You're lucky it's clones and not riders you're looking at right now."

"Those nags weren't worth the trouble," The Ghost scoffs. "We'd be barbecuing horse meat by now if you hadn't taken them off our hands."

Sven shoves The Ghost away from him in disgust. "Better watch that mouth of yours. I wouldn't want that getting back to the city. The riders adhere to cowboy retribution when it comes to horse thieves."

I lay a hand on Sven's arm. "Let it go. That's Jody's fight. How's your friend doing?"

"We stitched him up. He's resting in the Medical Sektor."

"Then let's head over to the Research Sektor and find Viktor," I say.

The Ghost grins around at us. "Now that I got shares on that galactic luxury liner, I'm in on the powwows."

Viktor looks up, startled when we walk in. "You made it."

"You didn't know we were here?" I raise my brows.

"The cameras are still down," Sven reminds me.

I frown. "Get someone on them right away. The security system has to be in working order by day's end. It's the first thing the Sweepers would restore. We need to start thinking like them if we're going to pull this off."

I turn my attention back to Viktor. "Is Jerome down in Terminus?"

"No." Viktor flicks a finger over his mole. "He's … sick. He must have picked up something from the deviations. Their immune systems were compromised by their stay in the city. They were never successfully enhanced so they're susceptible to everything."

I suck in a silent breath. "Where is he?"

Viktor blinks around at us.

I flinch when The Ghost suddenly slams his forearm to Viktor's windpipe. "Tell her," he growls, "before I squeeze it out of you."

"Medical Sektor," Viktor wheezes out. "He … needed fluids."

"I was there a few minutes ago," Sven says. "I didn't see him."

"He's in Sektor Sieben. We're keeping him isolated." Viktor drops his gaze, squeezing his hands in front of him. A sheen of sweat glistens on his forehead.

My stomach churns with dread. Whatever Jerome has, it has nothing to do with the deviations and everything to do with what Viktor's been hiding from us. I turn to The Ghost. "Stay here and don't let Viktor out of your sight until we get back."

Trout and I race through the gleaming tunnels after Sven. I'm not sure what Viktor's up to, but I only hope we manage to reach Jerome before it's too late. He must have found out whatever it is that Viktor's been trying to hide from us.

Sven punches the entry code into the keypad outside Sektor Sieben. The doors swing wide and we walk through the entry door. A scientist in a hazard suit and mask jumps up from behind a desk. "You can't come in here. We have a deviation in quarantine."

"Where is he?" I say, glancing around.

The cubicles are lying open, empty of their macabre participants, except for one. I race over and peer through the viewing monitor into the room. Dread fills my lungs like glue.

Jerome lies motionless on a gurney, eyes sealed shut, a single drip line in his arm. For a moment, I think he's dead. Then his chest rises and falls. My knees almost buckle beneath me with relief. "He's breathing," I whisper.

Sven pushes open the door. The scientist follows us inside, flustered and still protesting, but reluctant to confront Sven.

"Jerome! Can you hear me?" I shake his arm gently, but he doesn't respond.

Sven checks the bag of fluid and mutters something under his breath.

"What's wrong?" Trout asks.

"Bag's punctured," Sven replies. "They're not just giving him fluids. Someone's drugging him."

The scientist stares wide-eyed at the bag. "That's not possible."

"Who else has been in here?" I ask.

"No one. Just me and Viktor Kozlov."

Sven and I trade glances.

"Get the needle out of his arm!" I order the scientist.

She throws an uneasy glance Sven's way, then bends over and deftly disconnects the drip line.

"You must have something here to counteract the drug with," Sven says to her.

She gives a worried nod and retrieves a syringe and a vial from a shelf at the back of the room. Seconds stretch into eternity as we watch her turn the vial upside down, pull back the plunger and fill the syringe.

I step out of her way and grit my teeth as she sticks the needle into a vein in his arm.

Seconds later, Jerome lets out a gasp. His eye snaps open and fastens on me. His lips move, but nothing comes out.

I lean over him. "It's okay, Jerome. Take it easy."

"Viktor." He enunciates the name slowly like his tongue is thick and clumsy, finding its bearings again.

"What about him?" Sven says.

Jerome takes a long, rasping breath. "He didn't … intercept the transmission … he sent it."

Chapter 13

My brain fills with static.

Viktor set us up!

Trout glances at me, his eyes clouding with fear. "You know what this means."

I grimace. "There is no delegation and no audit. The Sweepers are coming for us."

I grab the scientist by the arm. "Stay here with Jerome. Don't let anyone in. We'll be back as soon as we can."

"If anything happens to him you'll answer to me," Sven warns her.

She gives a nervous nod, her face pale.

"We're screwed," Trout says, as we race back along the tunnels to the Research Sektor. "Viktor knows everything about our plan. Even the city's not safe now. He knows the entire layout, our security system."

"We still have a week before the Sweepers arrive to come up with a new plan," Sven says.

"Maybe not," I say. "If Viktor lied about why the Sweepers are coming, he might have lied about when they're coming too."

When we arrive back at the Research Sektor Viktor is slumped in a chair clutching the side of his head.

"He tried to access the CommCenter," The Ghost says. "I had no choice but to clock him one."

I walk over to Viktor, grab him by the shoulder and yank him upright.

"You sent a transmission to the Megamedes, didn't you?" I yell at him. "You told the Sweepers to come here."

Viktor's eyes dart back and forth, searching for Sven and The Ghost in his peripheral vision. "No! It's not what you think. I can explain everything."

Sven rolls up his sleeves and flexes a meaty fist. "Go right ahead, Doctor."

Viktor drops his gaze. "I sent a message to my son."

"Your son is on board the Megamedes?" Trout says, an incredulous look on his face.

Viktor shakes his head. "No. He's at an outpost. The Megamedes ordered a delegation from his outpost to conduct the audit."

"You mean the Megamedes isn't coming here?" I say.

Viktor shakes his head. "They'll remain in orbit until the delegation determines that there's no risk to the sovereign leader."

I lean back against the counter behind me, my heart sinking. "What did you tell your son?"

Viktor glances around nervously. "I told him the truth. He's agreed to go along with our plan and take me back with him when the delegation leaves." He hesitates. "I haven't seen Dimitri, my son, in over a decade. Family members weren't allowed to collaborate on classified research projects. They even changed his last name to Petrov so I couldn't trace him." He stares straight at me, his eyes moistening. "That's the real reason I hacked into Lyong's records—to find Dimitri."

"What kind of research was your son working on?" Trout asks.

Viktor raises his head and stares at him for a moment. "Ossification."

My heartbeat flickers. I can't help but throw a glance in Sven's direction. He furrows his brow, but he won't meet my eyes.

I turn back to Viktor. "You said there were rumors of a breakthrough?"

"Yes." Viktor throws Sven a wary look. "But no confirmation yet."

"Lyong was planning to take Sook there," I say. "That's all the confirmation I need."

The Ghost folds his arms. "Now who's getting ahead of herself? Don't forget about the audit."

Viktor gingerly touches the side of his head. "I think we can pull it off with my son's help."

"There's only one problem," I say. "I can't let you go back to the outpost with him afterward."

Viktor blinks rapidly. "But I haven't seen–"

"I know, but we agreed that you would man the CommCenter in case the Megamedes makes contact." I drum my fingers on the counter. "There may be another way for you and your son to stay together."

"How?" Viktor asks.

"We can inform the delegation that an order has come in requiring them to remain here and oversee the restoration of the Craniopolis to full operational capacity."

Trout frowns. "And what do we tell the outpost?"

"Exactly what they want to hear. We send them a glowing inspection report stating that everything is under control and that the delegation is returning."

I grin at Sven. "Then *you* can use Won's remote and your computer-hacking magic to stage a spectacular Hovermedes crash in the most inaccessible part of the Wilderness of No Return. After that, Viktor and his son, and the rest of the delegation can either join us voluntarily or remain here as our hostages."

Sven rumples his brow. "It's a bold plan, but it might just work."

The Ghost lets out a snort. "Or blow up in our faces. Why are you so gung-ho on helping the doc with his sappy family reunion anyway?"

Viktor twitches with apprehension as he eyes The Ghost's clenched fists.

"If we're going to save the clones, we need his son's expertise," I say.

Viktor rubs his brow, his eyes riddled with doubt. "The crash will have to be convincing. If the outpost suspects even for a minute that my son's alive, they'll stop at nothing to find him."

"Sven can be very convincing," I say. "In the meantime, I need you to get busy doing whatever it takes to put the Research Sektor back on track: scheduling shifts, updating records, repairing damaged equipment, restocking inventory, that kind of thing."

Viktor purses his lips. "Even if we pass the audit, they'll send another delegation once they realize the Craniopolis hasn't returned to normal operations."

"Then your job will be to supply them with a steady stream of bogus production reports and put them off for as long as possible," I say. "Now get started. We've only got a week to straighten this place out."

I turn to The Ghost. "Stay here and keep an eye on Viktor. Sven and I will work out the rest of the details with Jerome."

The Ghost bars his arms across his chest. "Not so fast. Either I go with you or you don't get your warm bodies for the Intake Sektor."

I mull it over for a moment and give a reluctant nod. I'm low on extras for this production, so I have little choice but to pacify him.

By the time we return to Sektor Sieben, Jerome is gone.

"He wouldn't listen to me," the distraught scientist says, backing as far away from Sven as possible. "As soon as he could stand without assistance he took off down the corridor to Terminus."

I turn to the others. "He still thinks Viktor betrayed us. We need to stop him before he does something he regrets."

"This way," Sven says, racing back out into the main tunnel. "Let's hope we get there in time."

The etched sign over the steel entryway to the deviations' living quarters reads *Terminus*. I shudder. A sadistic gesture on the Sweepers' part. An Optika module whirs into action, tracking our approach. I steel myself for what I'm about to encounter. I've only ever seen Terminus depicted in a hologram display, and that was disturbing enough. Even Sven's never been down here before. According to Jerome, over one hundred and fifty deviations call this place home, but the entryway has more of a mausoleum vibe than a welcoming aura. Sven taps a code into the key panel and the retractable doors slide apart.

Inside, the lighting is even more muted than in the other Sektors. Only the sound of our footsteps and an occasional groan disturbs the suffocating silence that envelops us. I know from talking to Jerome that this is how the deviations prefer it. Back in the city, they would often plug their ears or moan in distress when people burst out laughing or raised their voices. The deviations are sensitive to too much stimulation—one of many debilitating genetic impairments caused by the cloning process.

I glance around at the main living area. The pod chairs are made of the same material as those in the Biotik Sektor, but they're outfitted with an assortment of trapeze handles and lift mechanisms to assist the malformed deviations in and out.

Eyes follow us everywhere, bulging, bloodshot, misaligned, sunken hollows of sadness. Some of the deviations have a curious look on their asymmetrical faces, some seem perturbed by our presence, while others blankly track our movements across the room without any apparent recognition of what it is they're looking at. A few, like Jerome, have a higher than average level of intelligence, despite their macabre appearances, and some even exchange a greeting with us as we go by. I keep an eye out for the deviation who helped me when I lost my way during the fire in the tunnels, but I don't see her in any of the groups as we go by. A pang of sadness goes through me when I realize that she might have expired. I wish I'd had the chance to thank her properly. She was astute and kindhearted, despite her disturbing appearance and her struggle to articulate words.

I throw a curious glance over my shoulder at a deviation who's haltingly following a few steps behind us. At first, I can't figure out what it is about us that fascinates her so much, but then I catch her, head cocked to one side, ogling the artwork running up the side of The Ghost's neck. I suppress a laugh when I realize how uncomfortable her proximity is making The Ghost.

"She probably thinks you were cloned that way," I whisper to him.

His face flushes. "Vermin! The lot of them. They should be exterminated."

"They have better hearts than you or I could ever hope for. One of them saved my life."

The Ghost casts a scathing glance around. "If their insides are as messed up as their outsides, they don't even have hearts!"

"Not that different from them after all then, are you?" Trout pipes up.

The Ghost scowls at him.

"You're not heartless." I look The Ghost square in the eye. "You saved Izzy and Brock. I think you're afraid of the deviations' deformities."

He turns away before I can see what his eyes are saying.

"There's Jerome!" Sven interrupts. He points to the back of the room where Jerome is seated at the head of a large table, deep in conversation with several other deviations. Relief floods his face when he sees us approaching.

We pull up some more chairs and join him at the table.

"You scared us half to death disappearing like that." Sven squeezes Jerome's shoulder. "Are you okay?"

"I'm fine. I was worried about you," Jerome says. "We were making contingency plans to storm the Research Sektor and rescue you." He forks his fingers through his hair, a perplexed look on his face. "I can't believe Viktor betrayed us like that."

"It's not what you think," I say. "He told us everything."

The deviations seated around the table trade dubious glances.

"He sent a transmission to the outpost where his son works," I explain. "Viktor told him what happened here, and about our plan."

"What plan?" Jerome asks, frowning.

"The outpost is sending a delegation to conduct an audit of the Craniopolis. We're going to dupe them into thinking that Won staged a coup here. Viktor's son has agreed to go along with it."

Jerome scowls. "We can't trust Viktor. He drugged me up in Sektor Sieben like one of his wretched participants."

"He needed you out of the way temporarily." I sigh and rub my forehead. "He was afraid you were going to expose him for sending an unauthorized transmission. He knew you thought he ordered the audit. What Viktor did to you was wrong, but he was desperate to be with his son again."

Jerome pounds a fist on the table. "He treated me like one of his science experiments. We have only his word that it's even his son he's been talking to."

"I believe him," I say. "He was trying to hold back tears when he talked about him."

"We're wasting time," Sven says. "We need to commit to a plan of action before it's too late."

"All right." Jerome frowns. "Just keep him out of my sight. What do you want the deviations to do?"

"They can handle sanitation, maintenance, food preparation," I reply. "Put them back on a schedule servicing the Craniopolis."

Jerome looks around for approval at the other deviations seated at the table and then gives a reluctant nod.

"I'll put the cameras back online." Sven turns to Jerome. "I can access the system from here, right?"

Jerome scoots his chair out from the table. "Follow me."

Trout and I stand, and The Ghost gets to his feet as well. "What?" he says when I arch a brow in his direction. "I'm not staying here with these underworld creatures by myself."

I throw him a scathing look and follow Jerome and the others into a small office.

Sven gets to work bringing up an array of cameras on a large plexi-screen. He zooms in on Viktor hunched over his desk in the Research Sektor and chuckles. "He's working diligently on his chore list. That's a good sign."

He swipes his fingers across a projected keyboard and studies the screen for a moment. "This is interesting." He frowns. "Viktor really has been busy. He's declassified all the records."

Sven scrolls a little further and comes to an abrupt stop.

"What?" Jerome eyes him with apprehension.

Sven rubs a hand across his jaw. "I found our inception records."

Chapter 14

Jerome places a hairy palm on the hologram keyboard. "Don't do this."

Sven turns to him, his face rigid with shock. "I have a right to know."

Jerome shakes his head. "Why torture yourself with the days you have left?"

"His choice," Trout says. "I'd want to know if it were me."

The Ghost peers over Sven's shoulder. "What's the big find?"

"Inception records. They document the date we were cloned." Jerome grimaces. "No clone's ever had an expiration date past twenty-five units."

The Ghost's eyes glitter. "Can't say I'll be crying to be rid of the lot of you."

I glare at him. "No one's going to be crying at your funeral either."

Sven fixes his gaze on Jerome. "I want to know. It's important to me."

Jerome tightens his lips and reluctantly withdraws his hand. "Leave me out of it."

Sven hits a few strokes on the hologram keyboard. He frowns at the lines of records scrolling down the screen.

I stare at the baffling array of data hoping to catch a glimpse of Sven's name, but everything is numbers and code.

After a few minutes, Sven keys in a combination and the screen goes blank.

"Did you find it?" The words tumble out as I turn to him. My bottom lip trembles as an overwhelming fear grips me. "Do you–"

"Nineteen units," he says, flatly, a strange mix of emotions in his amber eyes.

I breathe slowly in and out. "That's good news, isn't it? You're still a teenager." I flash him a smile, but it droops a little as the reality sinks in. He's somewhere in the last six years of his life. He may not even make it to twenty-five. A machete-sized pain slices through me at the thought of losing him.

"We need to get back to the Biotik Sektor and check on the Rogues," Trout says, breaking the strained silence.

Sven gives a dazed nod.

"Let's go," The Ghost says. "I'm starved." He makes a beeline for the steel entry doors.

Jerome gets to his feet. "I'll stay here and get started on the deviations' work schedule."

Once the doors retract behind us, Sven lays a hand on my arm. "I saw Jerome's records."

I frown in disapproval. "He told you not to."

"I couldn't help it." An anguished look flits across Sven's face. "He's twenty-four units."

My pulse picks up pace as I try to mask the despair I feel at the news. "It's not too late. Viktor's son could turn it around."

"Don't get your hopes up," Sven says. "We may never get the chance. It won't be easy to fool the delegation."

We walk the rest of the way back to the Biotik Sektor in silence. I spend part of the time thinking about Jakob and Hannah, and Owen and Nikki. I envy their uncomplicated relationships. Boy meets girl, they fall in love and live happily ever after. None of this girl meets clone, fall down a rabbit hole of expiration dates and ossification. The fear of losing Sven is messing with my mind. But I can't deny my heart—he ignites something inside me that I didn't know was there before I met him, and I don't want to give up on it.

The Rogues have trashed the Biotik Sektor by the time we arrive back—it looks like they've sampled every lyophilized food combination possible and tossed the rejects at each other. The pod chairs are twisted around on their goosenecks, and muddy packs and gear are strewn across the floor. The Undergrounders shrug when I throw them a questioning look. "The Rogues are pigs, what do you expect," one of them says.

A flash of anger goes through me. There's a ton to do without having to clean up after the Rogues as well. I turn to The Ghost. "Tell your men to straighten this place up right away."

He sneers at me. "This ain't summer camp. My men don't like to be told what to do."

I stare coldly back at him. "They'll spend the rest of their lives being told what to do if we don't straighten this place up before the delegation arrives."

The Ghost shrugs. "We got time."

"We've got enough to do between now and then without adding to the workload. Are you with us, or not?"

The Ghost scowls, but he grabs a handful of trash and marches across to his men.

"Let's head into the office and go over a few things with Viktor while the Rogues sort this place out," Sven says.

We follow him inside and close the door, relieved to be rid of The Ghost breathing down our necks for a few minutes.

Sven gets to work at the CommCenter and fires up a projection display above our heads. A moment later a hologram of Viktor comes into focus.

"Everything on task?" I ask him.

"We have a problem." His voice wavers like he's under duress. "I just received a transmission from my son."

I curl my hands into fists and press my nails into my palms. Whatever bad news Viktor is about to give us, it had better not be that his son's backing out—he knows too much now. And he's the only hope we have of overturning Sven's and Jerome's looming expiration dates.

"What's the problem?" Trout asks.

"The delegation has brought their arrival date forward," Viktor says.

"What?" My heartbeat hammers wildly as the implications explode in my brain. "When?"

"Tomorrow."

Sven bars his arms over his chest. "Why the sudden change?"

Viktor blinks. "After reviewing the reports again, the Sweepers on the Megamedes felt the circumstances called for an immediate assessment of the situation."

Sven narrows his eyes. "If you're setting us up, Viktor, I'll find out. I can recreate every keystroke you've hit, dig up every transmission you've ever deleted."

Viktor frowns. "Why would I warn you if I was setting you up?"

My brain spins. Instead of a week to prepare for the delegation's audit, we're down to twenty-four hours. There's no time to put everything in place. We'll have to change our strategy and focus on a few priorities.

"Brief the scientists," I order Viktor. "I'll be there in a few minutes."

He nods and flat lines from view.

"I'll check up on the cleanup operation," Trout says, walking out of the office. "I'll get the Undergrounders to pitch in too."

I turn to Sven. "As soon as this place is put back together we'll take the Rogues down to the Intake Sektor. I told The Ghost we'd let the men familiarize themselves with the place. But we're out of time for those kinds of formalities now. They're going to be suspicious if we tell them the delegation is arriving early. The chances of one of them getting trigger-happy are high. We're going to have to figure out a way to lock them up without alerting them."

Sven raises his brows. "They'll go ballistic; you do realize that?"

I give him a rueful grin. "I hope so. Enraged extractees are a lot more convincing."

Sven chuckles. "I'll work something out. I can show them around and then slip out a side exit and lock all the doors from the computerized keypad. They can be activated from any CommCenter after that. The Intake Sektor is soundproofed so the delegation won't be able to hear the Rogues yelling. I take it you're not planning on joining them now?"

I rumple my brow. "I need to stick with Viktor while he's touring the delegation around, make sure he adheres to our plan. Trout and I, and the other Undergrounders, can pose as junior scientists. I think Viktor's come clean about everything, but he's fickle. He could be talked into something."

"It's risky," Sven says. "You don't know anything about their scientific research. One slip from you or Trout could trigger their suspicions."

"I'll leave the technical mumbo-jumbo to Viktor." I dig Sven playfully in the ribs. "Isn't it about time you rounded up the military clones and practiced goose-stepping in those dapper black fatigues?"

Sven reaches for me and pulls me close. "I know what it means, all this joking around. You're scared."

I shiver in the strong circle of his arms—arms that could buckle and warp into desiccated limbs at any minute, trapping me against his expired frame. I can't let that happen. I'll fight to the end to save him.

"We need to let Jerome know about this latest transmission," I say.

Sven nods and releases me. He reactivates the CommCenter, and a moment later Jerome's face comes into focus a few feet above us.

"Everything under control at Terminus?" I ask.

"All good. I'm working on the maintenance schedules," Jerome replies. "How about on your end?"

"There's been a change of plan. More of a timing issue, actually. The delegation's arrival has been pulled forward."

Jerome's face twitches. "When?"

"Tomorrow."

He runs a hand over his pitted forehead. "The deviations can't restore the Craniopolis to full operational capacity in twenty-four hours. Maintenance and cleaning are in disarray, laundry is piled up in every Sektor, trash for the incinerator is overflowing."

"It doesn't matter. Tell them to resume their old schedules and positions effective immediately and look busy. The most the Sweepers will do is throw a passing glance at a deviation pushing a food cart or a broom around. Our main goal is to convince the Sweepers that the Schutz Clones have restored security and that Viktor, as the new lead scientist, has resumed extractions and clone production. He's already dummied up the records the Sweepers are likely to inspect."

Jerome squares his jaw. "The deviations don't do well under duress and they don't like disorder. They might become disruptive—run off and hide, walk in circles, that kind of thing. It's not a good idea to put them back on shifts under these circumstances."

I frown. "There must be some way to keep them pacified for the few hours the delegation is here."

"We could say they've contracted a communicable virus and keep them quarantined inside Terminus," Jerome suggests. "It's a common enough problem with their fragile immune systems. I can operate a skeleton crew and only allow those who are stable to resume work duty."

"Do what you think is best," I say. "Just make it happen. Sven and I are taking the Rogues down to the Intake Sektor in a few minutes to lock them up. I'll check in with you in the morning."

Jerome inclines his head. Seconds later, he condenses and zips from sight.

"Let's do this," I say to Sven. We walk out into the main living area and survey the space. The Rogues throw us dark looks as we pass by, but they keep working under The Ghost's supervision and the watchful eyes of the Undergrounders. The place is already looking ten times better. Maybe all those years in the reeducation center engrained some kind of work ethic in them after all, or maybe they're just scared of The Ghost. I don't blame them. I'm trying not to think of what he'll want to do to me after the delegation leaves.

I wave Trout over. "You and the rest of the Undergrounders can stay here and finish putting the place back together. Sven and I are going to take the Rogues down to Intake now." I arch a brow at him. "*Some of us* will be back shortly."

He gives me a crooked smile. "Sounds more fun than trash pickup."

The Ghost gathers up his men and we exit the Biotik Sektor and follow Sven through a web of feeder tunnels. An uneasy feeling hits as soon as we step through the steel entry doors to the Intake Sektor. Inside, the space is laid out like a giant batting cage of sorts, sub-divided into sections separated by sixteen-foot high chain link fencing. A few mattresses and benches are scattered around the interior.

"This is just a temporary holding pen area for extractees," Sven explains to the Rogues. He points to some doors at the far end of the room. "Back there is where the extractees are medically and psychologically evaluated. After they're processed, they are moved into the living quarters—much more upscale, complete with a lyophilized food dispenser." He raises his brows at The Ghost. "You'll be in there when the delegation comes through. Feel free to look around. Through these doors. Follow me." Sven taps something into a keypad on the wall, waves the Rogues forward and with a subtle incline of his head signals to me to fall back.

I bend down and fiddle with my bootlace, peeking cautiously through my hair as the last Rogue disappears through the main door. I wait for several minutes, then exhale and get to my feet. Before I can move, someone steps up behind me and whistles softly in my ear.

Chapter 15

I gasp and spin around. The Ghost's steely eyes bore into me, unsmiling. "Getting a little behind the tour group, aren't you?"

"Just tying my bootlace." I jut out my chin, but inside I'm shaking. Any minute now Sven will reappear, but without The Ghost locked in the living quarters with the rest of the Rogues, our plan is useless.

He makes a sweeping gesture at the door. "After you." His lips tug upward, but his eyes are devoid of warmth.

I start toward the door, dragging my boots with every step. I punch in the code on the access panel and push on the door, but it doesn't give. Sven's secured it already.

The Ghost folds his arms across his chest. "Isn't this interesting? My men are locked inside the Intake Sektor, and coincidentally you're out here." He narrows his eyes at me. "Only one little miscalculation on your part—you forgot I'm not as dumb as the rest of them."

"Don't be stupid." I knock sharply on the door and make a show of peering through the viewing monitor in the door. "Sven doesn't realize we're stuck out here."

"He knows *you're* out here, just like you planned it." The Ghost tightens his grip on his M16.

In my peripheral vision, I catch a glimpse of Sven approaching. Something in my face gives it away because The Ghost spins around and aims his gun straight at Sven.

Without stopping to think, I swing the butt of my rifle hard and crack the back of The Ghost's head. He lets out a grunt and drops to the ground.

"Are you all right?" Sven asks, running up to me.

"I'm fine. Just get him secured before he comes back around."

Sven reaches for The Ghost's limp body and swings him over one shoulder. "I can't reopen the doors to the Intake Sektor for the next hour. They're on a timed lockdown. I'll put him in one of the holding pens for now."

"What if he starts talking when the delegation comes through?"

"Viktor can give him something to knock him out," Sven says, adjusting his load. "That's his specialty."

He takes The Ghost out to the holding pen area and lays him down on a mattress on the back wall.

"Pat him down for weapons," I say. "Drugs or no drugs, we can't take the risk of him grabbing a member of the delegation through the bars and holding a knife to his throat."

Sven retrieves a Glock and two blades and hands them to me. "I'll tie him up for now." He pulls out some rope from his pack and secures The Ghost's wrists behind his back.

"Hear that?" Sven asks, looking up.

A muffled din reaches my ears.

Sven grins. "Took the Rogues that long to figure out they were locked in."

I grimace. "Let's get Viktor down here before The Ghost wakes up and discovers *he's* locked in."

Sven walks over to a CommCenter and a moment later Viktor's face materializes above us.

"We need your help down here," Sven says. "The Ghost gave us some trouble. He's out cold for now, but we'll need something to keep him subdued until the delegation has left."

"I'll swing by Sektor Sieben right away and pick up some drugs," Viktor says.

He fades from sight, and I turn to Sven. "We're behind schedule, and this is going to hold things up even more. We should split up."

Sven gives a reluctant nod. "I'll set the military clones up with Schutz gear and assign them their positions."

"Okay," I say. "I'll take the Undergrounders to the Research Sektor and get them kitted out with lab coats. And I want to go over the reports with Viktor one last time."

Sven's face creases in concern. "I don't like the idea of you going back there without me."

"We have no choice. We're running out of time."

I spin around at a loud groan. The Ghost contorts in a coughing fit. He bolts up into a sitting position, lucid and livid, eyes like darkened slits as he takes in his surroundings. He jerks his wrists to test the strength of his bonds, but only Sven's hands will ever be able to undo the grip of those knots.

"You double-crossing punks," he snarls. "Trading us like meat to the Sweeper processing plant."

I walk over to the pen and wrap my fingers around the chain link fence. "No one's being traded to the Sweepers. The delegation's arriving early. They're suspicious of something. I knew the Rogues would opt to fight if they got wind of it. We had to lock them up to make sure they don't deviate from the script in the heat of the moment—take out a Schutz Clone or something. We only get one shot at fooling the delegation."

The Ghost eyes me coldly. "We agreed to the plan. You're the one deviating from it."

"Consider it a necessary modification," I say as Viktor sails through the door. I give a subtle nod in his direction. He takes a few steps toward the holding pen and reaches inside his lab coat for a dart gun.

The Ghost's eyes flash to me, comprehension flitting across his face. The dart hits him before his lips can move and he sags to the ground like an empty sack.

"How long will he be out?" I ask.

"I'll arrange for one of the scientists to dose him up again tonight," Viktor says. "He won't twitch for twenty-four hours."

I nod. "Good. Let's head back to the Research Sektor and go over your reports."

"Watch your back," Sven mutters, as I turn to leave.

I give him what I hope is a reassuring smile as I follow Viktor out of the Intake Sektor.

Trout and the other Undergrounders are already dressed in their lab attire by the time we arrive at Research. I stare unapologetically at Trout, his thick, brown hair parted and combed neatly to one side. Against the white scrubs, I realize for the first time how dark-skinned he is despite our years in the bunkers.

"Where's Sven?" Trout asks.

"Getting the clones fitted for Schutz fatigues." I arch a brow at him. "You know you don't look half bad in a lab coat. One of those Sweepers might take a fancy to you."

He makes a face and gestures toward the screen behind him. "I've run through most of the reports Viktor put together for the delegation. They look good."

I give Viktor an approving nod. "Nice work, given the short notice."

"I have my own selfish reasons for wanting to make those reports convincing," he says.

"Ten years is a long time not to see your son," I say, grudgingly.

He throws me a grateful look. "I need to wrap up a few things. I'll be at my station if you need me." He walks back to an array of screens and sits down.

Trout brings me a couple of different lab coats to try on. I reach for the smallest one, but when I stick my arms through, the sleeves ride up past my wrists.

"More Won's size." I laugh, as I shrug off the coat.

Trout hands me the larger one and I slip it on. "Perfect! How's this?" I swivel to show him.

"You're clean, for once," he says, grinning.

I try to punch him in the arm, but he ducks and walks off chuckling.

I spend the next hour familiarizing myself with Viktor's doctored reports, before Trout and I call it a day and head back to the Biotik Sektor with the other Undergrounders.

I sink into a pod chair clutching a lyophilized turkey and mashed potato dinner sachet. Without the Rogues tromping around, bellowing, the place has a surprisingly soothing effect on me, despite the fact that we're essentially in an oversized coffin.

It still shocks me that the Craniopolis exists. And that it stayed hidden from the world for so long. Big Ed says it used to be harder to hide things from the public when the world was made up of different countries: governments were always spying on each other and leaking things to the press. The media was one of the first things the world government abolished. They said the political fear mongering had become too disruptive to global progress.

Sven sits down beside me, rips open a sachet and pours the contents into his mouth.

"What's on the menu?" I ask.

"Cheesecake." He grins. "I ate a flatiron steak and a baked potato on the way over here. Alexander the Great would have loved the convenience."

I frown. "Who?"

Sven shakes his head. "Never mind. I forgot you didn't have school in the bunkers."

He stands and yawns. "Get some sleep," he says. "You've got the biggest performance of your life tomorrow." He hits the recline feature on my pod chair and I tilt backward, sinking into the luxurious matrix cushioning. I moan as the softness envelops me. "Tell Trout I said goodnight," I mumble.

I wake the next morning before anyone else and tiptoe across to the food dispenser to appease my growling stomach. One bacon and egg burrito later, I'm feeling satisfied enough to take a stroll and see if anyone else is stirring. I'm eager to be up and moving, and start preparing for the delegation's arrival, but it seems I'm alone.

Sven is in a deep sleep, his chest rising and falling in perfect rhythm. None of the military clones snore, a by-product of their flawless physique. Viktor and the other scientists are spread out across the room in various pod chair arrangements. I spot the Undergrounders sleeping in the corner of the room, but no Trout. After tiptoeing around the Biotik Sektor twice, and checking in all the bathrooms, a seed of panic starts to grow. Where could Trout be? I stuff my hands into the pockets of my lab coat and my fingers brush up against something I'm certain wasn't there last night.

I take a quick breath and pull out a scrap of paper.

Back soon. Heard something.
T

Chapter 16

I stare at the note, my mind racing through the possibilities. Did Trout hear someone moving around outside the Biotik Sektor? One of the clones? A deviation? Or did the Rogues escape? My skin crawls at the thought. I've no idea how long Trout's been gone. If the Rogues are on the loose, he's in real trouble, and so is our plan if they catch him.

I pick my way back through the pod chairs to Sven and shake him awake. "Trout's gone!" I whisper, waving the note in front of him. He squints at the words, then jerks upright, suddenly alert. "How long's he been missing?"

I shrug. "No clue. I just found this."

Sven rubs his hands over his face. "Trout and I were the last ones to bed down for the night."

"So he may not have gone to sleep at all." I stare at Sven, stricken by the implications. "He could have left hours ago."

"I'll wake the military clones." Sven gets to his feet. "We'll bring Viktor, too. He knows the layout of the Craniopolis better than any of us. The others can wait here until we get back."

We assemble in the main tunnel after doing one more thorough search inside the Biotik Sektor. There's no trace of Trout and no indication of which direction he went.

"Let's check Intake first and make sure the Rogues are still locked up," I say.

Sven wrinkles his brow. "There's no way they could have escaped, but if it makes you feel any better, we can."

There's no sign of Trout in the Intake Sektor or any evidence that he was here. The Ghost lies motionless in the hushed shadows of the holding pen, crumpled in the same position the dart left him in. We slip by his pen and peer through the viewing monitor into the Intake Sektor's living quarters. The Rogues are scattered around the room, fast asleep in pod chairs. Their chests rise and fall, but no sound of snoring seeps through the soundproofed doors.

"Let's go," I say. "Trout didn't come this way."

Viktor frowns. "It could have been deviations he heard. They're pretty adept at slinking through the tunnels."

"So why isn't he back yet?" I ask.

"Maybe they mistook him for a Sweeper," Viktor says, a grave look on his face. "He was wearing a lab coat after all."

I throw an anxious glance Sven's way. It never even occurred to me that Trout could be in danger from the deviations.

"The deviations wouldn't be able to get out of Terminus on Jerome's watch," Sven says. "But I'll swing by there anyway and make sure everything's in order. I'll check docking and the maintenance wing on the way too. You and Viktor take some of the military clones with you and search the mechanical rooms and factory area. We'll regroup in Research."

An hour later, we congregate at Viktor's desk after searching every nook and cranny in the Craniopolis, including the Sweepers' quarters. I look at the faces of the military clones as they troop back into the room, trying to curb my desperation. "No leads?"

"Nothing," Sven says. "Maybe we should head back to the Biotik Sektor in case he's returned."

"You mean we should give up." I glare at him.

Sven flattens his lips, but he doesn't take the bait. "If the Undergrounders wake up and find us gone, they might panic."

I give a dejected nod. "I'm sorry. I'm mad at Trout for pulling a stunt like this. He knows better than to wander off alone, but he just won't quit."

Behind us the CommCenter beeps, and a sequence of lights flashes along the dashboard. Viktor jumps into action. "Incoming transmission." He flicks a series of switches and looks up, a feverish glow in his eyes. "It's the delegation. Two hours to arrival."

A cold sweat wraps around me. We're almost out of time.

Sven turns to me, a questioning look on his face.

"We need to stick to the plan from here on out," I say. "Trout's on his own. Go back to the Biotik Sektor and get the clones in position. Send the Undergrounders up to me. I'll meet you at the docking station in two hours."

Sven gives a curt nod and turns on his heel, already in full military mode.

I run my sweaty hands down the front of my lab coat. "You and the other scientists will have to do all the talking," I say to Viktor. "Your son will direct the conversation to you, so he won't be a problem. If one of the other members of the delegation asks a question, it's your job to make sure it isn't directed at an Undergrounder."

A flicker of pain crosses Viktor's face. "I'll do whatever it takes to be with my son again."

The docking station is eerily silent, an unwitting participant in the waiting game we are playing. The two-hour arrival deadline for the delegation has come and gone. Six gleaming Hovermedes, restrained by cables, line the hangar floor like exotic insects pinned in place. Sven and his newly inaugurated Schutz Clones stand in formation, ready to salute the delegation. Tricked out in black fatigues and steel-toed boots, heavily armed, they strike fear in my heart every time I glance across at them, even though I know they are military clones loyal to Sven.

The scientists are dressed in their usual garb, but their faces betray the weight of the task at hand. We are all a part of the deception, but the scientists will be the front-line perpetrators. One slip from them and everything unravels.

A sound like metal grinding on stone jerks my attention to the roof of the steel-framed hangar. A pneumatic whirring follows, and the entire top section slowly swivels off its base, revealing a quartz-veined, stony sky. Icy gusts lash through the hangar, rattling aluminum sheets in the parts carts lining the back wall.

A short distance away, the low, sleek profile of a Hovermedes emerges from the clouds. A familiar shot of fear throws me back on my heels, and I fight the instinct to run. Blood beats in my temples. The years I spent evading extraction have carved a well-worn, flight-response circuit in my brain.

I throw a quick glance around at the others. The Undergrounders huddle together, spellbound at the sight of the ship bearing a delegation of Sweepers. I try to push Trout out of my mind and stay focused. Every time my thoughts drift to him, a wave of panic courses through me. He's supposed to be here by my side, an essential part of our smokescreen. I can't help worrying that something unthinkable has happened to him.

I take a deep breath and straighten my stance as the Hovermedes begins its approach. The ship slows its speed and moves into position above the hangar. I stare up at it with loathing—an enemy so silent it's impossible to detect its treacherous presence.

The Hovermedes drops in staggered intervals. I hold my breath when the landing gear touches down and the ship stabilizes.

The pneumatic door on the side of the Hovermedes slides open. Viktor steps forward with his team of scientists to greet the delegation. I fall in behind with the other Undergrounders. Sven doesn't flinch a muscle when I pass by him. My heart is shaking inside, but I keep my eyes down and press on toward the ship.

A tall, olive-skinned man appears in the ship's doorway. He moves down the steps with poise and walks straight up to Viktor. They engage in a curt, professional handshake, and then the man turns and introduces the rest of the Sweepers who follow him out of the ship, trailed by a squadron of Schutz Clones.

A bookish-looking, moon-faced Sweeper with thick-rimmed glasses steps forward, greets Viktor, and immediately wanders off from the main group. He throws a beady eye over Sven and the military clones and runs a hand down the side of the closest Hovermedes. He studies the tips of his fingers, his peaked brows squeezed into a nearsighted squint.

I drop my gaze when he stares in my direction. He's going to be trouble. No matter how well we've rehearsed our script, he's figured out that we haven't run the Hovermedes in the past few days. "We've got a hound dog in the group," I whisper to the Undergrounder standing next to me. "Keep an eye on him, but whatever you do, don't let him engage you."

The tall, olive-skinned man snaps his fingers and gestures to the Schutz Clones to take up positions alongside the ship. Sven and his men match their silent stance.

Viktor turns to us and introduces the tall man. "This is Doctor Dimitri Petrov, head of the delegation."

I suck in a breath. *Viktor's son!*

We murmur a greeting and fall in behind Viktor as he leads the delegation out of the docking station. "Regretfully, MagLev transport is still down, so we'll be conducting a walking tour of the facility," Viktor explains.

The moon-faced Sweeper's eyes sharpen. "Restoration of power should have been the first priority."

Viktor gives a nod of acknowledgment. "Indeed. However, the deviations have been hit with a virus. Most of them are unfit for work." He sighs. "After suffering such heavy casualties in the coup, my colleagues and I are severely understaffed. We barely have the manpower to restore the Research Sektor to full operational capacity, let alone address transportation or maintenance."

"Is the cloning program stable?" Dimitri asks.

"Affirmative," Viktor replies. "The Intake Sektor is still processing extractees."

The moon-faced Sweeper steps into Viktor's personal space, a cunning gleam in his eyes. "You have extractees, and yet the Hovermedes have not been run recently."

Viktor hesitates. A moment too long.

I step forward. "We saw no need. Shortly before the coup, we conducted a mass extraction from a Rogue camp a short distance from the Craniopolis. The Intake Sektor is already at maximum capacity which allows us to focus our efforts on repairing the damage to the Craniopolis."

Dark, beetle-like eyes rake me over through thick-rimmed glasses. "And you are?"

"Doctor Connolly." I wrinkle my brow. "I don't believe I caught your name either."

"Chen Fu. Head of Genetics. I specialize in mutations." He pulls his lips into thin bands that retract so quickly I can't be sure if he smiled or sneered. "And *your* specialty is?" he prods.

"Fu!" Dimitri Petrov elbows past me. "Your expertise is needed here to evaluate Dr. Kozlov's progress."

Before Fu has a chance to protest, Dimitri escorts him to the front of the group. Viktor raises his brows briefly in my direction, before returning his attention to the delegation.

I close my eyes, and let out a silent breath. Sweat pools beneath the collar of my lab coat. The delegation is surprisingly small, four men and three women, but the Sweepers have unleashed a relentless investigator on us. If we detain Fu here with bogus orders from the outpost like we planned, we run the risk of him sticking his nose into everything and asking all sorts of dangerous questions. I've got to do something about him. Sven can't leave the docking station as long as Dimitri has ordered the Schutz Clones to remain there, and Trout AWOL, I'm going to have to figure this out on my own.

When we arrive at the Research Sektor, Viktor busies himself showing off his extensive collection of fabricated reports. Dimitri plays along, expressing approval at our efforts to stabilize the facility and research programs.

Just when I'm beginning to breathe a little easier, Fu announces that he needs to collect some samples from Terminus to determine the strain of virus the deviations have contracted.

I bite my tongue and wait for Viktor to speak.

"That would be inadvisable under the circumstances," he says, after a moment. "The virus is highly contagious. Everyone inside Terminus is under quarantine."

"Nonsense!" Fu replies. "Our bio-hazard suits offer more than adequate protection. It's my role to report back on any new strains of virus detected at the outposts."

Viktor gives a guarded smile. "Very well. Let's finish up in Research first. We'll need to discuss our plans for Sektor Sieben now that our Head of Cybernetics is deceased."

Viktor's eyes flash a distress signal to me.

"I'll arrange for a bio-hazard suit for Doctor Fu," I say, stepping forward.

"Excellent," Viktor replies. He turns and escorts the group into the corridor that leads to Sektor Sieben. I wait until I'm alone, and then dash over to the CommCenter and set up a link to Terminus.

A moment later, Jerome's hologram floats into view. I grip the edge of the desk in front of me. "We have a problem," I say. "A Doctor Fu, head of genetics. He wants to go down to Terminus and test for our non-existent virus."

Jerome balls his hand into a fist. "Don't let him come down here under any–" His voice cuts off. Shock ripples across his face.

I suck in an ice cold breath when I realize he's looking over my shoulder at someone.

Chapter 17

The hair on the back of my neck prickles. I spin around. Fu is standing in the entryway, his eyes skewering me with a mixture of rage and satisfaction.

"Your bio-hazard suit is being brought up from the supply room," I say. "Is there something else I can help you with?" I throw a hasty glance over my shoulder, but Jerome has faded from sight.

Fu struts across the room and stops in front of the CommCenter, hands clasped behind his back. The blinking lights signaling the end of the transmission reflect off his yellow skin.

"No virus?" He says. "And yet the deviations are not at their workstations." He raises his brows at me.

"They were traumatized by the coup. We thought it would be in their best interest to protect them from the additional stress of an audit. You know how agitated they get."

"You seem a little agitated yourself." Fu laughs, a hard, stinging laugh that tells me he's enjoying watching me dig myself in deeper. His eyes narrow to dark dashes in his face. "I knew something was off as soon as I got here. Your little coup anecdote is fascinating, but it doesn't add up."

He takes a step toward me, his face contorting. "What really happened to Won?"

"He died in the coup like Dr. Kozlov told you."

I think about reaching for my gun, but I don't want to show our cards if there's a chance I can talk my way out of this.

Fu slams his fist down on a desk. "Won didn't try to overthrow Lyong."

I take a step closer making it clear he can't intimidate me. "You don't know what happened."

"I know *everything* about what goes on here," Fu shouts, his yellow teeth gnashing up and down in his face. "Won wasn't staging a coup, he was planning his escape. We had him under surveillance, but he gave us the slip."

My breath dries up. That explains why Fu started sniffing around as soon as he disembarked from the Hovermedes. If Fu tells the delegation that the virus is a hoax, we'll never get out of this alive. I have to find a way to contain him until I can figure out what to do about him. I slip my hand beneath my coat, but before I can pull out my Glock, Fu sticks a gun to my temple.

"Don't even think about it!" he shrieks in my ear. "Who are you anyway? You never did tell me what you specialize in, *Doctor* Connolly."

I scrunch my eyes shut, berating myself for not making a move sooner. My only way out of this now is to lull Fu into complacency and use my speed. "Please don't hurt me." I squeeze out a few crocodile tears. "I was forced into this."

Fu relaxes his arm and takes a step backward. "Pass me your weapon, slowly."

I nod and fumble inside my coat. The instant his lips relax in a smirk I dive to his left, roll, and take aim, but before I pull the trigger Fu slumps to the floor in front of me, the loud crack of his skull echoing around the room. I stare in disbelief as Rummy comes into view, gripping the barrel of his Glock in his right hand.

My jaw drops. "What … are you doing here?"

"You're welcome, Butterface," he says, holstering his gun. He jerks his chin at Fu. "Who is he?"

I throw a nervous glance over my shoulder. "A Sweeper. They're conducting an audit. Why are you here?"

"I followed the Rogues here. Still tryin' to find my brother, remember?"

"He's not with them anymore," I say. "The Ghost said he slipped away during the storm. I thought he was with you."

Rummy stares at me for a minute before his face splits in a grin. "So my little brother has half a brain after all."

I cast another glance toward the door. "Have you seen Trout anywhere?"

Rummy wipes a hand across his jaw. "Yeah, about that kid. He heard me climbing out of the tunnel and came to take a gander. I knocked him out before I got a good gander at who I was slugging."

I ball my hands into fists. "Where is he now?"

"I tied him up and threw him down in the tunnel. Didn't want him stirring up trouble for me."

The sound of footsteps approaching startles us both. "Quick!" I gesture behind me. "Hide in the storage area. Take him with you."

Rummy reaches for Fu and drags him by the arms across the tile floor. I shove the door closed on them just as the delegation returns.

Viktor raises his brows at me, his eyes infused with fear.

I give him a reassuring smile before turning to Dimitri. "Everything in order, I trust?"

"Yes." Dimitri rubs his hands together. "We've agreed to keep Sektor Sieben closed for the time being, at least until the other projects are back up to full capacity." He glances around the room. "Where is Doctor Fu?"

"He went down to Terminus," I say, my pulse hammering in my head. "He seemed eager to start on his work."

Dimitri eyes me curiously. "He's very dedicated to his research. A new virus is a gift to a geneticist."

The other Sweepers appear satisfied with my explanation and chat casually among themselves, but I can tell Dimitri knows something's amiss. It's reassuring that even though Fu disappearing wasn't part of our original plan, Dimitri is working with the script I'm feeding him.

"Excellent," Viktor says, visibly relieved. "Shall we proceed to Intake and inspect the extractees?"

"I'll meet you down there," I say. "I have to pull a couple of reports for Dr. Fu first."

When the delegation leaves, I dart over to the storage area and yank open the door. "You need to get out of here. Now!"

Rummy throws me a look of disdain and steps over Fu's motionless body.

"I just got here, who said anything about leavin'?"

"You can't be seen by the delegation." I rub a hand across my brow. "Or the Rogues either. They're in the Intake Sektor and The Ghost's out for your blood."

Rummy narrows his eyes at me. "You got them boys chained up?" He reaches for his gun and loads a round in the chamber.

A wave of panic rolls up from my gut. "Rummy! Listen to me! Forget The Ghost. Blade's not with him anymore. Now's your chance to go look for him while the Rogues can't touch you."

Rummy curls his lip at me. "How'd you lock 'em up? Them boys is edgy around pens."

"Sven took them into the Intake Sektor living quarters and slipped out a side door. The locks are computerized."

Rummy hikes an eyebrow. "What about their weapons?"

"They're armed, but the doors are bulletproof. They've only got each other to shoot at."

Rummy grins. "It's time an old friend paid them a visit. Speaking of friends, you might wanna untie Trout. I ain't going that way just yet."

I pull out my Glock and point it at him. "I can't let you do that. You don't understand what's at stake. If you blow our cover, this place will be overrun with Schutz Clones in a matter of hours, and then we'll all be dead, or worse, we'll end up in the lab."

"Take that gun out of my face unless you're gonna use it." Rummy scowls. "When are them lowlife Sweepers leaving?"

"They're not," I say, "but they don't know that yet. We faked an incoming transmission ordering them to remain here until the Craniopolis has been restored to full capacity." I gesture at the door with my gun. "They may not be leaving, but you are. Go, before someone sees you."

He stares at me intently as if trying to decide if I've toughened up enough to shoot him at point blank range. Something in my expression convinces him. He fishes his black beanie out of his pocket and pulls it low over his eyes. "If I don't find Blade alive, I'll be back for The Ghost."

"Untie Trout on your way out and tell him to meet me at Intake," I call after him as he disappears through the door.

I yank open and shut several heavy metal drawers before I find some plastic ties I can use to secure Fu's hands with. For good measure, I stuff a rag into his mouth, half-hoping it's got some chemical clinging to it that will finish him off. I drag a pushcart over to the storage area and haul Fu's limp body onto it and heap a pile of dirty lab linens over him. It's a slipshod arrangement, but there isn't time to finesse it. I need to take him someplace where I can contain him before the Sweepers return. I ram the cart out into the corridor and throw a quick glance in both directions. The wheels make loud squeaking sounds that echo off the tile floors as I roll the cart down the main feeder tunnel. The only place I can think to hide Fu until I figure out what to do with him is Terminus. The delegation won't go near the deviations as long as the quarantine is in effect. I grit my teeth and pick up my pace as I race along the corridor.

Outside the entry doors to Terminus, the Optika module zooms in on me and transmits a hologram inside. Seconds later, the doors retract and Jerome sticks his head out. He glances up and down the corridor, then pulls the cart inside. He tosses the lab linens aside and stares at Fu's motionless body. "How'd you pull it off?" he asks. "It didn't look like you had the upper hand last time I saw you."

"I was about to shoot him," I say, "but it turns out Rummy was hiding in there. He clocked Fu on the side of the head and saved me a bullet. He says he tracked the Rogues here looking for Blade."

Jerome's eye twitches. "Where's Rummy now?"

"Gone. I told him to leave. He's going after his brother."

"You believe him?"

I shrug. "He made it clear he'll be back if he doesn't find Blade alive."

Jerome runs his hands over his face. "*That* I believe. Rummy and The Ghost are gonna take this to the grave. It's only a matter of who goes first."

"Let's get Fu contained before he comes to," I say.

Jerome grabs the bar handle of the cart. "This way."

He wheels the cart back to a small windowless room with a steel door at the far end of Terminus and unloads Fu onto a mattress in the middle of the floor. "This is our cooling off station," Jerome explains. He slams the door shut and keys something into the computerized wall pad. "And he's going to need it when he comes around."

I shoot Jerome a grateful smile. "Thanks for hiding him. I need to get back to the delegation and figure out what I'm going to tell them when Fu doesn't reappear. They think he's down here collecting samples."

"Tell them the bio-hazard suit was defective and he got exposed," Jerome says. "It's a mandatory quarantine. They won't question it."

"Thanks," I say with a wink. "I was hoping you'd offer to put him up a little longer, but I would never impose a Sweeper on you."

A smile pulls at his lips. "Keep me posted on how the delegation reacts to their new assignment to stay here and oversee the rehab operation."

"It will only buy us a few more days at best. It won't take long for the delegation to start asking questions."

"Let's focus on buying a day at a time for now," Jerome says quietly. "It's all we have."

I nod, wondering if he senses his time is near.

I reach the doors to the Intake Sektor just as Trout comes round the corner. A huge wave of relief rolls over me. He's safe, and that means Rummy's gone. We embrace briefly and I punch him playfully on the upper arm. "Don't ever do that to me again," I say.

"It was a stupid risk to take," he says, sheepishly. "But everyone was asleep and I didn't want us getting ambushed. I was only gonna take a quick look, then *Bam*! The last thing I was expecting was Rummy's fist in the back of my head." Trout lets out a snort. "At least he didn't carve me up on his way back out. Good riddance to him."

"We searched all over for you," I say. "It never occurred to me to try the tunnel."

"Where's the delegation?" Trout asks.

I motion to the Intake Sektor. "Inside. They're taking the tour. Come on, I'll introduce you."

"How am I going to explain not being there when they arrived?"

I grab his sleeve and pull him toward the door. "If anyone asks, you fell asleep in the Biotik Sektor after working a double shift preparing for their arrival."

I activate the keypad to open the door and step inside. It takes me a second to process the fact that The Ghost's holding pen is empty.

Chapter 18

I aim my weapon in front of me and pivot slowly as I scan the area around the holding pens.

"What's wrong?" Trout asks, slipping his gun from his shoulder.

"The Ghost's gone." I walk over to the holding pen and step inside. "He couldn't have escaped; he was too heavily sedated. And there's no sign of the ties we secured his wrists with. Someone took him."

"The delegation might have moved him." Trout casts a furtive glance over his shoulder. "Where are they anyway?"

"No idea. Let me make sure the rest of the Rogues are still here." I hightail it down the corridor and peer through the viewing monitor on the door leading to the living quarters. A pierced tongue slaps up against the glass and a tattooed fist pounds soundlessly on the door. I jump back startled. "They're in there all right." I grit my teeth. "Temperature's rising by the looks of things."

Trout tents his eyes and peers in. "There's a Rogue lying in the middle of the floor. Do you think he's dead?"

I wipe a hand across my brow. "I don't know, but at least they're contained for now. We need to find the delegation and see if they took The Ghost somewhere. If he starts talking the game is up."

"What other Sektors has the delegation visited?" Trout asks.

"Just Research and Intake."

"Then they might be headed to the Biotik Sektor—it's almost dinner time after all."

I stare at Trout, my mind cranking furiously. The day's almost gone. The delegation will be getting ready to leave soon. We need to make sure Viktor sets up the incoming transmission.

We crisscross back through the tunnels to the Biotik Sektor, keeping a watchful eye out on the off-chance The Ghost is on the loose. Common sense tells me it's not possible. Viktor gave him enough of a dose to knock him out for several hours. It's more likely someone moved him. But who, and why?

When we arrive back at the Biotik Sektor, the Sweepers are seated in pod chairs eating a lyophilized meal. The Undergrounders have retreated to the far end of the room, no doubt to avoid being drawn into any conversation that might arouse the Sweepers' suspicions.

I make a beeline for Viktor and pull him aside.

"I was about to take care of the transmission," he says, flustered.

"This isn't about the transmission," I say under my breath. "The Ghost's gone."

Viktor's eyes dart to Dimitri and back. "I know."

"What do you mean you know? Where is he?"

Viktor furrows his brow. "He was gone when we arrived at the Intake Sektor. I thought you moved him."

A clammy fear grips me. I shake my head.

Viktor blinks at me, his expression deadpan. "So who took him?"

I balk at the unlikely but deeply unsettling option that comes to mind.

Rummy.

I turn to Trout. "Are you sure Rummy left through the tunnel after he untied you?"

"I didn't hang around long enough to watch." Trout scratches his head. "It's possible he doubled back after I left."

"He'll wait until The Ghost comes to, so he can find out where Blade parted company with him," Viktor says.

"*If* he parted company with them," I say. "The Ghost could have killed Blade. And I'll bet Rummy's thinking the same thing."

I let the picture sit in my mind for a few minutes. I helped Rummy escape once because I was afraid he would die at The Ghost's hands. Seems all I did was reverse the odds. The Ghost's too drugged up to even defend himself—something I'm responsible for.

"You'd better get back to the delegation." Viktor flicks his eyes in Dimitri's direction. "Be sure to hang behind our scientists so you're not asked any questions."

One of the Sweepers throws a curious glance our way. I avoid making eye contact and pretend to be absorbed in what Viktor is saying.

"I'm going to slip into the office and send a preliminary report off to the outpost," Viktor continues in a low voice. "I'll set up the incoming transmission to come through about thirty minutes from now. Whatever you do, keep the delegation out of the office until I'm done."

Trout and I stroll across the room to join Dimitri and the others. The conversation is highly technical and after a few mentions of recipient cytoplasts, germline genes and methylation of DNA, my eyes glaze over. Trout studies the floor, hands stuffed deep in his pockets.

I lean over to whisper to him that I'm as bored as he looks when one of the scientists brings up ossification. I stiffen, ears pricked to attention.

"Perhaps there may be time for a demonstration of your technique, Doctor Petrov," a Sweeper suggests.

Dimitri runs a hand over his jaw. "Without the specialized equipment at my outpost, it would take an inordinate amount of time to extract and re-splice the defective DNA from the clones, Weeks, months maybe."

My heart sinks. We may not have that much time before we are exposed.

"How many clones at your outpost have undergone the procedure?" the Sweeper asks.

"We have only just completed the clinical trials," Dimitri explains. "The next step is to attempt the corrective procedure on select subjects."

"How will those subjects be chosen?" another Sweeper pipes up.

"Impeccable health records, naturally. More importantly, they cannot be older than–

"Dimitri!" Viktor comes running out of the office. "Incoming transmission from your outpost. Would you like me to feed it through?"

Dimitri raises his brows, faking surprise. "Yes please. We should all be informed of any updates."

I look away, trying to keep my frustration under wraps. I didn't anticipate an age restriction on the procedure to reverse ossification. I'm guessing Sven's still young enough to undergo whatever it involves, but what if Jerome's too old? As soon as I get a chance to talk to Dimitri alone, I need to find out exactly what the cutoff is.

A holographic ticker appears above the CommCenter on the back wall of the room. My pulse quickens as I read along with the transmission.

Orders to the delegation under Doctor Petrov: remain at Craniopolis until such time as full operational capacity has been restored to all sectors within the facility, including Sektor Sieben.

The Sweepers murmur among themselves for a few minutes before turning to Dimitri. "We agreed not to reopen Sektor Sieben until the other research programs are at full capacity," one of them says. "It could take months to rebuild the participant program."

Dimitri rubs his hands together briskly. "My fellow colleagues, we have been entrusted with the task of restoring the Craniopolis to full capacity as a bastion of scientific advancement. Let us strive to accomplish our task and not disappoint in this worthy endeavor, no matter the time and effort involved."

I break into a round of applause, and Trout and the others follow my cue. The Sweepers clap politely, but few are smiling. My gut tells me they won't be eager to sign on with us once we give them the option of joining forces or becoming our hostages.

Viktor addresses the delegation next. "I suggest we all enjoy a lyophilized dessert together and refresh ourselves before retiring for an early night. There is much work to be done tomorrow in light of the new orders."

"What about Doctor Fu?" a Sweeper asks. "Shouldn't he be back by now? We need to inform him of what's transpired."

"Yes, of course," Viktor replies, blinking rapidly. "I'll contact Terminus right away." He scuttles across the room to the CommCenter and taps in a command.

Almost immediately Jerome's hologram pops up.

Beads of perspiration break out on my forehead. If anyone insists on speaking to Fu via holograph, our cover will be blown. I can only hope Jerome makes a compelling case.

"Greetings, Terminus," Viktor says. "We've received a transmission from the outpost. The delegation has been ordered to remain on-site until such time as the Craniopolis has been restored to maximum operating capacity."

"Excellent," Jerome says, smiling. "We welcome their expertise."

Viktor tilts his brows in a grave expression. "Did Doctor Fu complete his data collection on the virus yet?"

"I'm afraid I have some unfortunate news in that regard," Jerome says. "Doctor Fu's bio-hazard suit was defective and he was exposed to the virus. It will be necessary for him to remain in Terminus under quarantine for the time being."

As I look around at the Sweepers' faces I can't help but think that Fu is not a popular colleague. They almost seem relieved that he's been confined to Terminus until the virus scare is over, which works to our advantage.

Dimitri assumes a suitably shaken expression. "How could this happen? Surely quality control would have eliminated such a possibility."

Jerome bows his head in assent. "Ordinarily, yes. However, the events of the last few days resulted in destruction and disarray on a scale that we have never had to deal with before. Therefore, we welcome all the more the delegation's assistance in helping us refurbish and restore our programs."

Doctor Petrov folds his arms across his chest. "Perhaps it is for the best that we have been called upon to facilitate the recovery process. Doctor Fu can continue his research in Terminus as long as he is under quarantine."

"We'll notify you as soon as Terminus is clear of the virus," Jerome says. "In the meantime, please keep us apprised of your progress." When he fades from view, Viktor turns to the delegation. "I'll send a message to the Schutz Clones in the docking station to let them know you will not be departing this evening as planned. There's nothing more we can accomplish tonight. Please eat and relax. We will begin our work in the morning."

Trout and I take our lyophilized cheesecake and join the other

Undergrounders. A few minutes later, Dimitri and Viktor slide into two pod chairs beside us. We pick at our dessert in silence, all too aware that the other end of the room is full of ears.

Dimitri stifles a yawn. "I'm ready to turn in."

Viktor throws a wary glance across at the Sweepers. "We need to be up before our guests start sniffing around."

"I'm an early riser." Trout winks at me. "I'll wake you all before the Sweepers start stirring."

We hit the orientation modes on our pod chairs and tilt them into the optimal sleeping position. I stare up at the ceiling, my thoughts drifting to Sven and the military clones. I hope they're safe and that the Schutz Clones haven't become suspicious of them.

When the last of the Sweepers falls asleep, Dimitri whispers across to me, "We can't reasonably expect to dupe the outpost for more than a week or two. What's your plan after that?"

I sit up on one elbow. "Find the Megamedes."

Dimitri and Viktor exchange subtle nods.

"I know someone who can help," Dimitri says.

Chapter 19

I raise a skeptical brow. "Who do you know who can help us?"

"The woman who designed the computer system for the Megamedes," Dimitri says.

My jaw drops. "Is she on board the ship?"

"She's at the Superconductor," Viktor says, quietly. "She's my daughter."

I stare at him, bewildered at first. Then my mind flashes to the scientist who connected us to Viktor. I knew she was hiding something, but I never suspected anything like this. I chew on my lip, trying to wrap my head around the implications. "Can she hack into the Megamedes?"

Viktor cocks his head to one side. "Lyong kept a tight control on everything at the Craniopolis, but now it might be possible."

"Has she been in contact with the Megamedes?" Trout asks.

Viktor shakes his head. "No, but she's intercepted transmissions from the Megamedes to other outposts enquiring about geological readings. It's a good indication the sovereign leader is eager to return to earth as soon as it's safe."

A surge of anger goes through me. "We can't let that happen. I won't let him disappear under the radar to some outpost. He has to be held accountable for what he's done."

"It's true the experimental programs are completely out of control," Viktor says, a somber look on his face, "but maybe that wasn't his intent. The world government said all along they wanted to help humanity and prolong lives—restart life in the case of the brain dead. Power-hungry scientists could have forced his hand. After all, he was far removed from day-to-day operations."

"Yeah, in the safety of his ship," Trout retorts.

"Nothing you've said absolves the sovereign leader," I say. "He knew what was going on, but he didn't try to stop it."

"Derry's right," Trout says. "We need to get on board the Megamedes and find him. It's the only way to end this once and for all."

Dimitri nods, eyes gleaming. "The Megamedes is outfitted with state-of-the-art weaponry. If we can take command of the ship, we could destroy any remaining outposts in a single strike."

I stare at him, horrified. "We can't just kill everyone at the outposts."

"We can't let them continue to operate either," Trout says. "There could be Sweepers out there, even crazier than Lyong, developing entire armies of Schutz Clones for all we know."

"We can evacuate the outposts first and then destroy the facilities," Dimitri says.

Viktor sits back and wipes his fingertips across his brow. "Iskra, my daughter, could make contact with the Megamedes at any time. We need to be clear where we stand on going to war against the sovereign leader. Make no mistake, it will be a bloody fight to seize control of the Megamedes." He studies me intently as if sizing up my commitment to hold the sovereign leader accountable.

A shudder goes through me at the sheer weight of responsibility I feel for everything I've set in motion, and the chaos yet to be unleashed. There will be more bloodshed before freedom can be secured. But without it, we're doomed to exist in a laboratory or on the run for the rest of our lives. "We go to war," I say, looking around at the scientists and Undergrounders, "as soon as Iskra secures the Megamedes' coordinates."

True to his word, Trout is the first to rise the next morning and he shakes the rest of us awake before the Sweepers begin to stir. Viktor gets to his feet and stretches. "Dimitri needs to go to the docking station and brief the Schutz Clones on the new orders. We have to follow protocol so we don't raise any suspicions."

I nod distractedly. "I'll go with him. Sven can arrange for the Schutz Clones to sleep in the Sweepers' quarters tonight. They'll be more comfortable there."

"Count me in," Trout says.

"Don't engage the Sweepers while we're gone," I warn the Undergrounders. "Keep a low profile and let Viktor and the scientists do all the talking."

"I'll let the delegation know where we're going," Dimitri says to me. "I'll catch up with you in a minute."

"Stay alert in the tunnels," I mutter to Trout as we exit the Biotik Sektor. "We haven't accounted for Rummy or The Ghost yet. Rummy may well have gotten his hands on a weapon by now."

Trout throws a furtive glance over his shoulder at Dimitri who's engaged in a heated conversation with a member of the delegation. "Did you tell Dimitri there are Rogues at large?"

I shake my head. "He might send the Schutz Clones to search for them. We can't have them swarming all over the Craniopolis, in case they uncover something."

"Everything all right?" I ask Dimitri when he joins us in the tunnel.

He gives a tight nod. "One of the Sweepers is raising questions about all the private conversations you and I are having. If anyone asks, tell them we were discussing the ossification breakthrough."

My chest tightens. "I did want to ask you about that."

Dimitri raises his brows. "You're actually interested in my research?"

Trout gives me a teasing grin, and my cheeks grow warm.

Dimitri squints at me with a pained expression on his face. "Tell me this isn't about a particular clone."

My face grows hotter. "He's a friend. A friend who risked his life for me more than once."

Dimitri's expression softens. "It wouldn't be the first time a human has fallen for a clone. But, it can never work in the long run."

"Why not?" I ask. "You've resolved ossification. Anything's possible now."

Dimitri passes a hand over his face, hiding his eyes. "We have yet to attempt the reversal on a clone. And once we do, it could be years before we know for sure if we were successful or not—that's if the procedure doesn't kill them. There are no guarantees."

"But the clinical trials have been successful," I say.

Dimitri throws me a troubled look as we walk along the tunnel in the direction of the docking station. "He would be my first subject outside of clinical trials. It would be unlikely to work flawlessly the first time."

"Lyong believed in you," I say. "He was willing to let you do the procedure on his son."

Dimitri furrows his brow. "How does your *friend* feel about it?"

I suck in my breath, remembering Sven's haunting words, and the glow in his amber eyes when he looked at me.

Without an expiration date, you … I …

"He wants it too," I say.

"You'd better believe it." Trout shoots me a wicked grin.

Dimitri gives a somber nod. "I wish we had his inception date. The younger the genetic material, the greater the chance of a successful outcome."

A flicker of hope goes through me. "He found his inception records. He's nineteen units."

"Nineteen?" Dimitri frowns.

"That's good isn't it?" My heart beats faster. "He still has several years before his expiration date."

"I was hoping he was closer to your age. I've never worked with DNA older than fifteen units before."

Trout lets out a snort. "If nineteen's the new old, I'm screwed."

"It's old in clone years," Dimitri says.

I turn to him. "Please—"

The sound of a gunshot cuts me off, ricocheting through the tunnel. I flatten myself against the wall and pan the empty corridor.

"Which direction did that come from?" Trout asks, chambering a round.

"I don't know," I say.

"Were they shooting at us?" Dimitri asks, fear flickering in his face.

I grimace. "I don't know. There are a couple of Rogues on the loose, and each one wants the other dead, but they'd kill me too if they got the chance."

Dimitri's eyes widen. "How did they escape?"

"One of them came here to find his brother. The other one is—was—locked up in Intake."

Trout throws me a knowing look from beneath his brows. Viktor never got a chance to dose The Ghost a second time. He could be back on his feet by now, armed and dangerous.

"We need to eliminate them before someone from the delegation gets wind of this," Dimitri says. "If they find out the Craniopolis isn't secure, they'll order the Schutz Clones to tear this place apart to find the escaped extractees."

"And when they do," Trout adds glumly, "The Ghost will sell us out."

"Not if we find him first," I say.

Another shot rings out and I jump back against the wall.

Trout puts a finger to his lips. "That came from the direction of the docking station," he whispers. "Rummy might have dragged The Ghost in there before he realized the place was crawling with Schutz Clones."

"We need to end this," Dimitri says. "We can't have the delegation waking up to a gunfight."

I signal Trout to stay close by, and then pad silently around the corner in a crouched position, hoping I don't run into Rummy or The Ghost.

My heart thumps as I edge closer to the docking station. I listen for a few minutes, but no shots ring out inside. Tentatively, I reach out and punch in the entry code on the keypad. The double entry doors yawn open. I blink in disbelief. The Schutz Clones are gone. And so is Sven.

Chapter 20

I scan the deserted docking station in a daze. "The gunfire must have come from farther down the tunnel," I say, as Dimitri and Trout walk up behind me. "There's no one here."

"The Schutz Clones wouldn't have left their posts without my express order unless they were under attack," Dimitri says.

I furrow my brow. "Sven might have enlisted the Schutz Clones' help to go after the Rogues."

We turn our heads at the sound of boots tromping in rhythm toward the docking station.

"It's them," Trout says, a hopeful note in his voice. "With any luck, they've captured Rummy and The Ghost."

Sven and the military clones file through the door first. I briefly wonder where their helmets are, but then my heart trips when I realize they're weaponless. I fix my eyes on Sven, but he keeps his head forward and doesn't acknowledge me. The Schutz Clones march behind the military clones, barking out orders as they herd their captives all the way to the back of the docking station.

I feel hot and cold all at once. Beads of sweat prickle the back of my neck. I slip the strap of my rifle from my shoulder, unsure how I'm going to confront a squad of heavily armed Schutz Clones.

Trout grabs my elbow from behind. "Are you crazy? Let Dimitri talk to them first," he hisses.

Dimitri strides past us, face like thunder as he approaches the clones. "What is the meaning of this grievous breach in protocol?"

One of the Schutz Clones steps forward and salutes him. "Doctor Petrov, we have uncovered a plot. The Schutz Clones at this base have been murdered. These clones are imposters."

Dimitri takes a step back. He turns slowly to me. "Is this true?"

I force my face to register an equal measure of astonishment. "I'm as shocked as you are."

"They must have been supporters of Doctor Won's hostile takeover," the Schutz Clone asserts.

Dimitri walks over to Sven and peers at him intently for a moment. "Do you recognize this clone?" he asks, turning to Trout and me.

I nod, feigning a dawning comprehension. "I believe he's a military clone."

Dimitri sets his jaw. "How did you discover this deception?" he asks the Schutz Clone.

"Two escaped extractees showed up at the docking station. One of them addressed this clone by name." He gestures at Sven. "We ran his chip. He's military—052."

"Where are the escaped extractees?" I ask.

"We returned them to the Intake Sektor."

"Are they … together?" Trout asks.

The Schutz Clone looks at him blankly. "Yes, we secured them in a holding pen to await Doctor Petrov's orders." He turns to Dimitri. "What is your directive regarding the clones who participated in the coup?"

Dimitri rubs his chin between his forefinger and thumb, appearing to give the matter some thought. "Incarcerate them for now. We'll have to interrogate them."

A flicker of disappointment crosses the Schutz Clone's face. Maybe he was hoping for a swift execution. My stomach knots. I realize Dimitri has no choice but to play along with this farce for now, but I dread the thought of Sven and the other military clones being locked up anywhere near the Rogues. How are we ever going to get out of this mess? The rest of the delegation will side with the Schutz Clones when this comes to light. Head scientist or not, Dimitri has little control over the outcome. He'll be forced to report back to the outpost. I need to come up with a plan, and quickly.

Dimitri glares at me. "This is an outrageous failure on your outpost's behalf. You will escort me back to the Biotik Sektor as soon as we're finished here. I intend to get to the bottom of this and I will hold someone accountable."

"Of course," I say, adopting a suitably meek tone.

"Lock up the military clones in Intake and report back to the docking station for debriefing," Dimitri says to the Schutz Clone.

The Schutz Clone salutes and barks out an order to the rest of his squad who waste no time marching Sven and his men out of the docking station.

My heart aches to signal to Sven that everything will be okay, that I'll find a way to rescue him, but he doesn't even look in my direction. I watch him disappear through the double doors, knowing he's trying to protect me by not connecting us in any way.

We wait until the Schutz Clones are well out of earshot and then let out a collective breath.

"We're screwed," Trout says, sounding more desperate than I've ever heard him before.

Dimitri rubs his brow. "I'll be expected to transmit a full report as soon as I've debriefed the Schutz Clones. Reinforcements will arrive in a day or two. The scientists will be questioned. My father will be arrested and executed. We have twenty-four hours at most."

"We're not going to let it happen," I say. "We'll figure out a way to shut the Schutz Clones down."

"There isn't one." Trout rubs a hand across his jaw. "They're fighting machines."

I stare at him as the words sink in. *Fighting machines.* A crazy idea bubbles up inside me. But then crazy is exactly what we need. "I think I know how we can stop the Schutz Clones."

Dimitri raises his brows half-heartedly. "How?"

"We'll turn the Rogues loose. They're armed and they're itching for a fight—they already killed one of their own."

Dimitri frowns. "What's to stop them killing us?"

"They can't kill us if they can't find us," I say. "We'll set the timer to open the Intake Sektor doors after we flee to the city through the tunnel."

Dimitri mulls it over for a moment. "What about the deviations?"

"They're safer in Terminus than anywhere else for now," Trout chips in. "We can warn Jerome to stay under lockdown until the fighting is done."

"We just need to find a way to free Sven and the military clones first." I walk over to the CommCenter and activate the system to link to Terminus. Jerome's hologram floats into view.

"Checking up on our infected inmate?" he asks, with a grin.

"Not exactly."

His smile disappears. "What's wrong?"

"Sven and the military clones have been arrested."

Jerome rubs a hand across his jaw. "Does the outpost know?"

I shake my head. "Not yet. The Schutz Clones are on to us, but they don't suspect Dimitri is helping us. They're relying on him to manage the situation and transmit the appropriate reports."

"The Schutz Clones have to be eliminated," Jerome says. "It's only a matter of time before they discover the whole truth."

"We're going to release the Rogues and let them take their revenge on the Schutz Clones while we flee back to the city," Trout says.

"Do you want to come with us?" I ask Jerome.

"We can't move that quickly. We'll hunker down inside Terminus," he says, a grave expression on his face.

"And Fu?"

"I can handle him."

"I don't doubt it," I say. "Good luck, Jerome."

He bobs his head and disappears from view.

Trout gives my arm a quick squeeze. "He'll be fine."

I nod, grateful for the reassurance even though there is no guarantee we'll ever see Jerome again.

"We need to brief Viktor," Dimitri says, joining me at the CommCenter.

He taps a few buttons and waits. My breathing quickens as the minutes go by and nothing happens. Just when I'm about to give voice to my fear that the Schutz Clones have got to him, Viktor's face comes into focus.

"Sorry about the delay," he says. "I've been fielding questions from the delegation in your absence."

Dimitri's face tightens. "What kind of questions?"

Viktor frowns. "How the coup went down, how I managed to survive when Lyong and Won both ended up dead."

"What did you tell them?" I ask.

"That I was holed up in the Research Sektor. I can't put them off much longer though. When are you coming back?"

"The Schutz Clones are on to us," Dimitri says. "They know Sven and the military clones are imposters. They've taken their weapons and they're escorting them to a holding pen in the Intake Sektor."

Viktor's face pales. He passes a trembling hand over his face. Dimitri told us his father would be executed if we were exposed, and judging by the look on Viktor's face, Dimitri wasn't exaggerating.

"You'll have to go through the motions of arresting me." Viktor pulls a tissue from his pocket and brushes it distractedly across his beaked nose.

"I know," Dimitri says. "But we can hold them off until tomorrow morning. And by then we'll be gone."

Viktor knits his brows together. "How are we going to pull that off? The Schutz Clones will pursue us once they realize we've fled. We can't outrun them."

"We won't have to," Dimitri says. "We're going to turn the Rogues loose on the Schutz Clones while we escape through the tunnel."

"What about Sven and the military clones?" Viktor asks.

"We'll have to figure out a way to free them before we release the Rogues," I say.

Viktor looks dubious. "It won't be easy. The Schutz Clones will have guards posted at the Intake Sektor. They may not suspect Dimitri or you of double-crossing them, but they won't take a chance of more Rogues showing up unannounced."

"We can't risk gunfire," I say. "Can we tranquilize them with the drugs you gave The Ghost?"

Viktor nods. "I'll double the doses to be sure. Meet me at Sektor Sieben."

"We'll head that way as soon as the Schutz Clones return from the Intake Sektor," I say.

Viktor wipes a sheen of sweat from his forehead. "I'll be waiting."

The hologram melts away as the sound of the Schutz Clones' distinctive march reaches our ears.

Dimitri strides over to meet them at the door. He stretches out his hand and lays it on the shoulder of the lead Schutz Clone. "Excellent work exposing the imposters. We are all safer because of your diligence. Upon our return to the outpost, I will be recommending you for promotion."

The clone gives a clipped salute.

"I want your squadron to remain in the docking station tonight and guard the Hovermedes. Make sure no one attempts an unauthorized departure."

The Schutz Clone salutes again, overly eager to please. "I stationed two guards inside the Intake Sektor," he says. "The rest of us will remain on duty here."

Dimitri gives a somber nod. "No Hovermedes are to leave this station under any circumstances until tomorrow morning when we'll escort the prisoners back to the outpost."

The Schutz Clone throws a glance in my direction. I widen my eyes, doing my part to feign fear.

Dimitri waves a dismissive hand at Trout and me. "Juniors. They know nothing." He leans conspiratorially toward the Schutz Clone. "I will personally arrest Doctor Koslov in the morning and hold him responsible for allowing this to happen on his watch."

The Schutz Clone clicks his heels together, the only indication of his satisfaction at the news.

Dimitri leads the way out of the docking station. Trout and I follow behind, heads hung low like chastised children. The moment we round the corner, we break into a run and make a beeline for Sektor Sieben.

Viktor greets us at the door. He peers furtively down the tunnel, before hustling us inside. "Can you operate this?" he asks, fumbling with a sleek long-barreled gun. He blinks at Dimitri, ignoring Trout and me.

"It's a gun," I say, testily. "How hard can it be?"

"It's a rapid auto-loader dart gun," Viktor says, giving me a hard stare. "The darts are designed for instant impact sedation, but the sedative needs to enter the bloodstream right away. Intramuscular absorption would take too long."

I shrug. "I'm an excellent shot. Just tell me where you want it."

Viktor loads a dart and hands the gun and several additional darts to Dimitri. Evidently he doesn't trust me with the job. I can't help wondering how good a shot Dimitri is.

Dimitri slips the dart gun inside his coat and embraces his father. The gesture makes me uneasy like he thinks there's a chance they won't see each other again.

Viktor scribbles something on a scrap of paper and thrusts it at me. "This is the master code Sven set for the Intake Sektor living quarters." He gives a conspiratorial nod. "When you're ready to release the Rogues."

"I can probably handle punching in a code," I say, snatching the note from him.

We take our leave of Viktor and make our way through the feeder tunnels toward the Intake Sektor. Even though Rummy and The Ghost are supposedly back under lock and key, I throw the occasional nervous glance over my shoulder. The Ghost has an uncanny knack for showing up when I least expect it, and at times, I almost imagine I hear a faint whistling coming through the tunnel.

I breathe a sigh of relief when we reach the Intake Sektor. We edge around to a side door and peer cautiously through the glass. Two Schutz Clones patrol the area in front of the holding pens. The tranquilizing shots should be relatively easy to make if we can get inside without being detected.

Breath on pause, I key in the entry code on the keypad. The door clicks quietly and I push it open, gesturing the others inside. Dimitri fumbles with the gun, his hand shaking. I exchange a quick look of desperation with Trout, before snatching the gun out of Dimitri's hands. "Where?" I mouth at him.

"He points a finger at his neck and I nod. I take aim and wait until the two Schutz Clones are at the farthest point from each other before I pull the trigger. The Schutz Clone nearest to us collapses in front of the holding pen housing the military clones. The chain link fence rattles when they grab it, shoving each other aside to see what just happened. The second Schutz Clone, confused by the commotion, points his weapon on the clones in the holding pen, then keels backward as the second dart finds it target.

I stuff the gun in my jacket and bolt toward the holding pens. "Use the magnetic wand on the wall behind you," Sven yells to me. "It's a master key for all the pens." I yank it off the wall and wave it in front of the keypad on Sven's holding pen. The door clicks open and the military clones stream out and rush over to kick down the strongroom door and retrieve their weapons.

Sven wraps a giant hand around my waist and pulls me toward him. Before I realize what's happening he leans over and plants his lips firmly on mine. His warmth rushes through me, the softness of his lips sealing me in like a protective barrier from what lies ahead.

When we pull apart I see Rummy gripping the chain link fence of the neighboring pen with his fists, his eyes boring into mine. The Ghost steps up behind him and begins to whistle softly as he slashes a hand across his throat. My heart sinks. It's an unmistakable gesture. Someone in that pen is going to die if I don't do something. I can't leave this unresolved.

I walk across the foyer and toss my Glock onto a table by the entryway. "First one to the gun, boys," I say, waving the magnetic wand back and forth to unlock the Rogues' pen.

Their faces register a flicker of confusion, then comprehension. They barge through the open door of the holding pen and make a mad dash toward the table.

Sven throws me a stricken look and takes aim.

"I've got this," I say, curling my fingers tightly around the tranquilizer gun.

"Oops," I say, as I pull the trigger.

Chapter 21

The Ghost folds over and drops to the floor. I snatch up my Glock before Rummy can cover the last few feet to the table and grab it. He comes to a screeching halt and stares down at The Ghost's crumpled body.

"That's for taking care of Fu for me," I say.

Rummy looks up and smirks. "Sure wish you woulda used a dang bullet, but I guess you don't owe me no more, Butter–"

"Don't! Go, before I change my mind and dart you too."

He taps his fingers to the side of his head in a mock salute. "Until next time."

"There won't be a next time," I say. "I'm done trading favors with you."

He shoots me a mocking grin as he steps over The Ghost and retrieves the gun from a motionless Schutz Clone. He slings it over his shoulder and disappears through the door without a backward glance.

"Why'd you let him go?" Trout asks.

I blow out a heavy breath. "I owed him one last break. Let's put The Ghost back in the holding pen. He'll be trampled to death once we turn the Rogues loose."

"Good riddance!" Trout mutters, grabbing The Ghost by the leg.

"I gave Rummy a free pass," I say. "This is as much as I'm willing to do for The Ghost."

We drag him back inside the holding pen, and I lock the door with the magnetic wand.

"Don't you want it unlocked so he's free to fight the Schutz Clones when he comes around?" Sven asks.

"We'll leave that up to the Rogues to decide," I say. "Along with a note on the viewing monitor to tell them the Schutz Clones are in the docking station. They'll have the advantage of surprise at least."

I throw one last glance at The Ghost's sack like form as we leave, pushing down the foreboding feeling that niggles at me. If he survives, I've no doubt he'll come for his pound of flesh.

When we reach the Biotik Sektor, Dimitri pulls me aside. "Let me talk to the delegation for a few minutes alone. I'm going to try and persuade them to come with us voluntarily, but if they won't, we'll take them hostage."

I chew on my lip as I weigh our options. He's right of course. We can't leave them behind in the Craniopolis. They'll either be slaughtered by the Rogues, or escape in a Hovermedes and return with a legion of Schutz Clones. "All right," I say. "You have three minutes to convince them before we tie them up and move out."

Trout and I gather up our stuff, grab a handful of lyophilized meal sachets, and close up our packs.

I throw a couple of uneasy glances over at Dimitri and the other members of the delegation as the conversation grows louder. One of the Sweepers raises his arm, and, for a moment, I think he's going to take a swing at Dimitri. He gestures briefly in an animated fashion and stomps away from the rest of the group.

"It's a split decision," I say to Trout. "Brace yourself."

A few minutes later Dimitri walks back over to us, a resigned look on his face. "They don't trust me. They want to see Fu before they make a decision."

I shake my head. "Not gonna happen." I gesture across to the CommCenter where Sven is bent over the control panel. "Sven's setting the timer on the Intake Sektor doors. We need to go."

"Then we're going to be doing this the hard way," Dimitri says.

In the end, the members of the delegation don't put up too much of a struggle. They protest, but they quickly realize they don't have a chance with

Sven and the military clones at the ready.

I watch as the clones secure the delegation's wrists and separate them into pairs. I'm not excited about the prospect of yet another reluctant faction taking up residence in the city and adding to the tension, but for now, at any rate, I don't have a better place to take them.

Sven strides across the room to me, his face resolute. "We're ready."

"How much time do we have before the Rogues are free?" I ask.

"Ninety minutes. Enough time to get out through the tunnel and make tracks into the forest."

"Let's do this," I say.

"You know we won't be safe in the city for long," Sven says. "No matter who comes out of the Craniopolis alive, they'll come for us."

I grimace. "As soon as Iskra locates the Megamedes, I'm going to figure out how to get us on board. If we can take over the ship, we can end this." I hesitate and lay a hand on Sven's arm. "And then Dimitri can help you and Jerome."

"I'm not interested in being an ex-Sweeper's lab rat," Sven says. "Dimitri developed a theory for resolving ossification, but that's all it was."

I frown at him. "What do you mean?"

His shoulders heave up and down. "I talked to some of the other members of the delegation. The clinical trials were never completed. There were too many inherent risks that came to light."

I stare at him in disbelief, a sickening feeling swirling around inside. That's why Dimitri couldn't make any promises about the outcome.

It can never work in the long run.

Dimitri wasn't talking about a relationship between a human and a clone. He was warning me about the risks they uncovered. My eyes burn with unshed tears. I thought Dimitri could cure ossification, but he's been snatching at straws. I can't ask Sven to suffer needlessly for my sake. He has a right to enjoy the few years he has left. But I won't give up. There's still the Megamedes. None of us knows for sure what's on board, or what scientific advances the world government has made since the meltdown.

It takes a lot longer than we'd planned to get everyone out through the tunnel. The members of the delegation prove uncooperative once we're underway, arguing with our orders at every opportunity, and the military clones are forced to half-carry, half-drag them along at times. My muscles are cramping up by the time we reach the forest and climb back out into the cool evening air.

"We'll have to avoid the trails in case we're pursued," I say to Sven. "It'll be a tough overnight hike through some dense brush, especially with uncooperative hostages."

He nods. "The doors to the Intake Sektor should be opening about now."

Fear prickles like icy dew along my skin. My mind spins through the frightening scenario set to play out in the Craniopolis. "Who do you think has the better odds?"

Sven looks off into the distance. "The Schutz Clones are superior fighters, but they're grossly outnumbered. And opening those doors will be like letting the hounds of hell loose."

I shudder at the thought. I've seen first-hand what the Rogues can unleash when they've been crossed. Sven's right; incarceration has only ratcheted up their hunger for blood.

Rays of evening sunshine blink through the trees as we begin our long hike back to the city. A thick bed of leaves and fallen twigs crunches beneath our feet, an oddly comforting sound after the hard clacking of our boots on the gleaming Craniopolis floors. The lyophilized food we packed will save us valuable time, but even without stopping to eat, carving a path through the dense undergrowth is time-consuming and exhausting. Without Sven and his men clearing the way, it would be almost impossible.

I glance back over my shoulder. The delegation and the two military clones who are escorting them have fallen way behind, but I can still hear them moving through the brush. Viktor and Dimitri are somewhere at the rear of the pack, no doubt catching up on the past decade.

"The military clones are getting too far ahead of us," Trout says, coming up alongside me. "Shall I tell Sven to take it down a notch?"

"If only the delegation would quit dragging their heels," I grumble. "Tell

Sven he needs to keep us in sight. We can't risk getting separated."

Trout takes off into the brush and I lean back against a tree to wait for the delegation to catch up. My thoughts drift to the Megamedes. Even if Iskra locates it, we still have to figure out a way to get on board.

An angry yell from farther back on the trail startles me upright. I reach for my gun and begin plowing my way back through the brush, brambles tearing at my clothes and skin. I leap over a moss-covered boulder and collide with an ossifying clone tipped forward in the dirt. My heart lurches. I look up at the sound of someone thrashing toward me through the undergrowth.

"Go that way!" Viktor yells, pointing to his left as he runs by. "The delegation split when he expired." He dives back into the brush and disappears from sight. I surge forward into the undergrowth in the direction he pointed. My pulse pounds in my throat. I wonder how long it will be before Trout and Sven realize we're not following them anymore. The last thing I wanted is for us to get split up.

Up ahead I catch a glimpse of one of the members of the delegation. I grit my teeth and pick up the pace. We can't let them any of them make it back to the Craniopolis and escape on a Hovermedes. I edge closer and take aim with my gun. "Hold up or I'll shoot!"

He throws a harried glance over his shoulder, then ducks beneath a branch and disappears from sight.

I take off running after him again. "Last chance!" I yell as I skirt around the tree, weapon raised. His frightened eyes meet mine. Someone's already got a gun to his head.

Chapter 22

My legs almost buckle beneath me. Dark, metallic eyes in a shaved skull study me with a flicker of amusement. "This the skunk you're after?" Blade asks in a slow drawl. His lip twitches and the scar gouging the whole left side of his face writhes in concert.

I'm shaking inside, but I fight to hold my voice steady. "Him and a few other Sweepers. You could make yourself useful and help us find them."

For a moment, he looks mildly curious, but then he seems to remember something more important. He jabs the gun into the Sweeper's temple. "Where's The Ghost at?"

"How would I know?"

Blade eyes me skeptically. "Musta seen him. He tracked you to the Craniopolis."

I shrug. "Last I heard he was tracking you."

Blade's lips slit and tug up at one corner. "He ain't the type takes kindly to being made a fool of."

"Derry!"

I stiffen at the sound of Trout's voice.

"Derry! Where are you?" Trout yells more loudly.

"Don't answer," Blade growls. "Or the Sweeper dies, and then Trout."

I breathe slowly in and out. If I direct Trout this way, there's a good chance Blade will shoot him. But if I let him pass by, he'll waste precious time looking for me and run the risk of encountering Schutz Clones or

Rogues, either of which is a sickening proposition. I squeeze my eyes shut and listen with mounting anguish as the sound of Trout's voice grows fainter.

Blade nods in my direction. "All right, walk toward me and set the gun down at my feet, real slow."

The Sweeper's eyes dart helplessly to mine. I grit my teeth. Now he wants me to save his hide. But it's his fault we're in this mess to begin with. Whatever I do next, it won't be with his safety in mind. I take a few steps forward, and then bend over and lay my gun down on the pine needles. Instinctively, my fingers seek out the switchblade in my jacket pocket. I get to my feet and stare glumly at Blade. The moment his face relaxes in a victory sneer, I make my move.

I arc my right arm and slice the knife across his neck, knocking his gun upward with my other hand. Blood sprays me. Blade makes a guttural sound and staggers backward. Without a second glance the Sweeper bolts. I snatch up my gun and take off running low and hard, weaving my way through the brush, oblivious to the branches flaying my flesh. My only thought is to make it as difficult as possible for Blade to get a clean shot at me.

I can tell I'm making quick work of putting some distance between us. I'm faster and lighter than he is, and he's hurt. He's breathing heavily, cussing up a storm, thrashing through the brush. A shot rings out behind me.

I throw a terrified glance over my shoulder and leap over a boulder, landing on a slope of half-mulched forest litter. My feet slide out from under me and I roll, trembling, beneath a clump of ferns. Blade's footsteps tromp closer and I tense, waiting for his next bullet to find its mark. Instead, I hear a heavy thud as something hits the ground.

I listen intently for several minutes, but I don't detect anything more than the faint stirring of the wind through the trees and the occasional chatter of squirrels. I peek out from beneath the waving fern fronds. The evening shadows have lengthened, and I can just about make out a body lying ten or so feet from me in the brush. If it's Blade, his stalking days are over. There's an arrow through his chest.

I scoot along the ground on my belly until I get close enough to confirm that it's him. My mind races to one conclusion. *Lou.* Who else prowls around in the forest hunting Rogues with a bow and arrow? I call out her name several times, knowing full well it's a waste of time. She'll show up in her own time, on her terms.

I get to my feet and tentatively approach Blade's body. Lou's arrow has found its mark with deadly accuracy. I force myself to feel for a pulse. If I ever run into Rummy again, I can tell him I did that much at least. I stare down at Blade's face, eyes open, but strangely flat and bereft of emotion. I'll never see him again, and the thought cheers me.

"Derry!" It's Sven's voice, faint and frantic.

I jump to my feet, cup my hands to my mouth and yell repeatedly, directing him to me.

Seconds later he barrels out of the brush and wraps me in his arms. "Thank goodness you're safe."

"Blade was shooting at me but he's dead now," I say when we pull apart. I point at the body.

"Who killed him?" Sven asks, staring at the arrow.

"Lou's the only person I know who can shoot an arrow with that kind of accuracy, but there's no sign of her anywhere," I say. "Did you find the Sweepers?"

Sven shakes his head. "By the time Trout and I found out what happened, they were long gone. They must have doubled back in the direction of the Craniopolis. We gave up pursuing them once we realized you were missing."

"Too late to stop them now," I say. "We need to make tracks to the city."

The rest of the hike back is long and treacherous as night falls. The moon drips little light on our path as we slog through the forest and over gurgling streams. So much for the lyophilized food sachets–I don't even have the energy to tear one open and throw the contents down my throat. As dawn breaks, I finally make out the outline of Shoshane City, and I allow myself a sliver of hope. Up until now, I didn't think we'd make it. I kept looking over my shoulder all through the night expecting to see a horde of Rogues or Schutz Clones descending on us.

The container gates groan open upon our approach and we troop through, exhausted and famished. The Undergrounders and riders stare at us, wide-eyed and silent. At first, I'm not sure why we're such a spectacle. Then I glance down at my tattered clothing, spattered with mud and Blade's blood. Trout's covered in scratches like ruby-colored whip marks over his sunken face. Sven stomps along on my other side, eyes locked forward, his fatigues ripped and filthy. Dimitri and Viktor chicken walk behind him, eyes glazed over. The rest of the military clones, scientists, and Undergrounders take up the rear in similarly ragged shape.

I scan the faces as we go by, but there's no sign of Owen. I've been harboring some small hope that he would change his mind and return. Jody tilts the brim of her hat at me from her horse as we pass by. After a few minutes, I spot Rocco elbowing his way through the crowd toward us.

"What happened?" he asks, directing his question at Sven.

"The Rogues gave us away to the delegation. We left the Schutz Clones and Rogues to fight it out. Jerome is safe with the deviations in Terminus for now."

Rocco raises his brows. "Where's the delegation?"

"One of the clones who was escorting them expired on the way here. They split when they saw their chance."

"They'll never make it back to the Craniopolis," Rocco says.

Dimitri looks grave. "If they do, they'll board a Hovermedes and be back at the outpost in a matter of hours. We could have Schutz Clones descending on the city by tomorrow."

"You should have eliminated them when you had the chance," Rocco says.

"We hoped it wouldn't come to that," I say.

"Is everything stable in the city?" Sven asks.

"Some of the homesteaders returned a few hours ago," Rocco says. "They were afraid they wouldn't make it to the Deadwood River because of the storm."

"Was Owen with them?" I ask, fighting to keep my voice steady.

Rocco gives a quick shake of his head. "He's pushing hard to reach the river basin. He wants to have shelters built and food stocked before fall."

It doesn't surprise me to hear he's not giving up. Owen is too stubborn to admit this was a mistake. Leaving with so many unknowns, and with too few people to defend themselves. If they encounter Rogues or Schutz Clones, it will be an efficient bloodbath.

"How's Big Ed holding up?" I ask.

"The old man's close to expiring." Rocco corrects himself before I can respond. "Dying."

"Where is he?" I ask, my heart lurching in my chest.

"At the rider's barn."

"We need to go there," I say to Trout.

He nods, his eyes clouding over.

"Find Blackbeard and fill him in on everything," I say to Sven. "We'll be at the courthouse as soon as we can."

I turn to Viktor. "You and Dimitri head to the Superconductor. Find out if Iskra has made any progress on pinpointing the coordinates of the Megamedes. You need to man the CommCenter day and night until we make contact."

Viktor bobs his head and slips away through the crowd with Dimitri.

Despite my fatigue, adrenaline spurts through me as I hurry to the rider's barn with Trout. My thoughts are in turmoil. I knew the day would come when I would lose Big Ed, but I was hoping it wouldn't be anytime soon. If only the world wasn't so twisted, maybe the Sweepers would be able to save him.

We find Big Ed curled up in a bunk at the back of the barn, his chest heaving and falling, the ominous rattle of fluid the only background noise in the space. Tucker is stretched out across his legs, and for once he doesn't look overjoyed to see me. He lifts his head and stares at me reprovingly, before dropping it again. I rub his neck and hug him, grateful he's stayed close by Big Ed's side through this ordeal. He licks my hand once in response, a gesture that tells me I'm barely forgiven for leaving and bringing on this crisis.

I turn at the sound of the barn door opening. Hannah comes in and greets us.

I stare at her in disbelief. "I thought you and Jakob left with the homesteaders."

She sets down a basket of food and walks over to us. "Jakob didn't want to leave Big Ed in this condition. And he wasn't happy about Owen pulling out in the middle of the night without telling anyone either."

"What's wrong with Big Ed?" Trout asks.

Hannah grimaces. "The doctor says it's pneumonia. He refuses to go to the clinic. Jakob and I are taking shifts to make sure he's not alone."

Jakob and I. The words are innocent enough but telling. I look at her curiously as she adjusts Big Ed's covers, her blond hair tucked beneath a dingy cap, her faded skirt swishing above her boots as she moves.

"Jakob talks about you all the time." She smiles warmly at me. "What you did for us was unbelievably brave."

I nod and scratch at a non-existent itch on the end of my nose, blocking her clear-eyed gaze. Has she any idea what I've done? And how I feel inside about taking a life? How could she? The only blood on her hands is the blood of those she's saved.

Big Ed lets out a moan which dissolves into a sharp coughing fit. I swallow back a sob and lay my hand on his shoulder. He smacks his lips together and rolls over with another groan.

"Big Ed," I whisper.

His feverish eyes pop open and search the space around him.

I lean in closer so he can see me without his glasses. "It's me, Derry," I say, my voice breaking.

He blinks, staring past me as if trying to associate the information with some distant memory. But it doesn't come together. His eyelids drift closed again.

Tears trickle down my cheeks. Trout squeezes my arm gently.

"He doesn't even know me." I choke out the words between sobs. "I wanted to say good-bye at least."

"Give him a few minutes," Trout says. "He needs to orient himself."

We turn our heads at the sound of voices. A moment later, Sven barges into the barn. He pulls up short at Big Ed's bedside and signals to us to join him outside. I turn to Hannah. "If I'm not back in five minutes, take him to the clinic," I whisper. "He's too weak to protest now." I give Tucker a quick neck rub, before exiting the barn with Trout.

My blood runs cold when I see who's waiting for me.

Chapter 23

Rummy locks a hostile stare on me.

"He showed up at the gates a few minutes ago," Sven says.

"What are you doing here?" I say. "I gave you your freedom, you're on your own now. You don't belong here with us."

"I thought we were even," he says, in a menacing tone. "Seems we have unfinished business."

I glare at him. "What are you talking about?"

He shakes his arms free of his pack and tosses it on the ground. The military clones with Sven draw their weapons, but Rummy ignores them and unties the straps on his pack. He reaches inside for something, a dark scowl snaking across his face.

My mouth goes dry when he pulls out a broken arrow.

"This look familiar?" He runs the back of his nail along the wild turkey feathers.

"Why would it?" I say, my tone defiant.

He wipes his nose on his sleeve and studies me for a moment. "This here arrow killed my brother."

Shock ripples around the group but Rummy never takes his eyes off me—almost as if he knows I won't be surprised by the news.

"I could lie and tell you I'm sorry," I say. "But we weren't real close."

"Ain't that the truth." Rummy flicks the feathers on the arrow in an irritating fashion as he talks. "Thing is, see, I found Blade dead right after you passed by. Heck of a coincidence, ain't it?"

"The Sweepers got away from us. They must have killed him."

He laughs, but he doesn't sound amused. "Don't picture Sweepers hunting with wild turkey feather arrows." He bares his teeth before he continues. "This here was made by an Undergrounder and I reckon you know who."

I breathe slowly in and out. "Our business here is finished. You can leave of your own accord, or I can have you escorted out of the city."

Rummy's eyes narrow to slits. "You send me back out there and I'm a dead man." He takes a step toward me. "They're coming," he hisses. "They ain't far behind me."

My pulse creeps up a level. "Who?"

He gives a malevolent grin. "Well that's just it, ain't it? I didn't wait around to find out who put down the gloves. So we don't know if the Rogues or Schutz Clones are coming for us. And until we do, I ain't going nowhere."

I turn to Sven. "Lock Rummy up in the courthouse. We don't have time for this."

Sven signals to a couple of the military clones, and I watch as they restrain Rummy and march him off. "Much obliged for the hospitality," he calls back to me, grinning wide.

"Do you think he knows more than he's telling us?" Trout asks.

An ominous feeling grips me. "He practically begged us to keep him here, which means he doesn't think the Rogues stand a chance."

"Either way, we can't wait until morning to bolster our defenses," Sven says. He calls a couple of his men over and directs them to round up the rest of the clones and begin fortifying the barricade.

I'm torn about leaving Big Ed, but we need to prepare for an imminent attack. The Rogues wouldn't be able to march all night after fighting the Schutz Clones. But if the Schutz Clones prevail, they could be here in a matter of hours.

"We need to find Blackbeard," I say. "We'll put him in charge of organizing the Undergrounders to man the barricade while the military clones work on fortifying weak spots."

Trout, Sven and I make our way across town to the courthouse. The guard on duty directs us back to Jerome's office. Blackbeard gets to his feet when he sees us, hastily scanning our faces.

"Jerome's fine," I say, answering the question in his eyes. "He thought the deviations would be safer in Terminus than trying to flee."

"Flee from who?" Blackbeard says.

"We left the Rogues and Schutz Clones to fight it out," I say. "It's anybody's guess who'll prevail. But whoever does will come for us."

Blackbeard grips the edge of the desk and bows his head. When he looks up, his expression is grim. "You think they'll come all the way to the city?"

I let out a heavy sigh. "They might already be on their way."

Blackbeard straightens up. "I'll station reinforcements around the barricade." He yells for the guard and barks out a series of orders. "And put two squadrons of Undergrounders on the gate," he calls after the guard as he hustles out the door.

"You need to get some rest," Blackbeard says, eying us up and down. "Go lay down in one of the offices for a few hours. I'll wake you if anything happens."

I throw him a grateful look. My brain's barely functioning at this point, and I'm confident no one can fortify the city better against attack than Blackbeard. He and his men built the original barricade and container gate, and he and Jerome have spent months training the Undergrounders to defend the city in case this day ever came.

I drag myself into the office next door and curl up in a heap on the floor with my head on my pack. Sven and Trout follow suit and pull their jackets over their faces. The sound of Trout's snoring quickly fills the space. I slip blissfully into a fog of sleep.

My next conscious thought is that the ground beneath me is harder than the forest floor's supposed to be.

"Derry!" Trout says, an urgent note in his voice.

I sit up and rub my eyes, slowly piecing together where I am. Sven stifles a yawn and gets to his feet.

Trout gestures to the doorway. I stare in disbelief at Viktor and Dimitri, strained expressions on their faces.

"Is it the Megamedes?" I ask, my heart racing.

"Iskra's missing," Dimitri says.

I frown. "Missing?"

Viktor wipes a hand across his jaw. "When we got to the Superconductor the scientist on duty told us she disappeared during her shift yesterday and never came back. Dimitri and I searched the entire city, but no one's seen her."

I rub the back of my neck trying to wake myself enough to grasp the significance of what he's saying. Naturally Viktor's worried about his daughter, but we're running out of time to locate the Megamedes. And Iskra is our only hope of making contact. Wherever she is, we have to find her.

"My sister is a conscientious scientist. She would never abandon her shift," Dimitri says. "Something must have happened to her."

"She has to be somewhere in the city," I say. "We'll begin back at the Superconductor and track her last movements. Sven can pull the camera feed and review it. Most likely she fell asleep someplace. We're all exhausted."

Dimitri gives a resigned nod. Viktor looks like he's going to be sick.

"Stick your head into Jerome's office and tell Blackbeard we're going to the Superconductor," I say to Trout.

Trout slips out the door and I turn my attention back to Viktor. "Do you know what Iskra was doing when she disappeared?"

Viktor pinches his lips together. "I have a hunch she found the coordinates for the Megamedes. You think there might be a connection?"

"I'm not sure," I say, pushing down an uneasy thought. Did someone discover what she was doing and shut her down?

When Trout returns, we exit the courthouse and make our way across the rubble-strewn section of town to the Superconductor.

A distraught scientist greets us and ushers us inside. "I knew Iskra was worried about something yesterday," he begins without introduction.

"What do you mean?" I ask.

"I don't know exactly." He pulls distractedly at his collar. "She was jittery."

"About what?" Trout asks.

"I don't think it was *what* she was afraid of. It was *who*. I overheard her muttering to herself. *I don't trust him.*"

"Did she seem afraid of anyone in particular?" I ask.

The scientist shakes his head. "I don't think it was anyone who worked here. She kept throwing nervous glances at the door like she thought someone was going to walk in on her."

"Let's search the Superconductor one more time from top to bottom," I say. "Sven, can you pull up the cameras and see if there's anything unusual."

We work our way around the main command room, digging through piles of unused equipment in the storage areas, before fanning out to go through the smaller offices and research rooms. When we've combed every inch of the upper level we proceed down the metal, spiral stairway to the ground floor where the Superconductor is housed.

We repeat the same process, opening even the smallest storage compartments on the off chance that they might reveal some clue that will lead us to Iskra.

"Any luck with the cameras?" I call upstairs to Sven, still hunched over the CommCenter. He walks over to the stairway and runs his fingers through his hair. "I've reviewed all the footage. Nothing out of the ordinary. She left her desk a few minutes before she disappeared. According to the log, she went downstairs to do a routine check of the Superconductor gauges. That was the last sighting. No footage of her leaving the building."

I frown up at him. "But there's no way out down–" My voice trails off. *The tunnel.*

A look of comprehension flickers in Sven's face. He grips the handrails and bounds down the stairs two at a time. "There are no cameras on the tunnel entrance," he says. "She could have exited the Superconductor that way."

"But how would she have known about the tunnel?" I ask. "And why would she sneak out?"

Sven shrugs. "Beats me." He kneels down on the floor and searches around for the loose board to activate the trapdoor.

"Did you find something?" Viktor asks, frowning.

"There's a tunnel leading from here to the courthouse," I explain. "I'm not sure how Iskra would have found out about it, but it's possible she used it to escape undetected if she was trying to hide from someone."

Dimitri drops to his knees and begins feeling around with his fingers.

Sven locates the loose board and yanks on it. The trapdoor eases open and we stare down into the pitch-black space.

"I'll check it out," Dimitri says, climbing down into the tunnel before anyone has a chance to stop him. His boots clatter an eerie echo on the metal rungs as he makes a rapid descent.

I turn to Sven. "Wait here, I'll take a quick look and see if anyone's gone that way recently." I switch on my flashlight and clamber down the ladder after Dimitri, the tunnel walls closing in around me. I hunch over and assume an all too familiar shuffle along the dirt-packed floor until I bump up against Dimitri, stock-still on his knees in the middle of the tunnel.

"What are you doing?" I say, leaning over his shoulder. I let out a gasp when the thin amber beam of my flashlight illuminates the gaping eyes of his dead sister.

Chapter 24

"Iskra!" Dimitri chokes the word out, his body shuddering from the impact of his loss.

I lay a hand on his shoulder and squeeze it gently. There are no words to comfort him. He falls on top of his sister, sobbing unashamedly, giant waves of grief that echo eerily through the crypt-like space.

I peer down the dark tunnel, a foreboding feeling growing inside me. Death follows us no matter which direction we flee. Even our secret tunnel isn't safe anymore. There's a murderer at large in the city.

Viktor's features contort in a landslide of pain when Dimitri emerges from the tunnel carrying Iskra. His eyes reflect an even more shocking exposé of the grief he's wrestling with. He staggers over to Dimitri and gathers his daughter in his arms. "Lapushka," he whispers, then presses his lips to her forehead.

My eyes burn with tears at the softness in his voice. I avert my gaze and wipe the back of my hand across my lashes.

Sven comes up alongside me and motions me aside.

"What is it?" I ask.

He wets his lips. "Only a handful of people know about this tunnel."

My pulse picks up pace, my mind running through names. "You, me and Trout." I rub my brow. "Jerome's in the Craniopolis." I suck in a breath. "You don't think Blackbeard or his men–"

"No!" he whispers. "I told someone else about it."

My eyes widen. "Who?"

"I showed it to Rocco before we left for the Craniopolis—in case there was a crisis."

My jaw drops. "You don't think Rocco killed her, do you?"

Sven shakes his head. "I don't know."

"But you trust him," I say.

"I … did."

I frown, remembering what the scientist upstairs overheard. An icy tingle goes down my spine. "Sven," I whisper. "She said she didn't trust *him.* Do you think she was talking about Rocco?"

A flicker of anger crosses Sven's face. "If Rocco did this–"

I grab his arm, too late to stop him blurting it out.

Dimitri looks up, shock and disbelief ricocheting across his face. "You think … Rocco did this?"

"We don't know who it was," I say. "It could have been one of Blackbeard's men. But Rocco knew about the tunnel too, so we can't rule him out."

Dimitri balls his hands into fists. "If that clone murdered Iskra, I'll make sure he never has the privilege of reaching his expiration date."

I shiver at the words, and not just because of Dimitri's threat. I keep trying to forget that Sven's life is petering out in front of me and that I'm helpless to prevent it from happening.

"Tell the scientist upstairs we found Iskra," I say to Sven.

He nods and disappears up the spiral staircase in a couple of strides. I turn to Viktor who's sitting in a nearby chair cradling his daughter's body in his lap.

I clear my throat. "We need to … make arrangements … for Iskra."

He stares at me like a frightened child clutching a doll about to be taken away from him. Dimitri leans over his father and whispers something to him, then lifts his sister into his arms and heads for the winding metal staircase. Viktor glances around, tracking us blankly, before getting to his feet and following his son up the stairs.

We take Iskra's body outside, and Sven digs a grave inside the perimeter fence around the Superconductor in a matter of minutes. I don't want to risk taking her remains to the graveyard. Someone might see us burying her. If word gets out that there's a murderer on the loose, it will send the city into a panic, and right now we need to stay focused on the battle ahead. At Viktor's request, Trout erects a small cross to mark the spot. Dimitri says a few words over the grave, before putting an arm around his father and walking him back inside.

I don't know for sure what Iskra was working on when she disappeared, or who she was afraid of, but Sven will get to the bottom of it. Iskra may have been the brains behind the computer system on board the Megamedes, but Sven was engineered to hack into anything.

Trout and I retreat outside to the upper-level balcony to give Viktor and Dimitri some space while Sven gets to work on Iskra's computer. When he rejoins us a short while later I raise a quizzical brow at him.

"She made contact with the Megamedes," he says, a grave look on his face.

"That's great!" I say.

"No," Sven says. "It's not."

Trout narrows his eyes at him. "What are you getting at?"

Sven hesitates. "She betrayed us. From what I can tell from the transmissions, she told them everything. The Sweepers are probably already on their way."

"Iskra sold us out?" Trout throws me a horrified look.

"I don't understand," I say. "Why would she do that to her own father and brother?"

Sven shakes his head. "She may not have implicated them."

"Do you think someone discovered what she did?" Trout says.

"I don't know," Sven says. "But it's time we track down Rocco. If it wasn't him, we have to assume one of Blackbeard's men was behind it." He throws a quick glance over his shoulder. "I deleted the transmissions. I ... didn't want her father to know what she did."

"Good call," I say, eying Viktor hunched over, sobbing into his hands.

It's so like Sven to be moved by someone else's pain. From what I've seen so far, I'd say clones' hearts are just as tender as humans.

Jerome's office is empty by the time we get back to the courthouse. Presumably, Blackbeard is out checking on the fortifications around the barricade.

Sven walks out into the corridor and calls to a guard to fetch Rocco. "We'll get to the bottom of this one way or another," he says, sinking into a chair when he comes back.

My eyes skirt over Sven's bulging physique and pumped arms that have held me so tenderly. Rocco is a large clone, but I've no doubt who'll come out on top if he forces Sven into a showdown.

"The guard says all's quiet on the perimeter," Sven remarks.

Trout grunts. "It could change in a heartbeat. The barricade's too long for us to defend properly. If we're attacked on multiple fronts, we won't be able to hold them off indefinitely."

"There are more of us," I remind him.

Trout throws me a disgruntled look. "Yeah, but all the best shots are off on their merry homesteading way."

My heart skips a beat when I remember Owen out there forging a path to the Deadwood Basin. I only hope they don't run into whoever prevailed at the Craniopolis.

I glance up as Rocco and several other military clones file through the door. I study Rocco's face for any indication of guilt, but it's expressionless as usual.

He looks around the room. "We've shored up a large section of the barricade already. Something else you want us to jump on?"

"Sit down, Rocco." Sven pulls out a chair for him. "Derry and I want to ask you some questions."

Rocco raises his brows.

Sven gestures for me to begin.

"We found Iskra's body at the Superconductor an hour or so ago." I tilt my head to one side, inviting Rocco to respond.

He turns to Sven, frowning.

"She was murdered," Sven says. "During her shift yesterday."

Rocco leans back in his chair. "You want me to find out who's responsible?"

"We want to know if *you're* responsible," I say.

Rocco throws Sven a defensive look. "What is she talking about?"

"We found her in the tunnel beneath the Superconductor," Sven says, quietly. "You're one of the few people who knew about it."

"What about Blackbeard and his men?"

"Never mind them," Sven says. "I'm talking to you."

A dangerous glint appears in Rocco's eyes. "Are you accusing me?"

Sven half rises out of his chair. "I'm *asking* you."

"I'm your kind, remember?" Rocco says. "Maybe you should be asking Blackbeard."

Sven grabs him by the collar. "Just tell me the truth. Did you kill her?"

"She lied to me!" Rocco yells at him, spittle bouncing on his lower lip.

My jaw drops. The room goes silent. I glance across at Sven. He rubs a hand gingerly across his jaw, as though he took a blow to the chin.

"I thought I meant something to her," Rocco says, "but she was just like every other Sweeper!"

Sven frowns. "You two … were together?"

Rocco hangs his head. "I thought so until I overheard her transmitting to the Megamedes. She gave them counts of everyone in the city. She'd selected me for a program."

"What are you talking about?" Sven asks.

"Ossification trials," Rocco says. "They need guinea pigs—military clones who can withstand DNA re-splicing."

My pulse thuds wildly. A look of horror passes over Trout's face.

Rocco narrows his eyes. "I was an experiment to her. We all were."

Sven lays a hand on Rocco's shoulder. "I believe you, but why did you have to kill her? We could have arrested her. I swore to Dimitri and Viktor I'd find who was responsible for her death. I can't protect you. You're going to have to leave the city."

"I didn't want to do it, but she was dangerous." Rocco struggles to take a breath. He seems genuinely overcome with grief, as if it's only just registering what he's done. Which is all well and fine, but it doesn't change the fact that he's about to become an outcast in a world which has little sympathy for those without a faction, and there's nothing we can do to help him.

Sven gestures to the military clones standing behind him. "Take him outside the city limits. Give him his weapon and a supply of food and water."

Rocco gets to his feet, his face crevassed with grief. Trout bows his head. Sven folds his arms across his chest, his lips pressed together.

This can't be easy for Sven, but Rocco can't stay here after what he did. If word gets out that one of the clones killed a scientist, we'd have a riot on our hands. Viktor and Dimitri will demand his execution.

We follow the military clones and Rocco in what feels like a funeral march of sorts as far as the container gates. Sven and Rocco exchange one last embrace before Sven signals up to the guards to unlatch the gates. I wait for the familiar creaking to begin as the gates swing open, but instead a shout of alarm cuts through the air.

Chapter 25

"Hostiles spotted!" one of the guards shouts down.

My gut twists. *They're here already!*

The guards sound the warning horn in the watchtower. Within minutes, the barricade is crawling with activity. Undergrounders rush to take up their positions, their faces pinched with fear.

"Can you see who it is?" I yell up to the guard.

"Not yet." He peers through his binoculars for a few minutes. "It's Rogues!"

Trout and I exchange surprised looks.

"I can't believe they took out the Schutz Clones," Trout says.

I grimace. "They must have hiked all night. Get everyone into position."

"I'll lock Rocco up in the courthouse," Sven says. "We'll deal with him later."

I slide my gun from my shoulder and watch as two of the military clones march Rocco away. We could use his help now, but I can't trust him after what happened. Not to mention the fact that if Viktor or Dimitri run into Rocco there'll be war on both sides of the barricade.

Blackbeard strides over, his features rigid. "The riders and Undergrounders are ready. Most of the city has turned out to help."

"No one fires until I give the command," I say. "We can't afford to waste bullets until they're within range."

Blackbeard moves off down the barricade issuing clipped orders to his men. I join Trout and Sven beneath the guard tower and peer through the twisted steel and concrete at the ant-like figures in the distance. I rest the barrel of my gun on a tangled piece of metal and breathe in and out as I line up my sight. They're advancing slowly for an attacking force–too slowly. As they edge closer I can tell some of them are injured. I push down a repulsive thought. Surely they're not coming to us for refuge.

"White flag aloft!" a guard shouts down from the tower. "Hold your fire!"

I scrunch up my eyes and peer through the barricade. Minutes go by before I make out a long, white strip tied to a stick, fluttering in the cool breeze. Or maybe someone's waving it back and forth. It's impossible to tell without binoculars from this distance. My brain races to make sense of it. Is it a ruse to get inside the city? Or do the Rogues really want to surrender to us?

"Do you think The Ghost's dead?" I ask.

Trout throws me an uneasy look. "I don't know, but I don't like it. Knowing them, they're up to something."

I study the figures as they move closer and clamber over the debris. A small group, thirty Rogues at most. The losses at the Craniopolis must have been substantial. Unless this is some kind of trick and the rest of them are hiding somewhere.

"They're almost within range," Sven says, keeping his eyes forward. "What do you want to do?"

I smooth a few strands of hair out of my face. What I want to do is rid us of the Rogues once and for all. If we let them through the gate, they become our problem all over again. But I can't stoop to killing anyone carrying a white flag.

"We'll hear them out," I say.

Sven nods and walks off to spread the word.

I grip Trout by the sleeve when I spot The Ghost limping along to the right of the pack. "I can't believe he got out of there alive."

"I'm more shocked that he might be here to beg for mercy," Trout says. "Maybe they didn't defeat the Schutz Clones. Maybe they fled."

My heart thunders in my chest. "What if the Schutz Clones are pursuing them?"

"Bad idea all around to open that gate," Trout says.

The riders and Undergrounders along the barricade fall silent as the Rogues approach.

"Stay alert," Sven says, walking up to us. "They might try and mow us down once they're within firing range."

"They don't look like they're in any state to attack," Trout says.

Thirty feet from the barricade the Rogues come to a halt. Several agonizing minutes of silence go by before The Ghost calls out. "We had a deal, Connolly. I helped you stage the Craniopolis and fool the Sweepers."

"The land you wanted is yours. Go for it," I yell back.

"You left me and my men to die at the hands of monsters," he calls back in a tone that tells me the land won't be enough anymore.

"You blew our cover," I say. "We had no choice but to flee. I set you free to fight, something you keep reminding me you're good at."

"We killed every last Schutz Clone in the docking station," The Ghost says. "You owe the wounded refuge."

"I don't owe you anything. You've got your freedom now."

"There is no freedom," The Ghost says. "The sweeps have resumed."

A ripple of fear shoots through me. A heavy silence descends over the barricade like a shroud. I've been dreading hearing those words. The Sweepers must have deployed the ships as soon as Iskra alerted the Megamedes.

"How do you know?" I yell through the barricade.

"Half my men were extracted on the way here." The Ghost pauses to catch his breath. "We're too weak to run. If you don't give us refuge, we'll die out here."

Blackbeard appears at my side fingering his thick beard. "Do you think he's lying about the sweeps?"

"I don't know, but we can't take a chance," I say. "Send a message to Viktor and Dimitri to switch the Superconductor back on."

Blackbeard nods and flags down a couple of Undergrounders scuttling back and forth with ammunition.

I turn my attention back to The Ghost. "Tell your men to lay down their weapons. Then we'll talk."

The Ghost exchanges a few words with the Rogues. They disarm without hesitation and toss their weapons in a heap behind them, before shuffling the rest of the way to the barricade.

For a long moment, I stare out at their sunken eyes looking at me like I'm Caesar holding their fate in my hands.

I grit my teeth and give a thumbs up to the guards in the watchtower to open the gate. A familiar creaking breaks the silence. I keep one eye on the horizon to make sure there are no Schutz Clones bearing down on the city.

The Rogues traipse through the container gate exchanging wary looks with the Undergrounders who keep their weapons trained on them. The riders gallop past in the opposite direction to retrieve the discarded weapons.

I turn to Trout. "Go to the courthouse and warn the guards to keep Rummy out of sight. We can't risk The Ghost finding out he's here. Sven and I will take the injured Rogues to the clinic. It will give me an excuse to check up on Big Ed."

"I'll have my men take the rest of the Rogues to an unused building and set up a guard outside," Blackbeard says.

I give him a grateful nod. "Tell the guards in the watchtower to sound the alarm if they spot anyone else coming."

Sven and I separate out the Rogues who need medical attention and escort them to the clinic with the help of several military clones. I push open the door and peer inside. Hannah is at the far end of the room, mopping the floor, her hair neatly tucked beneath her cap.

"Hannah! We have wounded men," I call through the door to her.

She drops her mop and comes running, calling for assistance. Several other Undergrounders appear and help the Rogues into the examining rooms.

"Where's the doctor?" I ask.

"He went with Jakob to check up on Big Ed." Hannah throws me a look of apology. "Big Ed refused to let us move him to the clinic. He was pretty energetic about it too." She grins. "I think he's on the mend."

A smile breaks out across my face at the welcome news. It's a drop of hope in the sea of desperation we're swimming in. "Thanks for taking such good care of him," I say.

Hannah examines each of the Rogues, in turn, directing the Undergrounders to clean and bandage wounds as needed. I watch discreetly as she stitches up a Rogue's leg, talking quietly to him as she works.

"Hey! How 'bout I get some o' that lovin'?" a Rogue calls across to her. "He ain't hurt *that* bad."

Hannah rolls her eyes at me and I smile back.

All of a sudden there's a commotion at the door and a military clone bursts into the room. "Rocco's been shot!" he yells.

Sven jumps to his feet. "Is he alive?"

"Barely," the clone replies.

Sven grabs a stretcher and I toss some compresses and trauma dressing on it.

Hannah lays a hand on my arm. "I'll send for Jakob. He can take out the bullet."

I give her a grateful nod and hurry out of the clinic after Sven and the military clone. My mind spins with confusion. The only people who have any reason to shoot Rocco are Dimitri and Viktor and they're at the Superconductor. My thoughts gravitate to Rummy. He's at the courthouse too. Surely he couldn't have had something to do with this.

When we arrive at the courthouse Rocco is unconscious, cradled in Trout's arms, a blood-soaked rag pressed to his chest. The cell is splattered with enough blood to make me think he was hit more than once. A sign of unchecked rage. I clap my hand over my mouth, trapping the bile rising up from my gut.

Trout looks up with relief when he sees us. "We have to get him to the clinic before he bleeds out."

"Did you see who did this?" I ask.

Trout shakes his head. "I heard the shot and came running."

"What about the guards?"

"There's only one outside Rummy's cell. All the others are on the barricade."

Sven grabs a trauma pad and does what he can to stem the bleeding, before lifting Rocco onto the stretcher. Trout and Sven grasp the handles and lift their cargo. I follow a few feet behind as they charge down the main corridor and out through the front entry.

We make it to the bottom of the courthouse steps before Rocco's hulking frame recedes to gray, shrinking in on itself like a tiny mummified child.

Chapter 26

Sven falls to one knee and leans over the stretcher, his massive shoulders twitching with grief.

I want to reach out and comfort him, but I'm terrified to touch him in case he crumbles to dust too. The unrelenting fear I keep pushing down has surfaced with a vengeance. I can't stop shaking. All I can think about is that Sven could be next.

I take a deep, calming breath and try to pull myself together. "I'll find whoever's responsible," I say to Sven. "You stay here and take care of Rocco. I'm going to the Superconductor with Trout."

I nod to Trout and he falls into step beside me. I'm thankful he seems to realize without a word who it is I'm going after. If Dimitri and Viktor had anything to do with this, I'll track them down and have them arrested.

One harrowing scenario after another races through my head. The clones might attack the Undergrounders once they find out that Rocco's been murdered. And what if the Superconductor doesn't kick back on before the Hovermedes arrive? What if Viktor and Dimitri sabotaged the Superconductor and fled like fugitives? I swallow back a sob. I need Big Ed and his wise words now more than ever.

"You okay?" Trout throws me a sidelong glance.

I shake my head. "I can't put out the fires quickly enough."

"One blaze at a time," Trout says. "Let's find Viktor and Dimitri first."

When we reach the Superconductor, I breathe a small sigh of relief. The charged whirring sound assures me it's up and running again. One less thing to worry about. We enter through the main doors and race up to the second level. Dimitri is stationed at the CommCenter with another scientist, his forehead furrowed in concentration. He looks up when he sees us. His eyes are bloodshot from crying. "Derry! What are you doing here?"

"Where's your father?" I ask, fighting to keep the emotion out of my voice.

Something in my expression grabs his attention. He gets to his feet and scrutinizes me. "Is something wrong?"

"Is he here or not?" Trout asks.

"He went back to his quarters to lie down. It was too difficult for him to be here." Dimitri swallows hard. "I've been trying to locate the Megamedes. I have to finish this for Iskra. She was so close to finding the coordinates."

I throw a quick glance Trout's way. Dimitri's response seems genuine enough. If I had to hazard a guess, I reckon he doesn't know anything about what happened at the courthouse. "Rocco's been shot," I say. "He's dead."

Dimitri's eyes widen. He clutches the edge of the counter. "You killed him?"

"We arrested him. Someone else got to him in the holding cell."

"We don't know who," Trout adds. "The courthouse was unmanned except for the guard outside Rummy's cell. Anyone could have got in there."

Dimitri traces his fingers back and forth across his forehead. "Did he … confess?"

"Yes," I say. "I'm sorry."

Dimitri gives a somber nod. "He would have been executed anyway after he was tried by the Council," he says as if reasoning with himself.

I chew on my lip but don't respond. It serves no purpose to tell Dimitri we were planning on helping Rocco flee the city.

"Thank you for letting me know," Dimitri says. "I'll break the news to my father."

"We need to speak to him," I say.

Dimitri frowns. "Why?"

"We can't have vigilantes," Trout mutters.

Dimitri shoots a glance in Trout's direction. "You can't possibly think my father had anything to do with this. He doesn't have it in him."

"Everyone has it in them," Trout says, gruffly. "It's like a lock, just takes the right combination."

Dimitri staggers backward, as though contemplating the possibility. He snatches up his jacket and walks toward the door. "Let's sort this out right now. Come with me."

My stomach churns as I follow Dimitri out of the Superconductor. I hope we're not making a huge mistake. Viktor may not have had anything to do with Rocco's death. If we're wrong, it's a devastating accusation to make against a man who's just lost his daughter.

We're halfway between the Superconductor and the boarded-up office building in the old section of town where the scientists are housed when I spot Jakob going up the steps to the clinic.

"Wait here," I say to Trout and Dimitri. "I need to make sure Big Ed's all right."

"Jakob!" I shout as I jog over to him.

He turns and waits for me at the top of the steps.

"You look tired," I say, eying the puffy, purple ovals under his eyes.

He grimaces. "We could have used the homesteaders' help to treat all the injured."

If only Owen hadn't been so thick-headed.

He doesn't come out and say it, but it's a jab all the same, and I don't blame him. Owen left us short-handed.

"How's Big Ed doing?" I ask.

"Hard to believe, but he seems to be on the mend." Jakob rubs his hand over the back of his neck. "He's a feisty old goat, but Hannah can handle him."

"I like her," I say, after an awkward pause. "She's … capable, like you."

Jakob gives me a strange look. "You mean like *you*. I'm the one who stayed at the clinic while you went off to fight the Sweepers."

"I can't do what you do either," I say.

"You've changed so much, Derry." He gives me a rueful grin. "So much was thrust on you. And you've risen to the challenge. But then you always knew you were destined for more." He adjusts the peak of his cap and gestures at the clinic door. "They need me inside. I better get back to work."

I walk slowly back to Trout and Dimitri, mulling over Jakob's words. He's right. A few short months ago I was a girl with a dog and a handful of bunker chores. Now the weight of an entire city rests on my shoulders. But I don't regret the path I have chosen.

When we reach the building in the old section of town where the scientists are living, I push open the makeshift door and step inside. The stale, trapped air and musty scent of old newspapers hit me right away. Trout wrinkles his nose. "Smells like mold."

Dimitri shoves a decrepit office chair out of his way and peers around the deserted space.

"Viktor?" I call out. "Are you in here?"

A man tromps halfway down the splintered staircase at the back of the room and leans over the sagging railing. "We're upstairs."

Dimitri strides across the floor. Trout and I follow him up the staircase and nod in greeting to the scientists milling around an open seating area.

"Is Viktor here?" Dimitri asks.

"He came in a little while ago, but I haven't seen him since," one of the scientists replies, scratching his head. "He might be having a lie-down." He points down the corridor. "Bedrooms are that way."

I hurry out the door and down the corridor after Dimitri and Trout, taking a quick scout through each of the rooms as I pass by.

"We're in here," Trout shouts, sticking his head out from a doorway.

"Any sign of Viktor?" I ask when I join them inside the room.

Dimitri shakes his head without looking up from the bag he's rummaging through. "None of his stuff's missing. He's not exactly acting like a fugitive planning to hightail it out of here."

It's hard to miss the resentful tone in Dimitri's voice. I don't want to sour my relationship with the only person who might be able to help Sven, but I need to find Viktor as soon as possible. If he didn't shoot Rocco, it means there's an unidentified killer at large.

"Viktor has to be somewhere in the building," Trout says. "None of the scientists saw him leave."

"What about the roof?" I say. "Some of these old office buildings have a patio area up top. If he wanted to be alone that would be a good place to hang out."

Dimitri stops tossing items back into the bag and looks up, a frozen expression on his face. "Where's the roof access?"

"Fire escape would be my guess," Trout says.

Dimitri drops the bag and darts out of the room. Trout and I follow him to the end of the corridor. He clambers out through the empty window frame and onto the fire escape ladder and begins making his way up to the roof, his boots clanging eerily on the rungs with every step. I climb up the ladder after him and wait for Trout at the top. As soon as he appears, we follow Dimitri across the rooftop patio area, weaving our way through a jumble of crumbling concrete, twisted rebar and broken furniture.

"Viktor!" Dimitri calls out, disappearing behind a rickety chimney stack.

I skirt around it after him, and almost slam right into him when he comes to an abrupt stop in front of me.

He holds out his arm to keep me back, but I already know what he's looking at.

Chapter 27

Twenty feet away Viktor balances precariously on an uneven chunk of concrete overhanging the edge of the roof. His head is sunk low to his chest and his jaw moves up and down as though he's talking himself into the unthinkable.

Dimitri takes a tentative step forward, holding his hand up behind him to keep Trout and me at bay. "Papa!" he says.

Viktor doesn't even acknowledge that he's heard him. Cautiously, Dimitri closes the distance between himself and his father, calling out to him, but trying not to spook him.

Viktor's head swivels in our direction. His wild eyes sweep over us like beacons. I freeze, afraid even to flinch a muscle for fear he'll turn and take a forty-foot death dive to the ground below. Dimitri shrinks into a crouch as if this stance is somehow less intimidating to a man about to end his life. In reality, it's a terrifying posture, like a cougar stalking its prey. A sick feeling rises up from my stomach. "Please," I call to him. "Don't do this, Viktor!"

"Papa, I'm going to come over there now." Dimitri enunciates every word like he's speaking to a man with dementia.

Viktor stares at him with the kind of blank expression that tells me nothing's getting through anymore.

I hold my breath as Dimitri treads forward through the debris another half-step. Viktor keeps his head perfectly still, studying Dimitri's stealth-like movements like a curious bird. He lets Dimitri take several more steps toward him before a flicker of comprehension crosses his face. He turns away and shuffles several inches farther along the concrete ledge.

I grit my teeth. If Dimitri moves too quickly he'll spook him, too slowly and he might be too late. Beside me, I sense Trout getting ready to lunge toward Viktor, which would accomplish nothing. He could never make it across the roof in time to grab him. The only way Viktor's coming down off the ledge is if Dimitri can talk him off it—a familiar voice he can trust and someone worth holding onto life for.

Dimitri raises both hands in front of him. "Papa, I'll stay right here. Please, back away from the edge."

Viktor blinks. His head swivels back and forth. He peers over the edge like he's searching for something. Time expands until my brain feels like it's going to explode, each elongated minute stretching further than the one before. I close my eyes, but when I do a gruesome bloodied Viktor, sprawled unnaturally in the debris, springs to mind.

Suddenly, Viktor lets out a long, shuddering sigh, startling my already frazzled nerves. Trout grips my arm.

"It's okay, Papa," Dimitri says, his face blanched of color. "I know you don't want to do this." He holds out his arms to his father. "Just put one foot behind the other and shuffle backward. I'll be waiting right here for you."

Viktor looks up and locks eyes with him. He stretches out his fingers toward Dimitri and then tips silently forward and out of sight.

"Nooooooo!" Dimitri's scream burns like acid through my scalp. He stumbles across the debris in the direction of the iron ladder, clutching at the air like a blind man.

Trout and I lunge for him at the same time. "No, Dimitri," I say. "Let me go down first."

A shout from below tells me someone has discovered the body. A shiver goes through me as I reach for the ladder.

By the time I get down to the ground, Viktor's body has been covered up. I exhale a heavy sigh of relief. The other scientists gather around Dimitri when he appears, forming a barrier between him and the gruesome sight of his father's blanketed corpse.

"Let me see him!" Dimitri sobs.

"He wouldn't want you to see him like this," one of the scientists says. He drapes an arm over Dimitri's shoulders and steers him back inside their living quarters.

I turn to the remaining scientists. "Take Viktor's body and bury him right away. I don't want anyone else getting wind of this."

"What happened up there?" one of the scientists asks, eying me warily.

I pin a steely gaze back on him. "His daughter was murdered. He couldn't deal with it."

The scientist throws an uneasy glance around, but the others seem satisfied with my response and turn away. There's no benefit to telling them what Viktor did. It will only stir up more ill will between the clones and the scientists.

"That was rough," Trout mutters.

I grimace. "Dimitri's not going to be in any state to help us locate the Megamedes now."

"At least he got the Superconductor up and running."

"Don't get your hopes up," I say. "It won't save us if the Schutz Clones come on foot."

Trout and I watch as the scientists pick up Viktor's remains and lay them in a cart.

"Let's go," I say. "We need to get back to the barricade."

As we approach the container gate, I can tell there's something going on. The riders and Undergrounders are clustered around, talking and pointing through the barricade. I pick up the pace steeling myself to hear what I've been dreading most.

The Sweepers are coming!

I try to block the thought, but it circles like a shark in my mind.

Trout throws me a frightened look. "This could be it."

My heart flutters in my chest. "Come on!" I break into a panicked run and reach the barricade just ahead of him.

"What's happening?" I yell up to the guards in the watchtower.

"Some woman wants in. She's alone, but she won't surrender her weapons so we can't open up the gate.

I press my face up to the barricade and peer through the concrete and tangled steel girders, searching in both directions. My heart leaps when I spot a statuesque profile. "Lou!" I scream.

She turns in my direction and gives me a *good to see you too, now open the dang gate* kind of nod.

"Let her in!" I yell up to the guards. "I can vouch for her."

I hold my breath as the container gates swing wide and Lou strides through. She throws the guards a defiant look in passing and marches straight up to me.

I grin and embrace her. "You came after all."

Her eyes cloud over. "This isn't a social call. I came to warn you there are Sweepers headed this way."

My smile freezes, aching like an ice cream headache in my cheeks. The Ghost's ominous words flash to mind.

There is no freedom. The sweeps have resumed.

"How many?" I ask.

She balks like she doesn't understand the question, then leans in close so no one can overhear. "Ten ships so far. They're camped out a few miles northeast of the Craniopolis."

My mouth goes dry. Two hundred Schutz Clones, give or take. Along with any number of Sweepers. A considerable force to reckon with and more could be on the way.

"What's going on?" Trout asks.

I introduce Lou to him and give him the news.

He rubs a hand slowly across his jaw.

"The Hovermedes won't be able to approach the city as long as the Superconductor is operating," I say. "The Sweepers will have to deploy Schutz Clones on foot." I search Trout's face for the strength I need, but he's as terrified as I am. We can't keep fighting like this. We need an exit strategy, a final solution. It all comes down to finding the Megamedes.

"We need to arm everyone in the city." Trout says. "Even the Rogues."

"Not Rummy," I say.

Trout throws me a dark look. "We could always let The Ghost take care of him."

"Take *care* of him?" I raise a brow. "You mean kill him?"

"I mean let them work it out," Trout says, sounding disgruntled.

"You might as well put a bullet in his head yourself," I say. "That's not who we are."

"Your call. I'll set the rest of the Rogues up with weapons," he says and strides off.

Lou turns to me, a smile on her wrinkled lips. "I like that boy."

I grimace. "I do too when his head's screwed on right."

She makes a disapproving clicking sound. "You can't fight other people's wars for them. Sounds like that's what you're trying to do."

"You should meet Big Ed," I say. "He talks like you."

Lou swings her quiver over her shoulder. "Don't care much about meeting people."

"Neither does he," I say. "You'd get along great. But first, you and I need to go to the courthouse and let Blackbeard know the Sweepers are coming.

Blackbeard's eyes widen when Lou describes the fleet of Hovermedes camped outside the Craniopolis.

"We have to locate the Megamedes and get on board somehow," I say. "It's the only way to shut them down. Even if we manage to fight off this first wave of Schutz Clones, more will come."

"What about Jerome and the deviations?" Blackbeard asks.

"They're in no immediate danger. If the Sweepers discover them, they can feign ignorance of everything that went down in the Craniopolis."

Blackbeard looks unconvinced. "I'll head over to the CommCenter at the Superconductor and update Jerome."

"Got any water around here?" Lou asks.

Blackbeard gives a curt nod. "Follow me."

They exit the room just as Trout reappears. "I put the Rogues on the west side of the main gate," he says. "They're willing to fight—just thankful they made it to the city before the Hovermedes landed. Sven and some of his men are keeping an eye on them all the same."

I drum my fingers on Jerome's desk. "Do you really think I should let Rummy out?"

Trout looks somber. "We could use him. And The Ghost doesn't need to know he's here. We can put Rummy on the east side of the barricade with the riders."

I push my hands against the edge of the desk and slide my chair out. "Let's find out if he's up for war."

We make our way down the hallway to the holding cells. I can barely suppress a shudder as the memories come flooding back. Only a few short hours ago, Sven and Trout carried Rocco's ossified corpse along this same stretch of corridor. Yet, every time the grotesque image springs to mind, I see Sven's face.

I nod in passing at the guard outside the holding cell and step inside the room. Rummy gets to his feet and I waste no time relaying the news to him.

"A fleet of Hovermedes, eh?" A slow grin spreads across his face. "We got 'em running scared."

"You can help us if you're willing to do it on our terms," I say.

"I ain't gonna sit in here with my dang feet up. I'll fight 'em."

"Just to be clear," I say, handing him back his weapon, "if we survive this you need to leave the city afterward."

"That's a fair shake," he says, inspecting his gun.

"There you are," Lou's voice calls out from behind me.

Rummy glances up. The crossed cleaver tattoos on his neck twitch once. My blood chills at the darkness that comes over his face.

I swing around and my eyes light on the wild turkey feather tips peeking out from Lou's quiver.

Chapter 28

"I couldn't find you any—" Lou's voice trails off.

I turn in time to see Rummy raise his rifle. My heart booms in my ears. Trout yells something. My lips part but the only sound is a whooshing past my ear. Rummy grunts and collapses on the floor in front of me, an arrow protruding from his chest.

Lou slings her bow over her shoulder and walks over to him. She kneels and checks for a pulse. "He's gone." She gets to her feet and locks eyes with me. "Who was he trying to kill?"

I blink, taken aback by the question. Rummy wanted Lou dead for sure. But was he about to shoot me for hiding her? "I don't know for sure," I say. "You killed his brother. And I was protecting you."

"He kept the arrow so he could track you down," Trout says, holstering his gun.

Lou runs a hand over her lined brow. "Sounds like one of us had to die, sooner or later."

I stare down at Rummy's body. I'm not sure why I don't feel more relieved he's dead. Rummy and I had some strange connection in the end. He saved Curly's life, and he had my back a time or two. But I'm glad Lou's alive instead of him.

"If it makes you feel any better," I say, "You just solved a huge problem for me."

Lou raises her brows.

"If The Ghost had discovered I was hiding Rummy we'd have had a bloodbath on our hands before the Sweepers got anywhere near the city."

Lou nods thoughtfully. "It's going to take more than an arrow to stop the Schutz Clones advancing."

Her words snap me back into action. I turn to Trout. "Find Jody and tell her to send out some riders as scouts. I want to know as soon as the Schutz Clones are on the move. Lou and I will swing by the Superconductor and see if Blackbeard has made contact with Jerome."

I track down a couple of Undergrounders and instruct them to bury Rummy and mention it to no one. With any luck, people will assume he died in the battle to come.

The air outside the courthouse has a bite to it. Lou and I are halfway to the Superconductor when the first snowflakes land on us. I look up, startled to see the sky has turned a translucent gray. Several more white flakes drift gently downward. "Look!" I say to Lou. "I haven't seen snow since the meltdown.

Within minutes, the few remaining children in the city are in the street trying to catch the flakes in their outstretched palms. They shriek with delight, tasting the snow with the tips of their tongues like eager puppies.

The feathery snow melts as soon as it touches the ground, much to the kids' disappointment. I catch sight of Izzy running around in circles, arms outstretched to the sky, laughing hysterically. I smile, remembering the first time I set eyes on her grubby face, her spindly arms wrapped tight around Tucker's neck. I saved her once, I only hope the Sweepers don't take her in the end.

I turn at the sound of hooves and a moment later Jody and the other riders come into view, trotting in the direction of the main gate.

Jody waves across to us, her body seamless with the horse's movements.

I wave back, my stomach churning as the riders disappear around the corner. I should have known Jody wouldn't send her riders into danger without her. I'm asking a lot, sending them out on a precarious scouting mission, but we need to be prepared for what's coming.

Lou pokes me in the ribs. "Hey! I thought we were going to the Superconductor?"

"We are," I say, tearing my eyes away from the horses.

"Snow's an odd sight after all these years," Lou says, as we walk off.

"If it's snowing, the earth must be cooling, right?" I say.

She pinches her brow. "The last snow we had was right before the meltdown."

I throw her a look of alarm. "You don't think it's going to happen all over again, do you?"

Her sharp eyes appraise me. "The earth is disturbed. Anything's possible."

We walk the rest of the way lost in our thoughts. If the snow is an omen of another meltdown, we won't be safe in the city, even if we can defend it. Maybe we won't be safe anywhere ever again.

Inside the Superconductor, the air is cool and static. A low humming tickles the hairs in my ears. Across the room, Jerome's hologram hovers above the CommCenter. Blackbeard rests his palms on the desk, head bent, as though weighing something Jerome said. He looks up when he hears us enter.

"Everything okay?" I ask, glancing between him and Jerome's hologram.

Blackbeard tugs at his beard. "The Sweepers are planning to evacuate the deviations. We need to get them out of the Craniopolis."

"It's too dangerous," Jerome says. "There are hundreds of Schutz Clones camped outside, and an armed guard posted at the door to Terminus. We'll never get through."

Blackbeard draws his bushy black brows together. "They don't know about the tunnel. We could use it to evacuate the deviations. We just need to figure out how to eliminate the guards at the door to Terminus without alerting the rest of the Schutz Clones."

Lou pats her bow. "Consider it done."

Jerome rubs a hand across his jaw. "Has to be tonight. The Sweepers are going to begin documenting the deviations for transport tomorrow."

"We'll leave within the hour," I say. "That'll get us there by midnight."

"Even if we manage to get them out, it's a long trek to the city," Jerome says.

"What if we take them east of the Deadwood River to the homesteaders instead?" I say.

"We don't know if the homesteaders made it," Blackbeard says. "The Sweepers could be extracting them as we speak."

"Your call, Jerome," I say. "Talk it over with the other deviations before we get there. You don't have long to decide."

Jerome acknowledges with a nod and the hologram fades from sight.

I gesture to the other scientists at work around the room. "Has anyone made any progress on contacting the Megamedes?"

Blackbeard points to a bald-headed, lanky man. "Gustav picked up a weak signal about an hour ago. He's been chasing it ever since."

I cross the room to talk to Gustav. He runs his fingers through his hair and sighs. "I've sent for Dimitri. He's the only one who can lock the signal in."

"If he's able to function," I say. "He's in shock."

"I told him we picked up a signal," Gustav says. "He wants to do this for Iskra's sake."

Before I can respond, the entry door swings wide. Dimitri walks in, stiff-limbed and pale. A short, stocky scientist guides him by the elbow over to the CommCenter. He stares at the controls avoiding eye contact with any of us.

I walk over to him and lay a hand on his arm. "Thanks. I know it's hard for you to be here."

His feverish eyes search my face. "Iskra wouldn't be dead, and my father wouldn't have been forced into the decisions he made if it weren't for the Sweepers. I will find the signal if it kills me." He leans over the control panel and depresses a sequence of buttons. "Iskra would want me to finish what she started."

I tighten my lips. He doesn't know about Iskra's deception, and it's better that way. We desperately need his help to lock this signal in. I watch for several minutes, scarcely daring to breathe as Dimitri scans through row after row of data. His forehead glistens with sweat as he calls out occasional sequencing instructions to the other scientists. The minutes tick by and I wrestle to keep my doubts at bay that Dimitri can pull this off.

Lou grows restless and wanders around the room poking at equipment. I slump back against the wall. If Dimitri comes up flat, I have no plan "B" to save the city.

My eyes are beginning to glaze over when a harsh insistent buzzing fills the room. Lou jumps back from the monitor she was fiddling with. "Did I do that?" She looks around guiltily.

The scientists stare in unison at Dimitri. His fingers work furiously, adjusting knobs and gliding over screens until the buzzing sound evens out to a low hum.

"We did it, Iskra! We did it!" he whispers, his voice filled with awe. He sways forward so alarmingly that I grab him. He turns and looks at me. "I have the Megamedes!"

I glance around the room at the others. Trout grins across at me. The scientists exchange disbelieving looks with one another.

"Are you sure it's the Megamedes and not a Hovermedes?" Blackbeard asks.

Dimitri nods. "Positive. It's within a thousand mile range of here," he says, studying the screens in front of him.

"Why can't we hear anyone yet?" I ask.

Dimitri turns up the volume, then lowers it again when the loud buzzing sound starts back up. "Give it a minute."

I press my fingernails into my palms until Dimitri gives a sharp gasp. 'Listen," he whispers.

The other scientists gather around. I take a shallow breath, not wanting to drown out even the faintest murmur.

A moment later a loud crackling breaks the silence, and then a voice comes over the line. "… I repeat, do you copy, Craniopolis?"

"We read you," Dimitri responds. "Identify and state your position."

"This is the Megamedes. We have a contact bearing two hundred and eighty at four hundred and sixty miles and—"

The line sputters briefly and for a moment I think we've lost them.

"All surviving personnel evacuate to the Megamedes. I repeat, all surviving personnel evacuate to the Megamedes."

Chapter 29

The line sputters again. "Acknowledge orders, I repeat. Acknow–"

The lights on the CommCenter flicker and the line goes dead. Dimitri slams his fist on the counter.

"It doesn't matter!" I blurt out.

The shell-shocked faces in the room turn to me.

"We've got the coordinates now," I say, excitement swirling up from my gut. "We can launch the Hovermedes from the Craniopolis and land a raiding party on the Megamedes. The Sweepers will think we're part of the evacuation. They won't realize what's happening until it's too late."

Dimitri stares at me as if I'm some alien species he has inadvertently whipped up in his lab. "Are you out of your mind?" he asks.

"Not entirely. Sven and the military clones are trained to operate the Hovermedes. They can pose as Schutz Clones while you man communications from here between the ships. The Undergrounders can pass themselves off as scientists. Once we're on board we'll attack."

"Count me in," Lou says, giving an approving nod.

Gustav steps forward. "I can help Dimitri manage communications."

"There are six Hovermedes in the docking station at the Craniopolis," I say. "Enough to land a large raiding party. And we have the advantage of surprise."

Blackbeard grinds his jaw like he's chewing on something. "What about getting Jerome and the deviations out?"

"If we attack the Megamedes first, we may not need to evacuate the deviations," I say.

"I can send Jerome a message about the change in plan," Dimitri offers.

"No." I shake my head. "We'll tell him once we reach the Craniopolis. The deviations need to go ahead with their preparations to leave in case things don't go as planned on our end."

I turn back to Dimitri. "Are you sure you're up for this?"

He blinks, trying hard to hold back tears. "I've never been more sure about anything."

Gustav squeezes his shoulder gently. I give him an appreciative smile before turning to leave with Blackbeard and Lou.

"We need to pull Sven and the military clones off the barricade and head to the Craniopolis right away," I say, as we exit the Superconductor.

"What about the Rogues?" Blackbeard asks.

"They're under your command now." I look directly at him. "I need you to stay here in the city. There's no one Jerome trusts more to guard it in his absence than you."

"Just bring him back," he says in a hoarse voice. "That's all I ask."

"I swear to you I won't leave him behind."

Blackbeard's plea haunts me as we make our way across town. *Bring him back.* Maybe I can save Jerome from the Schutz Clones, but he's already twenty-four units. I can't keep him alive past his expiration date. His only hope of surviving beyond it lies with the secrets onboard the Megamedes.

Back at the container gate, Blackbeard moves some of his men into new positions around the barricade to free up those he's picked to supervise the Rogues. I'm not worried about leaving him behind with the Rogues. They're weakened and outnumbered, grateful we gave them refuge. The Ghost will have no takers if he tries to rally them to go up against Blackbeard and his men.

Sven and the military clones betray no emotion when Trout and I update them on the developments and brief them on our plan to attack the Megamedes. I'm reminded again that they don't fear war because this is what they were engineered to do. At times like this, Sven seems more machine than man, and yet I know by the way he looks at me when we're alone that he's capable of loving me as much as any man.

The Ghost watches the proceedings as the military clones fall into formation behind Sven, but he keeps his thoughts to himself. He's been subdued since he arrived back in the city with only a third of his men. I can't imagine he's thrilled about the shift in the balance of power. But for now, at any rate, he seems willing to toe the line.

I swing my pack over my shoulder and reach for my gun. All of a sudden the Undergrounders and Rogues start shouting to each other along the barricade.

"What's going on?" Trout yells up to them.

"Riders! Coming in hard," an Undergrounder shouts back.

I push my way through the crowd to the gate and wait with bated breath for word to come from the guards. It can't be good. Moments later, I hear the dreaded words. "Schutz Clones!"

My thoughts splinter inside my head. *It's happening!*

All around me men and women scramble up on the barricade, weapons in hand. Lou and Trout run to take up positions alongside the Rogues and Undergrounders. The container gates groan open and the horses bearing the riders gallop through, nostrils flared and heaving.

I press my face up against the shell of an abandoned car and angle my head as far as I can. When I scrunch my eyes up I detect a flicker of movement on the horizon. Minutes go by and the flicker turns into a steady crawl, like locusts darkening the earth. My blood runs cold.

The barricade fills up as more Undergrounders flock to help. The military clones resume their positions, faces set like steel. I spot Jakob and Hannah climbing into an abandoned truck built into the base of the barricade. Seems the entire city has turned out for the last stand. Men, women, and children old enough to hold a rifle, are tucked into perches all over the tangled steel and concrete wall. Lou kneels behind the burned-out cab of a truck beside me, bow in hand.

Sven walks up to me. "So much for attacking the Megamedes. We'll have to fight them here first after all."

"Keep everyone off the ridge line." I tuck my hair inside the collar of my coat and climb onto the barricade. "We don't give the Schutz Clones a clean shot."

Sven strides off giving orders to the military clones. I tent my hand over my eyes and study the shifting horizon for several tense minutes.

The black fatigue-clad troops come to a halt a quarter mile outside the city. Without binoculars or Sven's enhanced vision, it's hard to tell if the Schutz Clones are making camp or regrouping. I send a message down the line to the guards in the tower to let me know what's happening.

Blackbeard runs up to me with an update. "They're advancing again, but they've split into groups. I'm not sure what they're up to."

"Sven will know," I say, as he comes back into view. He strides over to us.

"What's going on?" Blackbeard asks. "Why are they dividing into groups?"

Sven grimaces. "To wear us down. They'll send in one wave of clones after another until we're out of firepower, and then they'll scale the barricade and take the city. The Sweepers don't want to obliterate us. They need our DNA."

"We haven't come this far to give up now," I say.

Sven smiles down at me. "I had a feeling you'd say that. Let's do this, Derry Connolly." His molten eyes search mine for some assurance I can't give him. I don't know if either of us will live beyond this day.

I pass the word down the line to hold all fire until the Schutz Clones are within range. We can't afford to waste any ammunition. I dig into my position a few feet from Sven and steel myself for what's to come.

When the Schutz Clones begin advancing again, my throat goes dry. They march in mechanical unison, gripping their guns tightly in their massive hands. A cloud of dread descends over me. No matter how many Schutz Clones we mow down, the Sweepers will churn out more. This isn't the battle I wanted to fight. I need to get on board the Megamedes.

The air is still and cold, and the sky a dirty white, but the snow has stopped falling now. I wonder what the Schutz Clones made of it. Tears prickle my eyes when I realize I never got a chance to ask Sven what he thought of the first snow he's ever seen—maybe now I never will.

I flinch when a single shot rings out. A Schutz Clone at the front of the pack drops to his knees and tilts forward on his helmet, ossifying like a sacrifice before the city gates. I didn't give the command to shoot, but everyone on the barricade opens fire, spraying the advancing troops with bullets. The Schutz Clones surge forward, firing back as they run. Lodged like bats in the steel and concrete barricade, we have the advantage of cover, and, despite their speed, the Schutz Clones make little headway. We mow them down them faster than they can reach the barricade.

Within minutes, it's over. An eerie silence settles over the carnage. The Schutz Clones' ossified corpses lie scattered around the barricade like macabre sculptures. I rest the barrel of my gun on a piece of rebar and pull out my water canteen with trembling fingers. Before I can raise it to my lips another shout goes out from the watchtower. I squint into the horizon. The second wave of Schutz Clones is on the move. "Sven!" I yell.

He crawls across to me. "Are you okay?"

"Yeah, just trying to work something out. If the Sweepers release a new wave of Schutz Clones after the first one has been decimated that gives us about fifteen minutes before they're within firing range, right?"

Sven hefts a questioning brow. "What are you thinking, power nap?"

I frown at him to keep from laughing. "If we let them get closer this time before we eliminate them, we'd have enough time to open the gates and retrieve their weapons before the third wave reaches us. With the increased firepower, we might be able to outlast the attack."

A somber expression comes over Sven's face. "The third wave of clones could charge us."

"We only need a couple of minutes. We crack open the gate, send out the runners—we'd be back inside before the Schutz Clones realize what's happening."

Sven rubs his jaw. "I'll station additional snipers at the gate to give the runners cover."

"Blackbeard can move some of his men over," I say. "And round up the fastest runners."

"No!" Sven lays a hand on my arm. "Send out the military clones. They're as fast as the Schutz Clones and they can carry a lot more weight than Undergrounders."

I grip his sleeve. "Not you."

He raises his hand and smooths my hair from my face before he gets to his feet. "I can't ask my men to do what I won't do."

I swallow the lump in my throat as he walks off. There's nothing I can say to that. It's how I operate.

Breath on pause, I watch as the second wave of Schutz Clones treads ever closer, the rhythmic pounding of their boots numbing us into silence. We hold our fire until they reach the marker we agreed on, a pile of corrugated metal siding overgrown with weeds. As soon as the first Schutz Clones steps over it, we let loose with a volley of bullets. Our fire is returned with a vengeance. The clang of bullets bouncing off metal fills the charged air. Undergrounders shout instructions to one another, scrambling and ducking for cover as they weave through the barricade like rats in a sewer. A piercing scream from above makes the hair on the back of my neck stand on end. A Rogue tumbles backward to the ground below. Perspiration beads on my forehead.

I spend my last three bullets, eject the clip and slap a new one in. That's when I see the kid on top of the barricade.

Chapter 30

I crane forward to take a closer look, but the kid hunkers down just out of view behind a steel girder on the ridge of the barricade. A moment later he pops his head back out and takes aim at the advancing Schutz Clones.

Brock!

The blood freezes in my veins. What is he doing? He's dangerously exposed. I have to reach him before it's too late. Heart pounding, I scramble to my feet. Adrenaline rushes through me, propelling me forward, but a lean figure bounds past me, scaling the barricade in seconds. I glance up in time to see The Ghost throw an arm around Brock's waist and pull him down, covering his body as a barrage of bullets pepper the girder.

When the volley dies down I leap over the last few feet between us and drop behind the metal girder.

"Get off me!" Brock yells, scrambling out from underneath The Ghost to retrieve his gun. His face is flushed with excitement. "I got this!"

The Ghost doesn't move. A creeping ameba of blood fingers its way out from under his torso. I yank Brock back down, hugging him to me as another hail of gunfire ricochets off the tangled metal we're crouching behind.

When the shots die down again I release my grip on Brock. He stares at The Ghost's body for a long moment. "Is he dead or something?" he whispers.

I nod, my eyes unexpectedly prickling as I check for a pulse to be sure. It's the second time today I've been moved by the death of a Rogue. "Yeah, he's dead," I say, reeling from the realization that whatever tune The Ghost was stuck on, he'll never whistle it again.

"I killed a Schutz Clone," Brock mutters.

"I'm sure you did." I squeeze his bony shoulder. His recklessness has cost The Ghost his life, but I think deep down he knows that.

I peer cautiously around the girder. The Schutz Clones are at the barricade now and several are scaling it with frightening speed. As quickly as the Undergrounders and Rogues pick them off, more take their place. But their reinforcements are dwindling. Without any cover, it's impossible for them to make it over the top.

To my horror, I spot a Schutz Clone squeezing through the barricade directly above Jakob and Hannah. Before he gets a round off, Hannah fires up at him. The Schutz Clone shudders and then ossifies in place, trapped between a chunk of concrete and a snarled roll of wire fencing. My heart slowly slides back down my throat. Hannah has blood on her hands now too, but she's still saving lives.

I focus my attention back on the remaining Schutz Clones and get a few more rounds off in between keeping Brock low and out of sight. Within minutes, the shooting dies away again and this time, it doesn't resume. I grab Brock by the arm. "Let's go." We scramble down the barricade to the ground and take shelter behind some corrugated sheeting.

My heart thuds loudly as I eye the groaning container gate. As soon as it creeps open a few feet, the military clones bolt through the opening and make a run for the abandoned weapons. Sven leads the charge, pounding over the debris that litters the ground outside the barricade. I swallow back the spiked lump in my throat. He has so little life left and yet he's willing to sacrifice it over and over. I'll never forget how he took Owen's place for my sake.

Brock watches, mesmerized, as the military clones pick their way through the ossified Schutz Clones' remains like vultures, stripping them of ammo belts and weapons.

One of the guards shouts something unintelligible from the tower. I look up in time to see the next wave of Schutz Clones thundering toward the city like a herd of elk. A tsunami of panic hits me.

"Run!" I yell. My voice is drowned out by the guards shouting over a loudspeaker to the military clones to retreat. All around the barricade Undergrounders scream the same urgent message. The military clones abandon what few weapons remain and flee toward the gate. I press my knuckles to my lips until Sven is safely back inside and the container gates are sealed. It doesn't surprise me that he's the last one through, but it does little to calm my fear of losing him before the day is done.

"Let's get you out of here before the next onslaught," I say to Brock.

He starts to protest, but I narrow my eyes at him. "You want to end up like The Ghost?"

Brock throws me a wounded look, but he shakes his head and gets to his feet. Seeing The Ghost's body was a wake-up call for him. A grim reminder that this isn't a game and that mistakes can be fatal.

"I have something important for you to do." I rest my hands on Brock's shoulders. "I need you to stay with Big Ed and defend him, no matter what happens."

He blinks, and then shrugs. "Sure, I guess."

"Take Lou with you," I say. "I want her to check up on Big Ed and let me know how he's doing."

He walks off and a moment later Lou strides up to me, a thunderous look on her face. Before she can say a word, I pull her close and whisper. "I need you to go with him to the rider's barn and tell whoever's there not to let Brock out of their sight until this is over." I straighten up as Brock comes walking back. "Brock will show you where the rider's barn is," I say, loud enough for him to hear.

I watch them disappear around the corner, but my relief is short-lived. Shouts alert me to fresh movement on the horizon. I climb back into position before the third wave of Schutz Clones begin their assault.

Over the next few hours, three more waves come and go. I sink down after the sixth attack ends and close my eyes, dreading hearing the sound of more boots crunching over the debris toward the barricade. I'm falling off my feet with exhaustion. I lean back against a stack of sheet metal, my eyes brimming with tears. How can we ever defeat a suicide squad like this? The

Ghost's bloodied body flashes to mind. We're all doomed. Even the Rogues are no match for this. I wish I could see Tucker one last time, but I'm glad for his sake that he's safe with Big Ed at the rider's barn. Lou returned with the welcome news that they're both doing great so that's one bright spot in this dark day.

"They're retreating," an Undergrounder above me shouts.

My eyes pop open. I scramble up on one knee and peer through the barricade. A sliver of black flickers on the horizon and then disappears. I blink, scarcely daring to believe that it could be anything other than a trick. I jump to my feet and run down the line to find Sven.

"Hey!" He waves down to me from the barricade.

"Are they really gone?" I call up to him.

"For now," he says, an ominous note in his voice. "But they'll return. It's just a matter of when. Tell everyone to hold their positions."

Hours go by and there's no sign of the Schutz Clones returning. "We can't sit around any longer waiting for the next attack," I say to Trout and Lou, as we munch on some jerky. "We need to come up with a plan."

I convene an emergency meeting beneath the watchtower and pass the word down the line to fetch Blackbeard and Sven.

"The Schutz Clones may not return for days, if at all," I say when everyone is assembled. "Let's go over our options."

Blackbeard frowns. "We still need to get Jerome and the deviations out before the Sweepers move them."

"First, we should work on fortifying the barricade," Trout says. "And we need to start building explosives out of whatever materials we can jury-rig together."

Sven folds his arms across his chest. "I say it's time to launch the Hovermedes and beat them at their own game."

I throw Lou a questioning look. "You're a neutral party. What do you think?"

"Secure the Megamedes," she says without hesitation. "You need to hit the bullseye to end this."

"She's right," I say, looking around at the others. "Everything hinges on finding the sovereign leader. I'll take half the military clones and a small group of Undergrounders with me back to the Craniopolis. Everyone else can stay here to defend the city." I nod to Blackbeard. "Under your command."

We exit the north side of the city using the secret passageway out through the abandoned school bus. If there are any Schutz Clones watching the container gate they have no idea that we're on our way to the Craniopolis.

The forest is cool and inviting after the intensity of the last few hours. Despite the respite it offers, I can't relax. We're heading into more danger than ever, the heart of darkness. Thick, scented pine branches undulate up and down like arms spurring me on as the enormity of the task ahead grows heavier.

The evening shadows lengthen around us and the trees take on the ghostlike greenish garb of night. Lou walks in front of me, her lithe movements never faltering as the light fades. This is her world and it embraces her like a daughter, a keeper of the secrets it shares with a chosen few.

"Keep an eye out for the scientists who escaped," Sven remarks.

Trout grunts. "If they're not back at the Craniopolis by now, they're already dead."

The words sound harsh and unfeeling, but the stark truth is that danger lurks everywhere in the forest for the inexperienced and unarmed, and the scientists fall into both of those categories.

"Take them alive if you find them," I say. "They may prove useful."

Shortly after midnight we reach the concealed entrance to the tunnel leading into the Craniopolis.

"Don't take any chances once we're inside," I say. "There could be Schutz Clones posted throughout the Craniopolis."

"The Sweepers don't know about the tunnel," Sven says. "They're not going to waste resources in the Biotik Sektor. We only need to worry about Terminus and the docking station."

"Leave the guards outside Terminus to me," Lou says.

Sven nods. "We need to hit the docking station before dawn. Hovermedes aren't designed to fly at night, so the Schutz Clones won't be expecting any action while it's dark out."

"Let's go," I say, climbing down into the earthy darkness. For once, I don't find the tunnel claustrophobic. I'm dreading leaving the safety of it. Terrified of what I've committed to do on the other end. But I'll find my courage and do it anyway like Big Ed taught me.

When we exit the tunnel, the Biotik Sektor is eerily silent, which I take as a good sign. We do a quick scout around to make sure there aren't any Schutz Clones lurking in the shadows.

"What's that?" Trout asks, frowning at a nearby pod chair. I turn and flinch. A glistening rust-colored patch streaks the back of the white chair.

Lou examines it. "It's fresh."

Sven puts the military clones on alert. He goes over to the doors leading out of the Biotik Sektor and peers into the main tunnel. "Clear out here," he says.

"Could be one of the escaped scientists," Trout says. "They knew about the tunnel."

"Then we're in trouble," I say. "If the Schutz Clones find out about the tunnel, we have no escape route."

Sven loads a cartridge into his gun, his face grim. "Whoever it was, they won't attempt to launch a Hovermedes until it's light out. Let's head to the docking station."

We exit the Biotik Sektor and creep along the main tunnel as silently as possible. My pulse hammers with each leaden step. The element of surprise we were counting on is no longer a sure thing. If even one of the scientists made it back to the Craniopolis, then the Schutz Clones are on full alert.

Halfway to the docking station Sven motions for us to hold up.

"What is it?" I whisper.

He points down a feeder tunnel. "The doors to the Sweepers' living quarters are open. Someone could be hiding in there."

"We can't go in blind," I say. "The place could be crawling with Schutz

Clones. Where's the closest place we can access the vents?"

"We just passed a mechanical room," Sven says.

I turn to the others. "Wait here."

Sven and I double back and slip into the mechanical room. He lifts me onto his shoulders, and I shimmy up into the vent and assume a half-crouch as I make my way along the shaft to the Sweepers' living quarters. My neck is cramping up by the time I reach the first grille. I flatten myself on my stomach and rub the feeling back into my neck as I peer through the mesh. My skin turns clammy and cold when I see what lies beneath me.

Chapter 31

The room is strewn with ossified Schutz Clones. I clap a hand over my mouth to trap the contents of my stomach that are halfway up my throat. My brain spins as I try to make sense of it. The Schutz Clones couldn't all have expired simultaneously. I furrow my brow as I weigh another possibility. Did the deviations attack them? I scrunch my eyes up and scan the room more carefully, searching for any evidence of dead deviations. There's only one way to tell their ossified remains apart from the Schutz Clones. To my relief all the shrunken piles of clothing are black—*Schutz Clone fatigues.* If there were any casualties on the other side, they've been removed. It seems unlikely the deviations could have pulled something like this off, even if they surprised the Schutz Clones when they were sleeping.

I cast one last bewildered look around and scurry back along the vent.

Sven reaches up his arms to catch me. I jump down and cling to him a moment longer than necessary to steady myself, savoring the comfort of his warm, muscular hands around me.

"What is it?" His eyes sweep across my face.

"The Schutz Clones are all dead."

He frowns. "Are you sure?"

"The place is full of ossified corpses," I say, breathlessly. "Do you think Jerome had a hand in it?"

Sven shakes his head. "The deviations wouldn't be able to take on the Schutz Clones."

"Did they turn on one another then?"

"There are no dissenters in their ranks. They're bred that way."

I give a wry grin. "Unlike military clones who can be very opinionated."

"Speaking of being opinionated," he says, "it's time we got back to the others."

Trout and Lou stare at me wide-eyed when I describe the macabre graveyard in the Sweepers' living quarters.

"Do you think whoever executed them might have eliminated the deviations as well?" Lou asks.

Trout glances across at me with dread in his eyes.

A heavy silence descends over us.

I feel sick to my stomach at the thought of Jerome and the deviations ossified inside Terminus.

"We need to find out what happened," Sven says.

He turns to the military clones. "We're going in. Keep your guard up for shooters."

We ready our weapons and begin inching our way along the tunnel to the Sweepers' living quarters. I slip through the open doors first, panning the room for possible targets.

"Told you they were all dead," I say after we've cleared the space.

Lou shakes her head in disbelief as we pick our way through the corpses.

Trout looks at Sven. "Ever seen anything like this before?"

"Never."

"Could it be some kind of virus?"

Sven shakes his head. "Impossible. Their immune systems are flawless."

Lou kneels down and picks up something from the floor. She holds it out in the palm of her hand. "It's a casing. If I had to guess, somebody ambushed them in their sleep." She gestures at their ossified remains. "Some of them are still curled up in the fetal position."

Sven lifts up the casing and examines it. "This didn't come from a Schutz Clone's weapon."

"There's no one else in the Craniopolis except for the deviations," Trout says.

Lou raises her brows. "This Jerome fellah's been busy."

Trout and I exchange skeptical looks. It's hard to imagine that many of the deviations can shoot straight, if at all. Some of them can scarcely carry out basic tasks.

"The escaped scientists might have had something to do with this," I say. "We still haven't explained the blood in the Biotik Sektor."

"We'd better make sure the deviations are okay before we head to the docking station," Trout says. "If there are killers at large in the Craniopolis, we need to warn Jerome."

Sven directs the military clones to collect the abandoned weapons and ammo and pile them up by the door. "We'll load the Hovermedes with the extra gear when we get back. We'll need every last round to secure the Megamedes."

Once we've finished sorting through the gear we're going to take, we make our way along the dimly lit tunnels to Terminus. True to her word, Lou disposes of the lone guard outside the entry door with deadly accuracy. The Schutz Clone topples forward, ossifying before he even hits the ground. Sven positions himself in front of the Optika module. Within seconds, the door is yanked open.

"About time!" Jerome says, peering anxiously over Sven's shoulder.

I let out a relieved breath. Until this moment, I wasn't sure I'd see him alive again.

He directs a couple of deviations behind him to drag the Schutz Clone's ossified remains inside. "I expected you hours ago," he says, ushering us through the door. "What happened?"

"Change of plans." I grimace. "We received a transmission from the Megamedes ordering all surviving personnel from the Craniopolis to return to the ship."

Jerome raises his brows and waits for me to continue.

"We were on our way to the docking station when we came across forty or so dead Schutz Clones in the Sweepers' living quarters."

"Know anything about it?" Sven asks.

"Nothing." Jerome frowns.

"We found fresh blood in the Biotik Sektor," Trout says. "There's someone else here."

"What about the escaped scientists?" Jerome asks. "Do you think they made it back?"

I nod, musing over the implications. "It's possible. But why would they execute the Schutz Clones?"

"It doesn't make sense." Jerome shakes his head. "The good news is that without the Schutz Clones, the Sweepers will be in no position to evacuate us tomorrow. We'll hunker down until you've secured the Megamedes."

He grips Sven tightly on the arm, and the two exchange a look that tells me they're not sure they'll see one another again. It doesn't do much to reassure me as we take our leave, but I knew this was a crazy plan all along.

Once the door to Terminus seals shut behind us, a grim determination grips us. We barely exchange two words as we make our way back through the main web of the Craniopolis. After the gruesome discovery in the Sweepers' living quarters, I'm dreading what we'll find in the docking station—hopefully, no ossified remains inside the Hovermedes. It's one thing stepping over the Schutz Clones' powdery corpses, but I don't want to have to touch them.

As we pass through a junction in the tunnels I catch a flash of someone or something disappearing into the Research Sektor just ahead. I motion to the others to be quiet and tread forward on the balls of my feet.

Sven comes up alongside me. "Did you see something?" he whispers.

I point to the Research Sektor. The doors are lying open.

Sven gives a curt nod and gestures to one of the military clones to move in. The clone noses around the doorway with the barrel of his gun and steps through, scanning the space with his enhanced vision. When he's satisfied it's clear, he motions us forward without taking his eyes off the room.

I aim my gun front of me, advancing in slow motion, as though a land mine might explode beneath my feet at any minute. Apart from the sound of my heart knocking against my ribs, I can't hear a thing. The place looks deserted.

"Sektor Sieben," I whisper to Sven, pointing to the door in the corner of the room leading to the participants' wing. I motion to Lou and Trout to stay put.

Sven follows me across the room. I press the keypad to open the door and slip inside the dim room. Cold steel presses up against my throat, and then I hear a gasp. The blade goes slack.

Sven steps through the door after me. His jaw drops.

I spin around and stare in astonishment at Owen. Over his shoulder, the rest of the homesteaders huddle together, faces pale and weapons drawn. My brain pounds against my skull. I throw myself at Owen and embrace him. "What are you doing here?" I blurt out.

"The sweeps have resumed." His voice sounds hoarse and tired. "They've extracted some of the homesteaders. We came to find them."

I wrinkle my brow, distracted by what appears to be blood on his shoulder. My brain fires on all cylinders. "Did you kill the Schutz Clones?"

He nods, his eyes boring into me. "Do you know where they've taken the extractees?"

The homesteaders behind him shift uneasily.

All at once I realize what he's saying. My skin crawls. "Nikki?" I whisper.

His face hardens.

I touch him lightly on the arm, eying his wound. "We'll find her, Owen, I promise."

"I've searched every inch of the Craniopolis." He runs his fingers distractedly through his hair. "She isn't here."

"They probably took them to the Megamedes," Sven says. "They're rounding up all the survivors in the Craniopolis."

"We're going to infiltrate the Megamedes," I add. "Sven and the military clones will man the Hovermedes as Schutz Clones, and the rest of us will pass ourselves off as surviving scientists being evacuated. We'll find Nikki as soon as we're on board." I search Owen's face, praying my plan has sparked some renewed hope in him.

"It won't work." He stares morosely at the floor in front of him.

"Why not?" I ask.

Owen lets out a heavy sigh. "Because we sabotaged the ships."

Chapter 32

I stare at Owen as it sinks in. Panic rises up inside me. "Are you out of your mind?" I yell.

"We needed those ships to reach the Megamedes," Sven says, grimly.

"I thought the Sweepers were using them to extract us," Owen says, his eyes flashing.

"Destroying them wasn't your decision to make," I say.

Owen gives a sarcastic laugh. "So now you own the Craniopolis?"

I glare at him, my breathing ragged. "Don't even go there. *I* led the uprising, and *I* lead the factions. *You're* the one who abandoned us in the middle of the night and risked the lives of the Undergrounders. After everything I did to rescue you from the Sweepers, you ditched me when I needed you most!"

Owen opens his mouth to respond, but Sven steps between us. "Knock it off! Both of you!"

Owen takes an uneasy step back and wipes his palm across his mouth. "Nikki risked everything to save me. I owe her the same."

"And what about me?" I say. "*I* risked everything to save you too."

Owen's face softens. "Yes you did, but you're not the one who's been extracted."

I take a deep breath to calm myself. "We can help you find her, but you can't play the lone wolf card anymore. Every decision you make affects all of us. It's time you pulled your weight in the same direction as everyone else."

Owen gives a wry grin. "You're right. I should have told you a long time ago you were right about a lot of things." He holds my gaze for a moment and I realize he's trying to tell me he's sorry for all the times he wasn't with me when I needed him before. But it doesn't matter now. It pushed me to become stronger, and for that I'm grateful.

"Mason always said you were a born leader," Owen adds. "You took the risks others cowered in front of."

"I only ever cared about what you thought of me," I say quietly.

Owen holds out his arms to me and this time he embraces me like he means it. "I'm sorry about the ships. I thought I was protecting us."

"We can find Nikki if we work together," I say when we pull apart.

Owen wipes a sleeve across his eyes. "You have a way of making people believe."

"Let me take a look at that shoulder," I say.

"It's nothing. A bullet grazed me."

"I'm guessing that was your blood on the pod chair in the Biotik Sektor?" Sven says.

Owen nods. "We stopped to get some lyophilized food. When we heard a noise, we took off thinking it was Sweepers. I guess it was you in the tunnel."

"We were afraid the escaped scientists had made it back here," I say.

"They didn't." Owen drops his gaze. "We had to eliminate them."

I bite my lip. I can tell by the weight in his voice that he wishes it could have been different. I don't press him for details.

"Maybe we can repair the Hovermedes if the damage isn't too bad," I say. "Let's round up Lou and Trout and check it out."

Once the military clones clear the docking station, we set about inspecting the Hovermedes.

"The damage is all on the outside," Owen says, a hopeful note in his voice. "We didn't have much time."

Sven takes a knee and examines the nose of the first ship. It's riddled with bullets and flattened like the snout of a hammerhead shark. "You did a thorough job," he says. "This isn't going anywhere in this condition."

Owen throws him a sheepish grin. "We found some crowbars by the parts carts."

Sven moves down the line of Hovermedes evaluating each ship in turn. "You ran out of steam right about here." He runs his hand over the body of the last ship. "The damage on this one might be superficial. The circuitry is deep enough that there's a good chance it's unscathed." He straightens up and moves around the side of the ship. "Only one way to know for sure." He presses a spot on the gleaming charcoal body of the Hovermedes. A sleek panel slides open and three steps float down to greet us.

Lou's eyes widen. "I've never seen inside one before."

"Now's your lucky day," I say, with a shudder. "Most people don't volunteer for the tour."

"I'll keep watch with Owen." Trout gestures to us to go ahead.

Lou and I follow Sven up the steps and inside the ship.

Lou whistles as she takes in the egg-shaped, pearlescent-white seats, lined with a matrix-like red cushioning, positioned on either side of the center aisle. "They're like the pod chairs in the Biotik Sektor."

I nod. "Except they're missing the sleeping mode that allows the chairs to tilt all the way back."

Lou walks all the way up to the cockpit and stares in awe at the staggering array of electronic gauges. "Looks like a rocket ship, not that I've ever been in one of those either."

She leans over, poised to press a button. Sven grabs her wrist. "Not the emergency beacon! If the electronics have survived Owen's wrecking ball marathon, it will send out a powerful tracking signal."

Lou grimaces. "Always was a hazard around gadgets."

"You're pretty handy with that bow, though," I say.

"You do what you gotta do," she says. She averts her eyes and examines the control panel on one of the pod chairs.

I bite my lip. She's used her bow more than once to save my life, but I wonder if the faces of those she killed haunt her like they do me.

"Bad news," Sven says. "The electronics are damaged. If I can locate the parts I need I can probably repair it, but it will take the best part of a day."

"We can't attack the Megamedes with only one ship," I say.

"It's all we've got," Sven says. "And even that's iffy."

"Then we need a new strategy," I say.

"What are you thinking?" Lou asks.

"Dimitri said the Megamedes was outfitted with state-of-the-art weaponry. If we can infiltrate the ship and seize control of it, we might be able to avoid an all-out attack."

Sven frowns. "I'll contact Dimitri and see if the ship's layout is somewhere in Iskra's files."

I nod. "It's our best shot if we're down to one ship."

We exit the Hovermedes and keep watch while Sven fires up the CommCenter in the docking station. A moment later, Dimitri's hologram appears. He stares at us, an incredulous look on his face. "You did it? Are the Schutz Clones dead?"

"The homesteaders ambushed them while they were sleeping," Trout explains.

Dimitri frowns. "What are the homesteaders doing in the Craniopolis?"

Owen and I trade uneasy glances.

"The sweeps have resumed," I say. "Some of them were extracted."

Dimitri passes a hand over his brow. "I'm sorry."

He says it like he's sorry he was ever a part of the Sweepers' agenda to begin with. And he probably is. It has cost him everything.

Dimitri presses his lips into a tight line. "The extractees are on board the Megamedes."

The nape of my neck prickles. "Are you sure?"

He draws his brows into a tight 'V.' "I intercepted a transmission confirming that all remaining extractees were being offloaded to the Megamedes."

"Did Iskra have the layout of the Megamedes anywhere in her files?" Sven asks. "If we can locate the weaponry on board, we could try and hijack the ship and disable the outposts at the same time."

"I'll transmit the plans, but they won't do you much good," Dimitri says.

I frown. "Why not?"

"I've been studying the engineering reports," he replies. "The Megamedes was never supposed to be in orbit this long. The directed-energy weapons onboard were designed to target attacking vehicles and disable them before they engaged. Unfortunately, the atmospheric conditions and weather created by the meltdown disrupted the infrared laser beams."

Trout cocks an eyebrow. "What does all that gobbledygook mean?"

"The defensive system has never been operational," Dimitri says. "You won't be able to disable the outposts from the Megamedes."

"So the galactic luxury liner is a lame duck," I say.

"The systems are failing. The survivors are going to have to return to earth before the ship fails entirely."

"Do you know for sure who is on board?" I ask.

Dimitri rubs his brow. "The world government and their family members. And the sovereign leader, of course."

I glance around at the Undergrounders, cataloging the fear and despair on their faces. *They need someone to believe in.* I flinch, almost as if Big Ed himself came up behind me and whispered in my ear. Thinking of him gives me the push I need.

"The Sweepers underestimated who took down the Craniopolis." I lift my chin. "They must have lost half their troops in the attack on Shoshane City, and they don't know yet that the Schutz Clones in the docking station are dead. We can take the Megamedes." I turn to Owen. "And free the extractees."

"The catch is that we don't have a ship that's flightworthy," Lou says.

I open my mouth to respond, but a flickering light on the CommCenter station catches my attention. I frown at Sven. "Are we losing Dimitri?"

Sven shakes his head. "It's another incoming transmission." He swirls a few sequences across the screen, then turns toward us, the color draining from his face.

"It's the Megamedes," he whispers.

Chapter 33

The Undergrounders exchange frozen looks of horror.

"What do you want to do?" Sven asks. "We can ignore the signal."

"Or we could answer them and pass ourselves off as survivors," I say. "We might find out some—"

Dimitri's voice cuts off my response. "No! They'll be expecting me to respond as head of the delegation. Patch me through to the Megamedes."

Sven throws me a questioning look.

I hesitate, second-guessing Dimitri's motives. Would he sell us out now after everything that's gone down? I push down my doubts. I have to believe he's in too deep and has lost too much to want to help the Sweepers any further. He blames them for Iskra's death, and avenging her is the only thing keeping him going.

"Can you make it appear as if Dimitri's transmitting from the Craniopolis?" I ask Sven.

"Give me a minute to redirect the signal." He swirls his fingertips over the screen and glances up at the hologram. "Okay, you're all set, Dimitri. We'll be able to hear you, but we won't be able to communicate with you until you terminate the transmission with the Megamedes."

"Understood," Dimitri replies, a strained expression on his face. I pace back and forth. I only hope he pulls this off. If he cracks, we're all lost.

Sven adjusts a few controls on the CommCenter dashboard, and then steps back.

Minutes tick by and everyone's breathing grows raspy to my ear. My heart feels as though it's swollen to twice its normal size. In the end, everything comes down to infiltrating the Megamedes, but it's become so much more complicated. We have to hijack a dying monster ship, free all the extractees, and land before the systems on board fail completely. It's a death wish, but there's no backing out now.

A snapping sound grabs my attention. A deep voice booms over the speaker. "This is the Megamedes transmitting. Does anyone read me?"

"Craniopolis responding," Dimitri says. "We read you loud and clear."

"Identify."

"Doctor Dimitri Petrov speaking, head of the delegation."

After a brief pause, the voice resumes in a more relaxed tone. "Doctor Amul Bhagat here. Is the Craniopolis secure?"

"Affirmative. What is your status?"

"Our CommCenter is failing and we are unable to make contact with the Schutz Clones or Hovermedes stationed outside the Craniopolis. We require additional Schutz Clones to oversee a number of hostile detainees. Request you send reinforcements to the Megamedes ASAP."

I squeeze my eyes shut. A direct invitation on board. The only hitch is that the Schutz Clones in the Craniopolis are all dead, and the Hovermedes inoperable.

"Copy that," Dimitri replies. "Ships are in maintenance mode. Several hours out."

"Expedite mainten–"

The transmission fizzles, snaps once and dies.

We wait for several more minutes, but the line remains dead. Sven flips a switch to reconnect us to Dimitri. Nothing happens. He lets out an exasperated sigh and fiddles with the dashboard. "Something's wrong with the CommCenter on the Superconductor end," Sven says. "If I can get the connection back up there's no guarantee it will last so make it snappy."

Finally, the line crackles and sputters back to life.

"You heard that," Dimitri says, rubbing his brow as he comes back into focus. "We just got summoned. Now, what?"

"We give them what they asked for," I say. "Sven and the military clones can don the black fatigues from the ossified Schutz Clones and goose step their way out of a Hovermedes."

"Except we don't have a ship fit to fly." Trout scowls across at Owen.

"Yes we do," I say, grinning. "We can take the Hovermedes east of here. You heard that Doctor Amul guy. They couldn't make contact with the Schutz Clones or the Hovermedes. That means we decimated the Schutz Clones who attacked the city."

"The Sweepers will put us straight to work if we go in as Schutz Clones," Sven says. "How are we going to hijack the Megamedes?"

I turn to look at Dimitri's hologram. "Is there a way to broadcast an emergency alert and feed it through to the Megamedes?"

Dimitri rumples his brow. "I don't see why not, now that we've locked into their signal."

"Good. When we're about to land I want you to send an alert to the Megamedes that the Craniopolis is under attack. Request the immediate return of the Hovermedes and all Schutz Clones on board."

Comprehension ripples across Dimitri's face. "Meanwhile, you disembark and the pilot flies back with an empty Hovermedes," he says.

"Exactly," I say. "We'll hide out in the Megamedes long enough to do some recon and figure out the best way to commandeer the ship."

"It's clever." Sven nods appreciatively. "The tricky part will be making it out of the docking station undetected. The Sweepers will have deviations working shifts and at least a couple of Schutz Clones overseeing them."

"We can take out a few Schutz Clones easily enough," I say.

"We should bring Jerome with us," Trout says. "If the deviations panic and alert the Sweepers, we'll be screwed."

"Good idea," Sven says. "The deviations trust Jerome.

I nod. "All right. We'll go by Terminus on our way out of here."

"One more thing," Dimitri says.

I turn my head in his direction.

He runs his tongue over his lips. "Big Ed–" Another loud crackle cuts off Viktor's voice.

My spine tingles. "What about Big Ed?"

The hologram flickers once and flat lines.

My skin crawls. I stare at the empty space over the CommCenter. "Do something," I yell at Sven. "Get him back on!"

Sven swipes a few practiced strokes across the screen. He shakes his head. "Connection's down at the Superconductor. I can't fix it on this end."

Trout lays a hand on my shoulder. "Don't assume the worst. Dimitri might have had a message for you from Big Ed."

Owen throws me a sympathetic look. "Trout's right. Nothing we can do now."

"That old boy's fine," Lou says, a mischievous sparkle in her eyes. "He was well on the way to recovery before we left."

I take several deep breaths. They're all trying their best to calm my worst fear; that Big Ed's dead and that I didn't get to say good-bye to the man who was closer to me than my own father. None of them knows what Dimitri was about to say, but they're bound and determined to keep me focused, and for good reason. We only get one shot at boarding the Megamedes, and they can't let me screw it up. Nothing I can do will help Big Ed now, one way or the other. If he's gone, I'll mourn him later. If there is a later.

We gather up our packs and weapons and make our way back along the tunnel to the Sweepers' living quarters to retrieve the Schutz Clones' fatigues. Sven and the military clones undertake the gruesome task of undressing the few shriveled corpses that remain among the piles of dust. A military clone turns over a boot and tips out the powdered remains inside. I turn from the sight, fighting the tang of acid in my throat. If the ossification bug can't be resolved, this will be Sven's fate sooner or later. In a strange way, the thought bolsters my courage. What we're about to do is the only thing to do in the face of the unrelenting evil that has taken over the world. Somehow knowing that makes it easier to believe we can win despite the odds against us.

"We're all done here," Sven says, walking up to me dressed head-to-toe in black Schutz Clone fatigues.

I repress a shudder. "Time to head to Terminus."

Jerome raises his brows when he sees Owen and the homesteaders.

I give him a wry grin. "We found out who took out the Schutz Clones in the docking station."

"What are they doing here?" Jerome asks, ushering us inside Terminus. His eye bores into Owen, seeking an explanation.

Owen clenches his fists. "The sweeps have resumed. They extracted Nikki and some of the other Undergrounders."

"Dimitri says they've been transferred to the Megamedes," I add.

Jerome runs a hand over his pitted face. "When will you attack?"

"We may not have to," I say. "The Sweepers sent a transmission requesting additional Schutz Clones to monitor hostiles, presumably the Undergrounders they extracted."

Jerome throws a questioning look Sven's way. "Let me guess. You're planning to pose as Schutz Clones."

Sven nods. "But we need your help. The docking station will likely be manned by deviations guarded by a handful of Schutz Clones. We can dispose of the guards, but we need you to persuade the deviations to smuggle us out of there."

Jerome frowns. "The Sweepers will expect you to report for duty as soon as you've landed."

"We've got that covered," I say. "Dimitri will broadcast an emergency alert through to the Megamedes letting them know the Craniopolis is under attack. He'll request the immediate return of the Hovermedes and all Schutz Clones on board. We'll infiltrate the Megamedes while one of the military clones flies the empty Hovermedes back here."

Jerome moves his jaw side to side as if weighing our odds. "All right, I'm in. Are you taking all six Hovermedes?"

"They're not operational," I say.

Owen throws Jerome an uneasy look. "We sabotaged them."

"We'll use the Hovermedes east of here," I say. "Most of the Schutz Clones died in the assault on the city. There may be no one left guarding them for all we know."

"We should get going before the Megamedes grows suspicious," Sven says.

Jerome exchanges a few words with some of the deviations and then gathers up his pack and gun.

I lead the way back out into the corridor and head south to the Biotik Sektor. My pulse races with the certain knowledge that there's no turning back now. Once the Hovermedes launch, death or victory await us.

When I round the final bend I come to an abrupt halt and gesture behind me to the others to ready their weapons. The steel entry doors to the Biotik Sektor are lying open. I grip my gun and inch toward the doorway. Scarcely daring to breathe, I tilt forward and crane my neck around the doorframe.

A hooded figure is hunched over the food dispenser hastily shoving sachets into a pack.

Chapter 34

I raise my gun and take aim, unsure if it's a Rogue or just a hungry deviation.

"Hands in the air!" I yell.

The figure swivels. I gasp at the gray, matted beard and wrinkled face inside the hood.

"Big Ed!" I shout, racing across the room. I fling myself at him and bury myself in the pine-scented folds of his flannel shirt.

I wipe a dangling tear of relief from my lashes when we pull apart. "What are you doing here?"

"I reckon I'm fit to fight," he says, staring at something over my shoulder.

I turn and see Lou approaching.

She beams at him. "Told you my special soup recipe would work wonders."

The pleats around Big Ed's eyes crinkle. "Sure beats this stuff." He gestures at the lyophilized food packets in his hand.

I shake my head in disbelief as Trout and Owen come walking up. "Can you believe this?"

Trout chuckles. "So that's what Dimitri was trying to tell us when the signal went down."

"He'll slow us down," Owen mutters.

I throw him a skeptical look as I reach for my pack. "You want to try shooing him back to the city?"

He gives a subtle tilt of his head in Lou's direction. "I wouldn't dare. I might end up with an arrow in my chest."

Jerome leads the way as we make our way along the now familiar turns in the dirt-packed tunnel from the Craniopolis to the forest. It's anyone's guess what we'll find when we reach the camp where Lou spotted the Hovermedes. If there are any surviving Schutz Clones, they could have moved the ships by now, or they might be waiting for reinforcements to arrive. Neither option gives me a warm and fuzzy feeling.

When we climb out of the tunnel, the sun glares down on us, a circle of red steel heralding a scorching hike ahead. Sven assembles the black fatigue-clad military clones into formation. I watch as they don their helmets, transforming themselves into the feared extraction force of a regime gone mad. The Undergrounders eye them warily.

Jerome locates a nearby spring and we take a few minutes to slake our thirst and fill our canteens. Big Ed rips open a lyophilized food packet with his teeth, spilling some of the powder into his grizzled beard. "It sure don't grease up the taste buds like the smell of meat roasting," he says, "but it's growing on me."

"Can't beat the convenience when you live life on the run," Trout remarks.

Lou pulls a face. "I want to live in a world with time to stir what I'm cooking."

"You will," I say, "once we take it back." *Or die trying.*

"Everyone ready?" Lou glances around at the others.

She takes the lead, heading east in the direction of the Schutz Clones' camp. Big Ed shows no sign of weakness, matching her pace effortlessly as they march. I'm flabbergasted at the recovery he's made. I suspect it has less to do with the soup and more with the soup maker. For a woman who prefers her own company, Lou seems to have plenty to talk about with Big Ed.

"How much farther?" I ask, coming up alongside them.

Lou points due east. "About a half mile in that direction. I can go ahead and do some recon."

Big Ed pulls at his beard. He won't try and stop her, but he'll want to go with her, and that's not an option. She's light and swift, and climbs like a monkey, but Big Ed's odds of outrunning a Schutz Clone are next to zero.

"No," I say. "I'll send Sven and the military clones ahead. It will look like Schutz Clone reinforcements arriving."

Big Ed beams at me. "Good idea."

I turn and make my way back to Sven and Jerome.

"The camp is a half mile from here," I say. "Might be best if the military clones lead the way from here."

Sven nods. "Once we clear the area, we'll fire up a Hovermedes and activate a beacon. That will be your signal to join us. We'll load up and be ready to take off as soon as you get there."

His amber eyes meet mine and a ripple of longing goes through me. The unexpected rush of the memory of his mouth on mine takes my breath away. I turn to leave, but Sven lays a hand on my shoulder. "Promise me you'll wait for the beacon."

I stare at his hand, the heat from it tingling all the way through me. *Promise me you'll wait.* We have so little time left together. Why does it have to be spent like this? I place my other hand on his and squeeze it, not trusting myself to speak.

Jerome eyes us curiously, one misshapen arm folded across his chest, the other palm resting on his corrugated cheek.

I look away, my heart filling with sadness for him. If Sven has the capacity for love, then, disfigured as he is, Jerome does too. Maybe the cruelest twist in the Sweepers' experimentation is the desire for love they couldn't eradicate from the hearts of even the most deformed deviations. I pull apart from Sven and nod good-bye.

When he marches off with the military clones, I keep my hands glued to my sides, fighting the urge to grab hold of him and beg him not to go. Once he's out of sight, I sling my pack aside and sink down on a tree stump. Every time we part, the thought that it might be the last time I see him cuts more than before. But, we can't stop now—not until we've found the sovereign leader and shut down the Sweepers' operation.

The waiting is torturous. No one is in the mood to talk anymore. Even Big Ed and Lou have fallen silent. I sit down in a clearing off to the side of the trail, my knees bent to my chin, my mind choking on chaotic images of Sven's demise. There are plenty of reasons why he may never come back, but I can't accept any of them. I want to believe that he can beat the odds and won't expire, but deep down I know it's a fantasy.

An hour goes by and my palms begin to sweat with a deathly fear that something's gone wrong. I'm debating whether to put together a search party to go after them when I hear Trout shout something. I jump to my feet, my heart straining at my ribs.

"It's them!" Owen yells, running up. He points behind me at a revolving beacon.

Relief floods through me. "Let's do this," I say. I tighten the straps on my pack and wait for Big Ed and Lou to load up. Jerome, Trout, and the Undergrounders have already assembled on the trail up ahead, their eyes betraying the rollercoaster of emotions going through them. I signal to Trout to take the lead.

The sun bears down on us now like a branding iron as we hike into the open. Sweat trickles down my face. I reach into my pack and rummage around for my water canteen. Somewhere in the recesses of my brain I register a familiar whooshing sensation. I glance up in time to see a cylindrical steel arm snake down through the trees and latch onto Jerome.

Screams fill the air. The Undergrounders scatter into the brush. Only Trout is close enough to hammer helplessly on the articulated metal tube before it retracts with its prey.

Jerome hovers above the trail like a blackened kill on a spit before the steel arm yanks him through the glare of the sun and into the belly of a waiting Hovermedes.

Trout falls to his knees and buries his head in his bleeding hands.

"Get up!" I shout. I rush toward him, panic flooding through me. What is he thinking?

He looks up as the second tube shoots down, too late to sidestep it before it locks onto him.

My heart slides up my throat, choking off my air supply. I stumble forward in slow motion, grasping in vain to reach him. I wince as the sun reflects off the menacing steel, whipping its way upward. I blink back tears, desperate to catch one last glimpse of Trout in the blinding sun. I sway back on my heels, dashes of darkness flickering across my field of vision like shadowy flotsam. *No! This isn't happening!*

Someone grabs me by the arms and yanks me into the brush. I fall to the ground and heave a few violent dry sobs. *Not Trout!* My eyes burn with salty tears. Big Ed, Lou, and Owen huddle around, peering at me anxiously.

"They're tracking us," I gasp. "Is there any other way to reach the camp?"

"We'll have to muscle our way through the undergrowth," Lou says.

"Do you think that beacon really was Sven?" Owen asks.

"I hope so," I say, getting to my feet. I wipe the back of my hand across my eyes. "We need to get to him before that Hovermedes finds us."

Weapons at hand, we begin the task of bushwhacking our way through a tangle of thorny brush and braided saplings. Without the enhanced strength of the military clones, it's an arduous task, branches flailing our faces as we weave our way forward. Every time I try to process what just happened to Trout and Jerome, the shock of losing them makes my knees go weak.

When we finally reach the camp perimeter, sweating and exhausted, Lou points through the foliage at eight gleaming Hovermedes lined up in a large clearing. "Two of them are gone," she says.

"They could arrive back at any minute," Big Ed says.

"Or they could be taking Jerome and Trout to the Megamedes," Owen says, his face creased with worry.

"Let's go," I say, parting the bushes in front of me. "Sven and the military clones must be on board the other ships already."

We step out into the clearing and jog toward the nearest Hovermedes.

That's when the Schutz Clones appear.

Chapter 35

Time stands still in the split second I have to make my decision. My senses heighten. Even the saturated hue of the pine trees spearing their way upward deepens. I scan the identical Schutz Clones coming around the side of the Hovermedes, picturing Sven's face beneath each helmet. There are no second chances. If we shoot, they die. I have to trust my instincts. I close my mind to any lingering doubt and squeeze the trigger. A hail of bullets from the Undergrounders hit the clones before they can lock their weapons onto us. They shrivel up and sink to the ground, deflating before our eyes like black balloons.

My heart squeezes like a sponge until I can scarcely breathe. I can't take it back. If I called it wrong, I'll live with the knowledge that I killed the man I love. Cautiously, Lou and I approach the ossified bodies. The barbed lump in my throat grows bigger. It's a sobering sight and I can never get used to it. What the Sweepers reduce the clones to in both life and death is unforgivable.

Lou lays a hand on my arm. "Let me check first." Her anguished tone tells me she wants to believe it isn't the military clones lying here, but that she fears the worst.

Big Ed and Owen come up alongside me and stare at the carnage.

"It's not the military clones," I say, in as firm a voice as I can muster. "They didn't identify themselves."

Big Ed takes off his hat and rubs a hand over his head.

"Sven said they would be in the Hovermedes," I add, my voice shaking.

Big Ed and Lou exchange nervous looks. Lou walks up to the nearest corpse, leans down, and lifts off the helmet. The skull crumbles like a sand castle washed away by a wave. Lou backs away, her face paling. "How can we tell who they were?" she asks, in a hushed voice.

"Search the pockets," I say.

I gesture to the Undergrounders to help. They venture closer, with obvious reluctance. For the next few minutes, we pick through the ossified corpses' pockets, searching for any identifying belongings.

"They're all empty," Owen says, with a shrug when he straightens up.

My heart soars. "It's not them."

Owen frowns. "How do you figure?"

"Sven carries Won's remote operating device for the Hovermedes in the cargo pocket of his pants," I say.

The others stare at me in silence. I can tell they think it's not enough to go on, that it might have fallen out of Sven's pocket or something, and they could be right. But the truth is Sven keeps something else in his pocket that I don't care to mention. *Our fortune. The greatest risk is not taking one.* It's reassurance to me that Sven isn't lying here.

"So where is Sven?" Lou glances around at the parked Hovermedes. "Maybe they took off in the other ship before we got here."

I frown. "Sven wouldn't leave without us."

Owen tents his hand over his eyes and peers at the horizon. "I see a Hovermedes coming our way right now. Could be the sweep that picked up Jerome and Trout."

My legs turn to jelly beneath me. "Quick! Inside," I yell to the Undergrounders. I activate the side panel door of the nearest Hovermedes and wait by the steps, peering anxiously over my shoulder as the Undergrounders pile through the entryway. With one last glance at the encroaching shadow in the sky, I bound up the steps and hurl myself inside the ship. Owen hits the keypad and the door slides shut behind me.

I shiver in the cramped space. It doesn't make sense. Sven wouldn't abandon us. I don't know where he is, or if he's even alive, but I have to find it in myself to keep going, with or without him.

"Be prepared to fight if the door opens," I say, looking around. I wish we had a better option to defend ourselves, but there's no time to make a run for cover in the forest.

My frustration mounts as I study the cockpit. Without Sven or any of the other military clones to pilot us out of here, we're essentially trapped. I look around at the strained expressions on the Undergrounders' faces. Big Ed stands with one arm draped protectively over Lou. We huddle in silent resignation, weapons at the ready as the approaching Hovermedes descends into position along the lineup of parked ships.

I watch transfixed through the darkened cockpit glass, scarcely daring to breathe. Retractable steel legs descend from the underbelly of the ship and grip the earth. The Hovermedes shudders to a stop. A moment later, the cigar-shaped body of the ship splits in two and the all too familiar black fatigue-clad figures begin spilling out. I slump back against the wall, my chest pumping so hard it feels like it might burst. We're sitting ducks, and I'm helpless to change our odds. I grit my teeth and ready my weapon.

"Derry! Look!" Owen nudges me, a thread of excitement in his voice.

"Military clones!" Big Ed says.

My jaw drops. I elbow past him and peer through the cockpit glass at the clones. It's the military clones all right—a couple of them have removed their helmets—but where's Sven? Dread seeps through me again. Something must have happened to him. He would never take off in the Hovermedes without me.

"Let's go," I say, as I activate the door panel. The slider retracts and I step through the doorway. I squint in the blinding sun and all of a sudden I see Sven striding toward the ship. My heart jolts. Without bothering to wait on the steps to extend, I leap straight to the ground and run to meet him. He wraps his brawny arms around me and rests his chin on my head. My whole body shakes with relief. I squeeze my eyes shut to trap my tears. I pinned all my hopes on a fortune cookie. But I was right to believe Sven wouldn't let me down. "Where were you?" I ask, looking up at him.

He grimaces. "We were waiting with the engine running when the extraction footage came up on the monitoring screen in the cockpit." A flicker of pain crosses his face. "I was afraid they had taken you too." We went after them, but they had too much of a head start."

"Dimitri said they're taking all remaining extractees to the Megamedes," I say.

Sven furrows his brow. "If they spotted our Hovermedes pursuing them, our cover may be blown."

"There's no time to waste." I tuck my braid inside my collar. "We have to move now. The extractees are in danger."

Sven takes my hand in his and brushes a strand of hair out of my face. "Whatever happens, I've lived the life I wanted to in the past few weeks."

I bite my lip to keep from crying. "Running from Sweepers? Watching good men die?"

"I was free," Sven says, "and the men I lost were free."

I lean up on my tiptoes and kiss him on the cheek. "It's not over yet. Let's do this."

Sven nods. "We'll take all eight ships. It will look like we're arriving with plenty of reinforcements."

We relay the plan to the others and distribute the clones and Undergrounders among the ships. When we're all loaded up, Sven takes the controls and our Hovermedes whirs to life and begins a vertical ascent. My stomach lurches as we rapidly ascend to cruising height. I glance across the aisle at Owen, sunken into his frame, staring at the chair back in front of him. His thoughts, now more than ever, are with Nikki. It's anyone guess if she's still alive, but hope has brought Owen this far. I peek out around the side of my chair and spot Big Ed and Lou, gray heads bent together in a private conversation a few rows behind me. I smile and lock the memory away. If they don't make it out, I want to remember them happy together at the end.

The military clones sit rigidly in their seats, clutching their Schutz Clone helmets in their laps. The Undergrounders pull their lab coats from their packs and silently don them. I reach into my pack and take out mine. I can't help wondering whose funeral we're dressing for, but I shake the thought. I can't give in to my fear. I have to believe we can triumph.

Sven turns on the ship's intercom. "I'm going to establish a link with Dimitri in a few minutes," he says. "That way he can monitor our approach and send out the broadcast alert to return to the Craniopolis. Any questions?"

"Do you think the deviations in the docking station will cooperate without Jerome?" Big Ed calls up the aisle.

"We'll overpower them if we have to," I say. "It's not my first choice, but we can't risk them alerting the Sweepers."

"How are we going to find the Intake Sektor without their help?" Owen asks.

"Dimitri sent us the engineering plans," Sven says. "We'll be able to navigate around with or without the deviations."

"Rescuing the extractees is the first priority," Owen says.

I throw him a sympathetic look. "Of course, but I need you to stick with the plan. We can't do anything to alert the Sweepers that we're on board until we're ready to make our move."

Owen nods, his eyes glistening.

Sven pulls up the engineering plans on a plasma screen in front of us. "Here's the docking station." He points out a large hangar at the rear of the Megamedes. "It leads directly into the mechanical wing. The deviations' quarters are also on this level. The Intake Sektor and the kitchen and infirmary are on the next level up. The upper deck houses the control station, Sweepers' living quarters and research laboratories."

I study the screen. "Our best bet is to hide out in the mechanical wing until we can work out a plan. We could take this side door out of the docking station to avoid any patrols in the main corridor."

Sven nods. "That will give me a chance to study the cameras and security system on board. I can do some rewiring in the mechanical wing so we can move around without being detected."

"Let's get Dimitri on the line now," I say.

Sven turns to another screen and logs in the coordinates for the Superconductor.

Moments later, Dimitri's voice fills the cabin. "Congratulations! You pulled it off."

"It wasn't without incident," I reply. "The Sweepers extracted Jerome and Trout."

"I heard the transmission to the Megamedes," Dimitri says, after a brief pause. "The good news is they didn't report being pursued."

A glimmer of hope goes through me. At least we still have the element of surprise.

"How far are we from the ship?" I ask.

"Fifteen minutes from docking," Dimitri replies. "As soon as you touch down, I'll broadcast the emergency alert."

"We need you to contact the Megamedes once the pilots make it back to the Craniopolis," I say. "Tell them the attack was just a few stragglers with explosives who took out the Schutz Clones, but that everything's under control again."

Dimitri gives a curt nod. "Good luck with the landing." The image turns fuzzy and he fades from the screen.

Sven throws a quick glance over his shoulder. "Make sure everyone's strapped in. If something goes wrong and the Megamedes starts firing at us, I might need to make some sharp evasive maneuvers to get us out of there in one piece."

I pass the word down the aisle to the military clones and Undergrounders before securing my own seat harness. My pulse races when I think about everything that could happen next. I'm afraid, but whatever this thing called life means, it's worth fighting for.

"I see the Megamedes," Sven says, quietly.

I stare through the cockpit glass for several more minutes before a looming gray frigate comes into view. I gasp at the staggering size of it.

Sven reduces the power. Several lights flicker across the control panel. "We're cleared to land," he says, maneuvering the Hovermedes into position. The back section of the Megamedes slowly hinges open to reveal an expansive, gleaming hangar housing Hovermedes of varying sizes. Sven guides our ship through the opening and into position, before extending the landing gear.

I cast a glance around the deserted hangar. "Where are the deviations and

Schutz Clones? They're expecting evacuees, aren't they?"

"Something's not right," Sven says, through gritted teeth. "Stay alert."

The instant we set down, a loud beeping breaks the eerie silence. Dimitri's voice echoes through the hangar. "We are under attack. Repeat, the Craniopolis is under attack. All Schutz Clones massacred. Request immediate return of Hovermedes and all on board."

Sven hops up out of his seat with the ship still running and a military clone slides behind the controls in his place.

"Everybody out!" I yell, activating the door panel.

We jump out into the hangar and run for the side door leading out of the docking station. The military clones and Undergrounders from the other ships follow suit. Behind us, the Hovermedes lift off in quick succession.

Following the layout on the plans, we make our way into the mechanical wing of the Megamedes. The claustrophobic space is nothing more than a giant network of wiring and pipes with a narrow passageway to walk through. Sven immediately gets to work. "I'll rig the camera system onboard to play on a loop for the next several hours," he says. "That should give us all the time we need."

The military clones stand guard at the entry doors while Sven works. Owen offers some jerky around, but I can't eat. I go over our route to the control station in my mind until I feel like I've walked it a thousand times. When Sven finally finishes, I jump to my feet.

"We have just under three hours before the cameras kick back on," he says. "I set an override code of 0978 to allow us to lock or unlock the access doors to the various sections of the ship. Everyone needs to memorize it."

We gather up our packs and weapons. I lead the way out of the mechanical wing into a dimly lit gleaming corridor connecting to the deviations' quarters. Silently, we slink our way along until we come to an airtight door. I pull the handle and step inside the airlock. Sven follows me into the cramped space that houses a control panel. I reach for the handle on the second steel door, but Sven's hairy hand closes over mine. "Check the viewing monitor first," he says, a note of concern in his voice. "There's a reason the deviations weren't on duty in the docking station. They could be under quarantine." He traces his fingers across the panel in the door and a sequence of lights flickers as the monitor powers up. I squint at the image on the screen, struggling to grasp what it is I'm looking at as it. My throat swells with fear.

Chapter 36

A sea of ossified corpses litters the room. The sight takes my breath away.

"What happened to them?" I gasp.

Sven grimaces. "I have a hunch, but let's find out for sure." He turns and punches something into the control panel.

I swallow back a sob. I'm thankful Jerome isn't here to see this.

"Just as I suspected," Sven says. "The air's been turned off in the deviations' living quarters. The Sweepers weren't lying when they said the onboard systems are shutting down. They're conserving oxygen for the sections of the ship they deem critical." He stares at the control panel. "No surprise the deviations didn't make the grade."

Big Ed sticks his head through the door. "Everything all right?" His eyes widen when he sees the image on the viewer. He steps inside and quietly removes his hat.

"They switched off the oxygen," Sven says.

"How can anyone be so heartless and twisted?" I say.

"There's them that cross a line into darkness and never return," Big Ed says. He thumps his chest. "Nothing in here anymore." A troubled look flits across his face. "What will you do when you find the sovereign leader?"

I bite down on my lip. I've tried not to think too hard about what I'll do when I come face to face with the man who's responsible for so much suffering. I loathe the sovereign leader with every fiber of my being, but if he surrenders to us we'll be forced to put him on trial. He'll almost certainly be sentenced to death by the Council, but at least his blood will be spilled in justice and not revenge. "We'll take him alive if at all possible," I say. "He should face judgement by those he's wronged."

Big Ed looks visibly relieved. He turns to Sven. "Is the air off in any other Sektors?"

Sven gestures at the control panel. "No. This is it."

"So far," I say. "But if the ship's systems are shutting down, there's no limit to how many more people the Sweepers will kill to save themselves."

Big Ed throws a quick glance over his shoulder at the Undergrounders. "If Owen gets wind of this he'll take off to find Nikki."

"Don't mention anything for now," I say. "We need to keep everyone calm until we're ready to make our move."

I push open the airtight door, and we walk back out to the others.

"How many deviations are in there?" Owen asks.

"Too many to bring with us," Big Ed says.

"First, we free the extractees," I say.

Owen shoots me a grateful look.

"We don't know how many guards are stationed at the Intake Sektor," I say, "but we do know the Sweepers are short-handed so it should make getting in there easier."

Lou gestures to her bow. "I can handle the guards."

I nod in her direction. "We'll back you up. Once we've freed the extractees we'll head for the upper-level control station. If we can take command of the ship, we'll give everyone on board the chance to surrender."

"And if they don't?" Lou asks.

The gruesome image of the ossified deviations flits to mind. I tighten my lips. "We eliminate them."

"What are our options for reaching the Intake Sektor?" Lou asks.

"Only one," I say. "We play the roles we came dressed for and walk proudly down the main corridor as a group of Schutz Clones and Sweepers."

Owen frowns. "Why don't we go through the deviations' quarters and avoid as much exposure as possible?"

I exchange a subtle glance with Sven. He steps forward. "Too risky. If we agitate the deviations, they might give the game away."

"All right," Owen says, with some reluctance. "Let's not waste any more time."

We make our way to the nearest stairwell, our mood somber as we climb the first flight of stairs. When we reach the door leading out to the second level, I give a tight nod. "You all know what to do."

Sven keys in the code on the control pad by the door. We walk through to a long, smooth white corridor. I glance around curiously. The passageway is bare of cameras or ducts, or even any access doors or windows. The hull is softly lit, but there are no apparent light fixtures. The military clones fall into Schutz Clone formation, goose-stepping, guns hoisted.

I smooth down the front of my lab coat and fall in behind them. We can't hide our weapons well, but our disguise isn't meant to fool anyone for longer than the few seconds it will take to eliminate them. As I walk, I make out the faint outline of the occasional door in the luminescent wall and a touchpad beside it. It's next to impossible to see the access doors unless you stare closely. My heart races. At any minute, someone could step out into the corridor and surprise us.

All of a sudden, I hear the sound of boots approaching from the opposite direction. Owen and I exchange worried glances. Sven and the military clones don't falter their rhythmic pace. My stomach churns. I'd almost rather fight than endure the strain of trying to pull off this hoax. We round a corner and a squad of four Schutz Clones march toward us. Our weapons are shielded from sight beneath our lab coats, but the minute they draw alongside us, they'll see we're hiding something. We'll have to be ready to do what needs to be done.

I test the trigger on my gun, my fingers slick with sweat. The Schutz Clones salute Sven and his men, then take an abrupt left and disappear through an access door before they reach us. My shoulders sag with relief. Owen and I exchange dazed looks.

"Keep moving," Sven calls over his shoulder. I increase my stride to keep up with the unrelenting pace set by the military clones. The sooner we reach the Intake Sektor, the better. I only hope we're not too late.

The military clones finally come to a halt by an access door. Sven keys in the code and we slip through into a narrow feeder passageway.

"Before we go any farther, let's go over this one last time," Sven says. "The Intake Sektor is around the next bend in the main tunnel. There are likely to be two Schutz Clones posted outside the doors."

I turn to Lou. "Can you silence both of them before they get a shot off?"

"Should be straightforward enough," Lou says. "Sven can strike up a conversation and shield me from immediate view while I take down the first guard. By the time the second one realizes what's happening the arrow will be in his chest."

"Let's do this," Owen says, a feverish look in his eyes.

Big Ed sandwiches Lou in his arms and bows his head on top of her long, gray hair. "Be careful." When he releases her she kisses him on the cheek and slips her bow from her shoulder.

"I'll take Lou and Derry, and half the military clones," Sven says. "The rest of you wait here. A smaller group will make it appear like a routine visit to Intake."

Sven taps on the control panel, and the access door to the main passageway slides open. He steps through and gestures to us to fall into formation behind him. We resume our somber march down the gleaming corridor. I suck in my breath when we turn the corner. On either side of the entry doors to the Intake Sektor stands an expressionless Schutz Clone. The squad of military clones comes to a halt in front of me. Sven walks up to the guards and exchanges a salute with them just as Lou's first arrow whizzes past his shoulder. It finds its mark with deadly accuracy, hitting the Schutz Clone square in the chest. I wait with bated breath for him to crumple, but instead he raises his weapon in Lou's direction and begins marching toward her.

"Hostile detected, hostile detected …" he repeats in an eerie voice that my instincts tell me is neither clone nor human.

Chapter 37

The second Schutz Clone falls in step behind the first one. They tromp right past Sven as if they assume he's one of them, their attention firmly fixed on Lou.

"Run!" I yell, a burst of adrenaline surging through me. We turn and leg it back down the corridor to the access door where the others are waiting. The Undergrounders greet us with terrified looks as we hurl ourselves through the doorway. Trembling, I punch in the override code. When the door slides shut I close my eyes and breathe out a sigh of relief.

"What happened?" Owen shakes me. "Did you get in?"

Lou stares at me, wide-eyed. "I don't understand. My arrow hit its mark."

"We couldn't kill the guards." I look around at the others. "Whatever they were, they weren't regular Schutz Clones."

Big Ed frowns. "Where's Sven?"

"They think he's one of them so he's safe, at least for now," I say. "But we're not. Even if Sven manages to delay the Schutz Clones, it won't be for long. We need to go."

The Undergrounders and military clones waste no time gathering up their gear. I lead the way down the feeder passageway, searching desperately for another exit.

"See that?" Owen points at a pulsing orange light running along the base of the wall.

"I think those Schutz Clones triggered some kind of alarm," I say.

"So we've blown our cover," Owen says.

"Not necessarily. A hostile could mean an escaped extractee for all the Sweepers know. They don't know we infiltrated the ship."

Owen looks unconvinced. It's weighing on him that we couldn't get Nikki out. But for now at least freeing the extractees will have to wait.

"There's a door up ahead," Lou calls to us.

"I've no idea where this leads to," I say when we join her. "This isn't the route I memorized from the map."

"Let's check it out," Owen says. "We can't stay in here."

"We may have to fight when that door opens," I say, once everyone is assembled. "But we're sitting ducks in this passageway anyway."

Big Ed nods. "Let's stick with the plan and look for the control station. That's where Sven will head."

I ready my weapon and punch in the four-digit override code. To my relief, it still works. I was half afraid the Sweepers might have discovered what we'd done and deactivated the code. The door slides open revealing a lustrous white tubular stairwell. "Looks like we're going up again," I say.

Owen draws his dark brows together. "The question is whether it leads to the control station or into the Sweepers' quarters?"

"It doesn't matter." I lock eyes with him. "We have to fight them now, regardless of where it plays out."

I nod to the Undergrounders and military clones and step through the doorway. We make our way quietly up the stairwell and into another clinical white passageway. The pulsing orange lights are still visible along the base of the wall. I wonder if the Sweepers are watching us. Maybe the entire luminescent wall is a giant viewing screen and we're nothing more than lab rats skulking down corridors all leading to the same trap.

Owen gestures to get my attention. He points up ahead at an unmarked door. We're in the general area of the control station, but I'm not sure what's behind this door. I signal back to the others to be ready and tiptoe forward to the keypad. I take a quick breath and punch in the code. Before the door slides fully open a volley of fire erupts from within. I dive to the floor and roll away from the doorway. We return fire, shooting blindly into the room while crouched on either side of the door. I can't tell if we're shooting at Sweepers or Schutz Clones, or how many of them we're up against. I let loose a few more random shots and wait for another round of return fire, but it doesn't come. I signal to the others to hold their fire. Minutes tick by, but I don't hear anyone moving around inside. Owen throws me a questioning look. Tentatively, I peer around the doorframe and pan a small section of the room. No one in sight. I crane forward and angle myself to secure a better view of the space. It's a laboratory of sorts, outfitted with steel tables and miscellaneous scientific equipment, but it's deserted.

"What do you see?" Owen whispers.

I shake my head. "Nothing. They're either hiding somewhere or they took off through another exit."

"We need to go after them," Owen says. "They'll alert the rest of the ship."

"We can't just go marching in there," Big Ed says. "They'll blow our heads off."

I throw a glance at the military clones. They have more chance of making it to cover inside the room than any of us, but I can't ask them to risk their lives and go in there first. That's Sven's call, and he isn't here. My stomach churns when I think of him. Those Schutz Clones guards at the Intake Sektor didn't realize he was a threat, but how long will it be before they uncover the truth? We need to get to the control station and make sure he and the other military clones got out okay.

"I'll check the place out," I say. "The rest of you cover me as best you can."

I take a shallow breath and peer around the doorframe again. I study the room for several minutes for any sign of movement and then nod to the others. I tense my muscles, ready to spring, and count to three. Clutching my gun tightly I dive into the laboratory and roll behind the nearest steel work bench. My heart thuds wildly, but no one fires. When I've gathered my wits again, I chance a glance around the side of the bench. From my new vantage spot, I can see another door at the back of the room. I'm guessing the shooters went out that way.

I get to my feet and signal to Owen and the others to join me. They file into the room, panning their weapons in all directions. To my horror, I hear the thud of boots in the corridor heading this way. We freeze and exchange panicked looks. We do the only thing we can and take up positions behind the work benches. We're in a vulnerable spot, stuck between two doorways with the potential of being attacked on both fronts, but for now, we have to focus on the more immediate threat. I furrow my brow in concentration, as the footsteps draw closer. A moment later two Schutz Clones march by the laboratory and continue on down the main corridor. I exhale slowly. After the unkillable Schutz Clones we encountered outside the Intake Sektor, I'm all for avoiding another confrontation.

I gesture with the barrel of my gun to the doorway at the back of the room. "Time to flush out whoever's hiding in there," I say. "If it's an exit, we've already lost them, but be prepared for anything." We pad the rest of the way across the room and position ourselves outside the room. I type in the override code on the keypad and take aim as the door slides open.

"Don't shoot!" several voices scream in unison.

I stare, dumbstruck, at a small group of scientists huddled together in a supply room, hands raised high. They peer out at us with confused expressions on their faces. "Who are you?" a short man with a thick mustache pipes up.

"I'll ask the questions," I say. "All you need to know is that this ship is under our control now."

The man blinks around nervously at the rest of our group.

"How many Schutz Clones are on board?" Owen asks.

The man shakes his head. "Most of them expired. The others were shipped out to attack Shoshane City. We operate a squad of robot clones for routine security."

"Robots!" Lou exclaims. "No wonder I couldn't kill them with an arrow."

"Where's the sovereign leader?" I ask the man.

"We haven't been able to contact him since the alert about a hostile was triggered."

I study the man's face, but I see nothing to indicate that he's lying.

"Which way's the control station?" Big Ed asks.

The man balks, throws a nervous glance over his shoulder at his colleagues. I gesture to the military clones. They step forward, grab him by the arms, and haul him away from the rest of the group.

"The main passage!" the man screams, his eyes filling with fear as he takes in the helmet-clad clones. "Take the next right."

I turn to the military clones and select two from the group. "Stay here and guard the prisoners. The rest of you come with us."

"One last thing," I say, turning back to the man. "What's the pulsing orange light along the bottom of the corridor?"

"Oxygen is running low," the man replies.

Fear flickers across Owen's face. "We need to go, *now.*"

I nod to the two military clones. They herd the scientists to the back of the room and aim their weapons at them. The scientists exchange uneasy looks. I see no reason to tell them their guards aren't really Schutz Clones. Maybe if they think we're leaving a pair of killer robots to supervise them they won't try anything.

We turn and make our way out through the deserted laboratory and back into the main passageway.

"The sovereign leader's got to be in the control station," I say.

"We should search for Sven and the rest of the military clones before we storm the place," Owen says. "There may not be enough of us to overpower them."

"You heard the scientist," I say. "The Schutz Clones have all expired, or been shipped out. We can take on the Sweepers."

Lou throws me a dubious look. "We still need Sven. None of us can fly the Megamedes."

I frown. "Dimitri can direct us if need be." It's not my first choice to proceed with the plan without Sven, but we're running out of oxygen, and that means we're running out of time to save the extractees.

We take a right and creep forward in the corridor until we're close enough to read the sign on the steel door up ahead. *Control Station.*

I take a choppy breath. "Ready?" I mouth to the others. When everyone's in position, I key in the override code. The door slides open to a collective gasp.

I slowly lower my weapon and stare in disbelief at the Schutz Clones piled on the floor in front of us.

"That scientist wasn't kidding," Owen says.

I furrow my brow. Something about this doesn't sit right with me. Why didn't they ossify like the deviations? Does it have to do with the air in this part of the ship?

At the far end of the room, a sea of screens surrounds a gigantic cockpit. I scrutinize the space, searching for the Sweepers. The station's deserted, but someone must be captaining the ship. I hone in on an oversized pod chair with its back to us. I pull my brows together and study it more closely. I can't tell if anyone's sitting in it, but some sixth sense tells me we're not alone. A moment later, my suspicions are confirmed when the chair swings around to face me. A current of fear shoots up my spine. The sovereign leader rises to his feet and stares dispassionately across the room, his eyes coming to rest on me.

"Derry Connolly, I presume."

I swallow hard. "How … how do you know my name?"

He curls his lip disparagingly. "Let's just say a mutual acquaintance was persuaded to be of assistance." He clicks his fingers and two Sweepers appear dragging a limp Schutz Clone between them. He lifts his head and glances in our direction. My heart jolts. *Sven!*

A searing pain goes through me. What have they done to him? I take a quick, steadying breath. My mind scrambles to put together a plan. We can easily take out the two Sweepers and the sovereign leader. They're vulnerable, even with a hostage to barter with. I throw a subtle glance at Owen. I can tell he's thinking the odds are in our favor too. The tricky part will be keeping Sven alive while we do it. And there may be other Sweepers waiting in the wings.

"Let him go," I call up to the sovereign leader. "Your ship is failing and your Schutz Clones have expired. There's no way out of this. If you surrender now, you'll be given a fair trial."

The sovereign leader throws his head back and laughs heartily. "*You* would dare to judge *me*! My foresight has spared your generation from extinction. The programs I authorized ensure that we will continue long beyond whatever apocalyptic event strikes earth next. Vats of embryos have been sent to our stations on other planets. Cloning technologies will allow for rapid repopulation in times of natural disaster, and scientific pruning of the gene pool has made certain that only the fit and intelligent strains of life will be allowed to seed the next generation."

"You tortured people!" I try to restrain myself from charging at him and grabbing him by the throat. Rage bubbles up inside me. Despite everything I said about giving the sovereign leader a fair trial, I'd like nothing more right now than for him to give me an excuse to shoot him. I aim my gun square at his chest, my finger toying with the trigger. A soft clicking sound distracts me from my target. My blood chills. It's coming from the Schutz Clones at my feet.

Chapter 38

I stumble backward in a fog of disbelief. Before my eyes, the Schutz Clones unfold their bent limbs and pick themselves up from the floor. Their movements are eerily synchronized as they unhinge and fall into formation, blocking the sovereign leader from view. With one accord, they begin marching toward us, their lips moving up and down in a mechanical chant. "Hostiles detected, hostiles detected, hostiles detected …"

I shoot, even though I know it's useless. The bullets zing off the metal torsos of the robots. They keep coming toward us at an unrelenting pace. We abandon any attempt to fight them and beat a hasty retreat out into the passageway.

"Remote!" Sven gasps, slapping the cargo pocket on his pants.

I realize immediately what he's trying to tell me. I peer through the line of advancing Schutz Clones and take aim at the Sweeper holding a black remote control. Sweat beads on my forehead. I pull the trigger, knowing that if I miss we're all going to die. The Sweeper grunts and tumbles forward. Before he even hits the ground, an arrow takes out the second Sweeper. I pan the room, heart pounding, but no one else appears. I duck between the line of robots, some of whom continue walking aimlessly into the wall. The military clones rush to pick Sven up off the floor. I aim my weapon square at the sovereign leader's chest as I approach him.

"It's over," I say. "Surrender peacefully or you'll die at my hands without a trial."

He sinks back down in his pod chair and fixes a reptilian stare on me. "You're a misguided idealist in an expansive universe. What do you know of who lives or dies beyond this moment?"

"I know your reign of terror's over," I say, my courage soaring as several of the military clones come alongside me.

The sovereign leader laces a sardonic grin across his face. "And what, pray tell, will you reign over in my absence, a colony of savages?"

"A free world."

He raises his right eyebrow. "Then let me be the first to exercise my freedom in this new world order."

In a flash, the pod chair spins away from me. A single gunshot echoes through the space. I stand rooted to the spot. For a brief second, I wonder if I've been shot. But I feel no pain. I walk forward in a trance and turn the pod chair back around to face me. The body of the sovereign leader is slumped to one side, the brains behind the Sweeper operation splattered across the plush white cushioning.

I stagger backward, bile rising up my throat. In all the nightmare scenarios I envisioned, it wasn't supposed to end like this. Big Ed comes up behind me and grabs my elbow to support me. Silently, he removes his hat.

"What did you do that for?" I say, angrily. "The coward escaped judgement. He doesn't deserve your respect."

"I ain't fit to judge no man," Big Ed says. "Some things are best left to God."

"I hope you're right about that," I say, turning away from the grisly sight. I'm weary of death and retribution, but, in the end, I can't help feeling there was too little blood spilled to atone for what the sovereign leader did. Finding him and holding him accountable was the whole goal of our mission, and now that opportunity is gone forever.

I make my way over to Sven, slumped in a nearby chair, and smooth my hand over his forehead. "Are you all right?"

He grimaces. "Those robot clones can pack a punch. I'm fine, though. Nothing broken." He signals to one of his men. "Set the course on the ship. We're heading back to earth."

A spontaneous cheer goes up around the control station. I pan the room taking in the pale, but jubilant faces of the Undergrounders. So many have sacrificed so much throughout this struggle, but we've finally toppled the sovereign leader. And they're satisfied with his death. Now, at last, we have a real chance to rebuild the world the meltdown took from us.

Sven gets to his feet, unsteadily. "I'll steer us back. This ship will be a bear to bring in smoothly."

"Owen and I will go down to the Intake Sektor and release the extractees," I say.

Sven nods. "I'll make an announcement over the intercom that we've taken command of the ship. But take some of the military clones with you in case there are stragglers who choose to fight."

"Lou and I will come with you too," Big Ed says.

I give him a grateful smile. If anything has happened to the extractees, I'll need him there to help me deal with Owen.

We exit the room and begin retracing our steps along the main passageway.

"We'd better check in here too," I say, gesturing at a door marked *No unauthorized access.* "If I remember the ship's layout correctly from Dimitri's plans, this is where the Research Sektor is located."

Owen throws me a worried look. "Let's make it quick."

I punch in the code to activate the door and step into the cool, gleaming space. Big Ed, Lou, and Owen tread in after me. There's no one behind the monitoring station. At the far end of the room, I see a familiar orbital viewing monitor on a steel door. My stomach tightens. Is there a Sektor Sieben on board the Megamedes too? "I hope that's not what I think it is," I say. "I don't want to see any more rewired participants."

"It's probably empty," Owen says. "The Sweepers weren't transferring the brain dead to the Megamedes, only the extractees."

Lou shudders. "Let's hope you're right."

I walk across the gleaming floor and steady my nerves before peering into the orbital monitor. The breath leaves my lungs.

I pull back from the monitor and lean against the wall. "One of the beds is occupied," I say. "What are we going to do?"

Big Ed scratches the back of his neck. "Nothing we can do for that poor soul now. We'll deal with their remains once we return to earth."

I wipe a weary hand over my brow. "We need to make sure whoever's in there isn't alive."

Owen activates the keypad to open the door. We slip through and make our way over to the metal frame sandwiching the participant inside. An assortment of wires runs from the motionless body to a bank of screens and equipment. I flip the switch to rotate the participant. I step back in horror when a gargoyle-like face comes into view.

Lyong!

Owen swears softly under his breath. "So this is where they brought him."

I stare, dumbstruck at the shrunken face on the bed in front of us. I can't believe it. Of all possible endings, why has it come down to this? I never wanted to see him again. I could crush what's left of his disfigured face with my fist, but it wouldn't change anything. He's gone, and yet in some macabre way he clings to the edge of the precipice of life, refusing to let go—it's like he's forcing me to pry his fingers off the ledge and send him over the brink.

"I wanted to kill him so badly back in the Craniopolis, but this is too easy," I say.

"That sucker's already gone where he's going," Big Ed says, a somber look on his face. "I'll unplug him if you want."

I furrow my brow. "No, this isn't something I can put on you or anyone else. I was responsible for his death. I told Nikki to take that shot. I need to finish this."

I walk back to the bank of machines and force myself to flick the switches off one by one. A soft whirring fills the deathly silence and then the machines power down. Lyong's body doesn't flinch, and no final breath escapes his lips. I lift a sheet from a nearby bed and pull it over his remains. It's more dignity than he afforded the living, but it feels like the right thing to do.

Big Ed gives an approving nod and replaces his hat. Lou brushes her fingers across my face in a motherly gesture that almost brings me to tears. I've had to do so many hard things in the past months, but it never gets any easier.

I turn abruptly to Owen. "Let's get Nikki out."

We head back into the main corridor and continue retracing our steps to the stairwell. We make our way down to the second level of the ship and out into the passageway leading to the Intake Sektor. The discovery of Lyong's body has dampened the jubilant mood we were in when we left the control station earlier. I can tell by the anguish in Owen's face that he's reliving memories he'd rather not have to face. Memories we've never discussed. I only hope we can all recover from what we've been through.

When we reach the final bend, I peer cautiously around the corner. My eyes widen. Two Schutz Clones are standing guard at the entry door. "The robot clones are back," I whisper.

"Who's controlling them?" Owen asks, a puzzled expression on his face.

"Could be Sweepers inside the Intake Sektor," Big Ed says.

"Or they could be preprogrammed to guard the entrance and detect hostiles," Lou adds.

Owen paces back and forth. "The question is how do we destroy them?"

"Maybe we don't," I say. "Maybe we lure them away instead. If one of us can lead them back to the control station, Sven could shut them down from the mains."

Big Ed steps forward. "I'll do it."

"No." I shake my head. "You're not fast enough to outrun them. I can make it back to the control station. I'll follow the route we took last time. You and Lou stay here and help Owen get the extractees out safely. Bring everyone to the upper deck."

Big Ed tugs at his beard. "I don't like the idea of you acting as bait. Too dangerous."

"Leaving the extractees in there any longer is dangerous too." I stuff my gun inside my lab coat. "The oxygen supplies are depleting rapidly. We need to move everyone to the upper level so we can seal off these decks.

Owen pulls me to him and hugs me. "If anyone can do this, you can. I'll see you back in the control station."

My eyes sting with tears. Knowing that Owen believes in me makes me want to pull off the next-to-impossible all the more.

I walk briskly down the passageway, around the corner and past the doors to the Intake Sektor. The robot Schutz Clones don't flinch at the sight of a scientist walking by. I head straight toward the door leading into the stairwell and enter the code. From behind the doorframe, I pull out my gun from under my lab coat, take aim at the clones and open fire through the opening. The Schutz Clones lock onto me with a laser-like stare and begin marching toward me chanting, "hostile detected, hostile detected … "

I punch in the override code to close the door behind me and take off up the stairs at full speed. I don't dare look back over my shoulder when I hear the door slide open behind me. Somehow they've cracked the code, which wasn't part of my plan. I don't know how quickly the robots can move, or whether their guns are equipped with any kind of heat-seeking laser beam, but I've no intention of hanging around long enough to find out. I push open the door at the top of the stairwell and bolt back the way I came, knowing my life depends on reaching the control station before the robots make it into the corridor. All of a sudden, a tremendous shudder goes through the ship. I lurch forward and skid across the floor. Panicked, I scramble to my feet and take off running again without as much as a passing glance over my shoulder.

When I reach the door to the control station I punch in the override code and burst into the room. "Robots!" I yell.

Sven turns to the controls and scans through the commands. The door to the control station slides open and the two robots march into the station. They raise their weapons and aim directly at me.

"Got it!" Sven yells.

The robots freeze in position. I hold my breath, half-expecting a burst of gunfire to escape from their weapons regardless. After a protracted moment of terror, I sink back against the gleaming white wall, my heart pounding. Sven's timing was impeccable.

"Are you okay?" Sven calls over his shoulder, flicking switches on the control panel in front of him.

I walk unsteadily over to him and sink down in the chair next to him. "Just take me back to earth," I say.

A second violent shudder goes through the ship. I cling to the armrests to keep from being flung out of my seat. "What's happening?" I yell.

"The ship's systems are failing. I need to shut off power to the lower levels immediately." He hesitates. "And the oxygen pump."

I stagger to my feet. "Owen and the others aren't back yet."

Sven looks me square in the eye. "If I don't do it now, no one will make it back to earth."

Chapter 39

My pulse jabs in my temple like a pickaxe. I shiver at a vision of the Undergrounders gasping for air halfway up the stairwell to the upper deck. "Give them five more minutes," I say, pacing behind Sven's seat as he adjusts the controls. The words have barely left my lips before a tremendous force rips through the room. I cling to the back of Sven's chair as the ship makes a dramatic dip, catapulting packs and gear across the room. One of the Undergrounders goes flying backward and crashes into the door. Several more are thrown to the ground. Even the military clones jockey to keep a footing. The ship rocks violently, shaking its contents like an undigested meal

"Stay down!" I yell over my shoulder.

I struggle to strap myself back into the seat nearest Sven. He throws me an anguished look. "I have to kill the power. There may be enough oxygen on the second level to last until I land, but if I don't stabilize the ship, there won't be a landing."

I give a reluctant nod. "Shut it off."

Sven bends over the controls again, his forehead lined in concentration. I close my eyes and picture the extractees' faces. I only hope they're close enough to the control station to make it before the air supply runs out. The disturbing image of the ossified deviations, trapped in their living quarters, comes back to haunt me. At least we still have the freedom to fight for our lives. It's more than the deviations were given.

I open my eyes and watch through the cockpit glass as Sven slowly swings the crippled ship around. "I've set a course for earth," he says. "We should touch down outside Shoshane City in about thirty minutes."

Before I can respond a siren blares behind me. Flashing red lights ripple across the ceiling and fade away. A sinking feeling comes over me. "What was that?" I turn to Sven.

"Oxygen alert," he says, tersely. "We're running on reserves in the control station now."

I flinch when a series of sparks arc out from a monitor to Sven's left. "Are we going to make it?" I ask, my heart drumming wildly. A strange pressure is building inside my chest, and I'm not sure if it's panic or oxygen deprivation.

"Power's reducing by the second," Sven says. "Anybody's guess if we'll survive the impact."

A shout comes from the doorway. I crane my neck around just as Owen and Nikki burst into the room. A moment later I spot Big Ed's matted beard bobbing among the other Undergrounders. Lou waves at me from his side. I undo my seatbelt and lurch my way back to them. "Where's Trout?" I ask, frantically searching the faces piling through the doorway. "And Jerome?"

"They're safe, they're behind us," Big Ed says.

I squeeze between the Undergrounders and stagger out into the passageway, fumbling for the walls each time the ship pitches.

"Trout!" I yell as he comes into view ahead of the military clones and the scientist hostages. Jerome trudges along beside him, his black skin gleaming in the luminescent light. He doesn't even crack a smile when he sees me. I've been dreading telling him about the massacre of the deviations, but by the look on his face, I'm guessing Big Ed might have already broken the news to him.

I help usher the Undergrounders inside the control station and direct them into pod chairs for the landing before I weave an unsteady path back to Sven. "The ship's listing badly to the left," I say, as I drop back into my seat.

"I know." He frowns. "I'm trying to route all remaining power to the control station."

The sound of an explosion reverberates up through the decks. Goosebumps prickle along my flesh.

"Might be too late," Sven says, wiping the sweat from his forehead.

I chew on my lip, gripping the sides of my seat with both hands. "I want you to know," I say, my voice cracking. "If we don't make it, the time we had together—"

"We're still together," Sven interrupts. He turns to me, his amber eyes fierce. "Keep believing."

I reach over and squeeze his huge hand. "I do believe."

"Then that's all I need." He sets his jaw. "We're beginning our final descent to Shoshane City. I'm going to try and make contact with the Superconductor." He fiddles with the controls to open up a channel. "Dimitri, do you read me?"

For a few seconds, there's silence before Dimitri's voice comes through.

"This is Dimitri Petrov. Identify."

"This is Sven 043. Our ship is crippled, I repeat, the Megamedes is crippled. Coming in hard. Only the upper deck is pressurized. Seals are holding so far, but it's becoming more difficult to breathe. Crash landing imminent."

The line crackles and Dimitri responds. "Understood. Will conduct initial search for survivors on the upper deck."

"We are on approach," Sven says. "Three minutes to land. Prepare to aid us if we don't implode at impact."

"Copy that," Dimitri says.

"Over and out." Sven kills the connection and turns to me. "Our reserves are depleted. I'm shutting down the computerized landing system and going in manual. It's our best chance of making it. Brace yourself." He grips the joystick and twists it until he brings the Megamedes level.

My heart flutters in my chest. Strange clanging sounds are coming from the underside of the ship. I tell myself it won't hurt; death will be instantaneous, but deep down I'm not ready to give up.

"The landing mechanism is jammed," Sven yells over his shoulder. "Prepare for a crash landing. Heads between your knees."

I bite my lip. I'm not about to duck and miss what could be the last sight I'll ever see. I especially don't want to close my eyes on Sven when he needs me most. "You can do this," I say to him.

He grimaces. "The speed we're coming in at gives me only a window of milliseconds to time the landing."

Sweat trickles down his face as he begins the maneuvers to land the Megamedes. The muscles in his powerful arms flex and I realize with a start I've forgotten all about the possibility of him expiring. It seems like a moot point now. And, yet, if by some miracle we pull this off, his expiration date will come back to haunt me.

"Even if the ship withstands the impact, the danger won't be over," Sven says, keeping his eyes fixed on the controls.

I turn to him, frowning. "You mean it could explode?"

"I mean it *will*. The Megamedes was designed to self-destruct if more than seventy-five percent of its systems malfunction—to prevent the weaponry from being hijacked. We may have only minutes to disembark."

I lurch forward in my seat as the ship sways from side to side. There's a loud popping like gunfire, then grinding sounds, like parts of the ship are breaking off. Trees rush toward the cockpit glass. Despite my earlier resolve, I scrunch my eyes shut.

We slam into the ground with a force that shakes every ligament inside me. Only the cushioning of the pod chair saves me from crushing every bone in my body. I brace myself through a violent aftershock and then the ship starts sliding. We skid for what feels like several agonizing minutes before coming to a shuddering halt. I stare through the cockpit glass in horror. Smoke billows out from the ship in every direction. Heat is already building inside the control station. I undo my belt and grab my gun.

"Let's go!" I yell to the others, leaping from my seat.

I lead the survivors out into the passageway where a gaping hole on the far side of the hull provides the welcome sight of blue sky above and the forest floor below.

With the help of the military clones, we slip and slide our way down the searing hot mangled exterior of the Megamedes and take off running for our lives in the direction of the city. Adrenaline pumps through my veins, but instinct tells me we won't be fast enough to evade being torched alive. We're already choking on the fumes coming from the wreckage. Sven and the military clones might be able to make it to safety if they break away, but they're keeping pace with the rest of us. Sven won't leave me behind, and I won't let him carry me despite his repeated pleas to do so. I won't abandon the Undergrounders.

"Riders!" someone yells.

I blink through the smoke at a rising cloud of dust up ahead. My hope soars. I never thought I'd see the day when I'd welcome another death-defying ride on the back of the riders' stallions, but right now I could cry with relief.

Within seconds, the riders have drawn up alongside us. They reach out leather-gloved hands and swing the Undergrounders up on horseback.

"Go!" Sven shouts to his men. The military clones take off at the speed of greyhounds toward the barricade.

I lock my arms around a rider's waist and grit my teeth as we gallop for our lives, leaving behind the suffocating smoke billowing out from the carcass of the Megamedes. When we reach the container gates I turn my head in time to catch the brilliant explosion that incinerates the hub of the Sweepers' bloody operation.

The horses slow to a trot as we enter the city. I release my death grip on the rider in front of me and rub my burning eyes, too numb from shock to even acknowledge the Undergrounders who run to greet us. Sven appears at the side of my horse and wordlessly lifts me into his arms. Somewhere deep in the recesses of my brain I register the creak of the container gates closing behind us before everything goes black.

Chapter 40

When I drift back to consciousness, I'm curled up on a bunk in the riders' barn, deliciously limp and snug. I let out a loud yawn, and the blanket over my legs moves. A slobbery tongue trails across my cheek. I jolt upright.

"Tucker!" I fall on his neck, sobbing and hugging him to me, inhaling the familiar scent of him. He licks the salty tears tracking down my face and swishes his tail contentedly back and forth. I sink back down on the bunk and snuggle him to me, savoring his healing presence that demands nothing of me in return. I close my eyes and try to go back to sleep, but my mind keeps replaying the clip of the explosion. I sit up with a sigh and swing my legs over the edge of the bunk. My stomach growls, reminding me that I haven't eaten anything in the past twelve hours. I reach for my boots. Time to remedy that.

The following days are a blur of activity as we try to come to terms with everything that's happened. I still can't believe the sovereign leader is gone, his remains, thankfully, incinerated in the explosion. For the most part, the Sweeper hostages from the Megamedes remain subdued and cooperative. The members of the world government will stand trial for what was done in the name of science under their command. Despite their insistence that what they did was for the advancement of humanity, the deviation holocaust and the wretched abuse of the participants in Sektor Sieben is more than enough to condemn them in the eyes of the Council.

In the end, it has cost a lot of blood to live the life we believe in. But Big Ed reminded me that if we can't live free we're not fully alive to begin with. We all agree we would pay the price again for every Undergrounder, clone, and deviation we saved from the Sweepers' regime.

Other than the select few who saw him, no one knew Lyong was on board the Megamedes, which is a good thing. His is a face best forgotten. The biggest loss in my mind with the destruction of the Megamedes is the fact that we won't be able to use the weaponry to destroy the outposts like we'd hoped. The sovereign leader's death leaves them isolated, but still with the potential to continue the cloning experimentation. It's a problem we'll have to deal with at some point, but today's agenda is all about integrating the new arrivals.

Jerome comes into his office in the courthouse where I'm going over housing arrangements with Trout and Big Ed. Tucker lifts his head and eyes Jerome with a doleful look as he sizes up the situation. He shadows me everywhere I go, committed to keeping me within licking range at all times.

"I wanted to stop in and say good-bye," Jerome says. "I'm heading back to the Craniopolis to take care of the deviations."

"How long will you be gone?" I ask.

"As long as it takes to persuade them to relocate to the city. We can set them up in their own section and integrate them more slowly this time, like we discussed."

"I'm sorry we couldn't save the deviations on board the Megamedes," I say.

Jerome casts his eye downward. "The best I can do to honor them is to pour my energy into the living."

"Can you stay for the celebration?" I ask.

He nods. "I'll leave in the morning."

I talk to Big Ed and Trout at length before I feel prepared to address the city. There's so much to say at tonight's victory celebration, and so much that's best left unsaid. Big Ed agrees I need to focus on the future rather than seeking retribution for the past, especially when it comes to the decimated Rogues.

"More blood won't change their hearts," he says.

Who knows how calloused the remaining Rogues are without Rummy, or Blade, or The Ghost at the helm. They've been cautious since their battle with the Schutz Clones, but when their wounds heal and their egos recover, they may try to usurp us, despite the presence of the military clones.

"Do you think I should let the Rogues stay here or tell them to move on?" I say.

"You'll figure it out," Big Ed says. "Show mercy and speak truth. That's all I got."

Regardless of what's gone down, including the deaths of Undergrounders from my own bunker, I want to reach out to the remaining Rogues and offer them a home here. Some, no doubt, will move on, disgruntled by the presence of former foes. Those who choose to remain will have to learn to live in a way that respects the freedom of others. It won't be an easy process, but my dream is for Shoshane City to become a sanctuary to anyone who comes in peace.

The Sweepers and members of the world government are scheduled to stand trial next week. It's pretty much a given that the Council will return a guilty verdict, but any vote on the death penalty will likely be contentious. If I've learned anything in my time as a leader, it's that freedom is messy, which is probably why the world government seemed like a good solution at first.

"We should go," Trout says, interrupting my thoughts. "Everyone's waiting on you."

I scrub my hands over my face and get to my feet. I know how to rally a crowd to war; now it's time to test the power of my rallying cry for peace.

My eyes widen when I see the throng of people clustered around the makeshift wooden platform that the military clones erected by the container gate. Tables piled high with food are stacked along the barricade, and I hear the strains of guitars and singing. As I scan the crowd, my heart swells. This isn't the same segregated group I faced before inside the courthouse. Undergrounders, Rogues, clones, and scientists are interspersed throughout, engaged in conversation, sharing food, and laughing with one another. I'm not so naive to think it will always be like this, but it's a beautiful sight while it lasts.

I position myself on the wooden platform and survey the faces pressing in around me. At the front I spot Izzy twirling on her toes, clutching her brother by the hand. I smile to myself. I can't put a price on the value of one life. Even if all of this had only been to save Izzy, it would have been worth it.

I raise my hand for silence, but suddenly someone starts clapping. Bursts of applause erupt from the crowd, followed by a series of loud cheers and whoops. I glance uncertainly at Big Ed. He removes his hat and bows his head. I look around, confused at first, but then I realize everyone's clapping for me. Tears well up and slide down my face. I don't deserve this unconditional outpouring of their praise. I'm inadequate in so many ways, but it's enough for them that I acted.

When the applause dies down I wipe my eyes on the back of my sleeve and clear my throat. "Tonight we celebrate victory, *our* victory. We fought hard for the freedom that is once again ours." I hesitate and swallow back the sob still stuck in my throat. "Ours has not been an easy journey. We have made mistakes and decisions that cost us along the way. But we fought a good fight. Our knees buckled beneath us at times, but our hearts never failed us." Whistles and more clapping drown me out for a moment. "Today," I continue, "we celebrate the end of tyranny and a new beginning with freedom for all, regardless of life expectancy, ability, or past wrongs. With this freedom comes responsibility, and we all play a part." I pause, and they seize the opportunity to raise jubilant fists in the air and start cheering again. Only this time they don't quit. I grin at Trout who's doing some kind of crazy jig with Izzy. It's all the confirmation I need that it's time to stop talking and let the party begin. I jump down from the platform and join them. Maybe, just maybe it will be possible to build something beautiful out of the ruins of Shoshane City.

Epilogue

When spring comes, I take Mason's ashes up to Elk Creek Rapids. I hike alone, despite multiple offers from Sven and Owen to accompany me. This is something private between Mason and me, a tribute I've wanted to honor him with for a long time, perhaps in some small way to atone for the jealousy that kept me from getting to know the real Mason until it was almost too late. Fiercely loyal and protective, he was an insanely brave man who risked everything to escape the Craniopolis and save us from the Sweepers. A man who should have grown old and told his story to his grandchildren.

The sun sears my skin as I reach into my jacket and pull out the worn pouch I've carried around with me for months. "Thank you for your strength and courage, Mason, and for believing I could lead them when I scarcely believed it myself. I'm sorry I was such a pain." I blink back tears as I release his ashes into the foam that crashes and peaks in the sea of granite teeth below. This time, he won't return in the flesh.

I wipe my sleeve over my eyes. I know Mason would be pleased with the spot I chose to scatter his ashes in. This is where he proved to me I could trust him, and revealed to me who he was, and this is the place he came back from. In a strange way, it gives me hope that I'll see him again, in another realm.

I hike back to the city feeling lighter than I've felt in a long time—like I've been forgiven. Wildflowers perfume the canyons and there are more birds nesting in the forest than I've seen in years. The world is beginning to heal from the meltdown, and the Undergrounders are finally beginning to heal from war.

There have been no more sightings of Hovermedes despite the numerous scouting missions Jody and Ida regularly conduct on the city's behalf. With some reluctance, the Council finally ruled it safe to shut down the semiconductor andbegin building settlements outside the barricade. The homesteaders are gearing up to leave at the end of the month. Jakob and Hannah, along with Owen and Nikki, will accompany the group, but this time, they'll leave with my blessing.

They tried to persuade Trout to join them, but after some consideration, he chose to remain in the city, and I have to admit I'm relieved. He's been a dear friend to me through all of this, and I couldn't bear to lose him too. His common sense and dry wit got me through some of the toughest days of my life. And I'm not the only one he's been a tonic for. He's become like an adopted son to Dimitri. I think they understand each other's deep losses better than most.

Big Ed and Lou are inseparable. I never truly understood the meaning of soulmates until I saw those two together. Whatever thoughts Big Ed had of succumbing to his bout of pneumonia, they're long gone. He's walking with a whole new spring in his step that tells me he plans to be around for some time to come. The two of them disappear into the mountains for weeks on end at times, but they always show up again to dispense their wisdom on whatever issues the Council is facing.

Jerome has entrusted the city to me when he expires. At twenty-four units, and then some, his day is drawing near. I may not even have time to recover from everything we've been through before I'm called upon to take on that mantle of responsibility. The deviations have resettled in their own section of the city and some of them, with Jerome's encouragement, enjoy a limited amount of interaction with us. Most, however, are too traumatized to ever fully heal. They remain content with their own company, and we respect their wishes. I assured Jerome I'd do everything in my power to protect them when he's gone. Dimitri and the other scientists have sworn to devote the rest of their lives to finding a cure for ossification, but the truth is they may be too late to save any of the remaining clones or deviations. The best we can do is to stop it ever happening again.

As for my beloved Sven, I don't know if he will make it to twenty-five units, or even to twenty, but I know without a shadow of a doubt that whatever time we have left together will be enough for us. He has proven his love for me time and again in his selfless acts of sacrifice and bravery. And I've even seen him shed a tear or two, proving he's more man than machine, not that he ever gave me a reason to question it.

At my request Big Ed and Lou have made a special effort to be in town this week. I can't stop smiling. It's finally happening. Big Ed even let Lou trim his beard for the occasion. At sunset tomorrow, on the steps of the courthouse in front of every faction in the city Sven and I will seal our promise to love each other until death do us part. I hope his expiration date never comes.

If you enjoyed the book I would REALLY appreciate a short review. Your help in spreading the word is invaluable. Your review makes a BIG difference in helping new readers find the series, and that makes it possible for me to keep writing stories. THANK YOU!

Visit below to download a free illustration of Shoshane City.
http://normahinkens.com/embattlement-city/

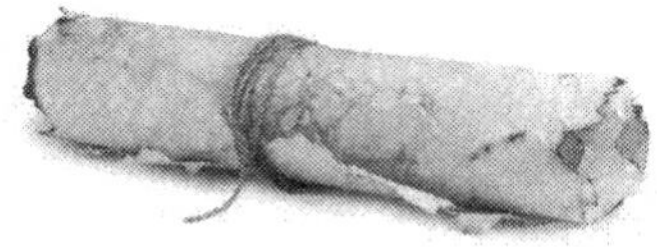

Join my **VIP Reader Club** to be the first to to stay on top of new releases, receive exclusive promotions and giveaways!
http://eepurl.com/bGSLlb

Connect with me on Facebook, and LIKE my page for giveaways, cool stuff & more!
https://www.facebook.com/NormaHinkensAuthor/

Check out my blog for inspiration and information to supercharge your own writing journey!
http://normahinkens.com/blog/

Made in the USA
Middletown, DE
09 December 2016